I0832171

GOBLAND

GOBLAND

by **Dr. Marcus Aurelius Roe**

AP Fiction
AuraPura Publishing

United States of America

ISBNs:

978-1-967916-96-2	—	(Hardback)
978-1-967916-97-9	—	(Paperback)
978-1-967916-98-6	—	(Ebook)
978-1-967916-99-3	—	(Audiobook)

Other works by Dr. Roe:

Your Fight (YourFight.Club)

24K Journal of Virtues Science (24k.cc)

virtues.blog

... find more at AuraPura.org

This book is dedicated to the truth seekers.

Cover art: 'Haywain Triptych' by Hieronymus Bosch

CHAPTER ONE

SOLIPSIA'S REPOSE

Through ice and darkness, focused on singular edge of mind and blade, swung Drake, son of the kingdom's now lost hero, Eldred. He trained as his father had, in preparation for the moment of his own ultimate trial. Every night and through to the morning was the routine, regardless of the season.

Dawn crept over Solipsia, light stealing glances at her beauty. The light, a timid suitor, wiggled exploring fingers through the stark silhouettes of trees and the frost-kissed shrubs below. Shadows clung to snow, as if reluctant to yield their nightly dominion, retreating slowly into gorges and hollows where they would linger.

Silence was thick in the waning winter, broken only by breezes slicing past bare branches and snowy pines dripping in icicles. He stood in the small clearing of receding snow, hemmed by old trees stretching toward the heavens like calloused hands seeking solace and warmth from the sun. Loam, sap, and pine permeated his senses, each of Drake's misty breaths drawing in more frozen essence of Solipsia.

Drake's father had saved the kingdom from goblin aggression. Eldred also developed an entire system for notating fighting forms and battle strategies. The many lessons were always with Drake, "Music notations follow sets of five lines, each set indicating definite separations of vibrancy patterns across a central one, in a spectrum. It is a map of frequencies as distinct moderations, which is little different from what we do with our defensive motions, sword strokes, and strategies. We judge the tension, strength, and timing against the distances, environment, and the actions of our opponents." Drake was Eldred's greatest student, passed down as his teachings were, most fervently.

Training his sword song through the night prepared him for the coming of the darkness once again, and it was well known to him. Drake was yet hardened beyond his years, as product of his father's persistent care in upbringing and focus on inner strength first. His face was the frame of resolute determination rather than innocence, the rightful property of his given years. Storm-filled eyes bright beneath brows drawn tight in concentration, the thoughts behind them ever resident and present on this inheritance in deed.

Drake's breath plumed before him like spectral banners of purchased nobility, vanishing into the cold as swiftly as they appeared. In his hands, he grasped his father's own sword, a relic from an age when heroes walked unhesitatingly towards perilous destinies. The blade bore no adornments save for the scars of battles long past and the patina of time etched deep into its metal. It whistled as he swung, winding a melody through the song of his steely purpose.

His grip tightened. The sword moved in arcs against the dawning sky. Each stroke was deliberate and precise. This was a dance honed by countless hours of ceaseless practice. Drake's body flowed through well-rehearsed patterns, muscles' memories guiding him as surely as any map for a ship navigator, or sheet music for a conductor.

Drake's blade moved with pure force and imposition upon anything he struck, like fire through ice. With each swing, Drake felt power released from a coiling within, as he had been trained. Sweat beaded on his brow despite the biting cold, tracing paths down flushed cheeks. This was his life, every day without end. He had tried and failed to get others to take this all as seriously as he did, as his father had taught him.

Grimness set deeper into his soul as he pushed onward through the pain, "saving it for the rain," as his father would say. Many questions remained past his father's mysterious death. A tremendous legacy loomed, a burden wrapped in motivation, entwined tightly. Drake felt compelled ever more to hone himself into a weapon as formidable as the sword he wielded, preparing himself to replicate what his father had done in battle.

The whistling crescendo of steel upon wood mingled with the rhythmic crunch of boots against snow and frozen earth. Each motion reaffirmed resolve, every breath fueled the inferno within that scorched away doubts and fears alike. This was meditative ritual as much as exercise and martial forms.

His foot slipped on packed ice, a mistake. He was able to correct for it at the last second and land with sword in defensive position, just as trained. He took special pleasure in moderating himself, as his father had taught him. Each end, no matter how small, was an opening to the beginnings of still greater moderation. Each mistake was an opportunity to develop correction.

Drake squatted, breathing deeply now. His gaze swept over the clearing, as though to check if anyone had witnessed his foul. He closed his eyes and rehearsed again, avoiding the packed ice that was there this time in his mind as well, before rising and trying again.

In moments of stillness like this, Drake invested in himself. He held glimpses of iron will and progress. Thoughts of triumphing over his wicked foes filled his mind. Reflections of his father, in personal visions greater and more embedded than the tales now in bards' retinues across the land. There were other shadows here too, stranger recollections shared by his father that nipped at these moments in peace.

Goblins were gone from Solipsia, banished by the actions of the heroes, yet questions remained which only multiplied with remembrances of his father's words. "The goblins came from the shadows, boy. Swarming like locusts, darkening the fields. Yet we stood, against the darkness and anything else."

Eldred had said that they would return, as he always knew they were still out there in the larger world.

It would take the whole kingdom by surprise. They were forced to wait for evil to rear its ugly head again, instead of preparing for it as a kingdom, pleas falling upon deaf authority. Therefore,

"Only action mattered," as Eldred would often say. Drake's actions were born of duty and would be finally executed in steel.

He resumed the martial dance from memory, sword singing once more. Every fiber of Drake's being screamed defiance against the creeping dread, each swing was a declaration of intent.

The sun ascended higher over Solipsia's frozen landscape. In Drake's exertions, his father's old tales would drift through his mind wildly. He strove towards this as if to capture all remaining warmth from an extinguishing fire, and the last embers of a dying light. Each strike with his sword against wood was a jarring reminder of extreme violence and its results, the steel to eventually meet flesh and bone.

The scents filled his lungs, high up there in the mountains. His body burned like a torch, slick with sweat despite the chill. Muscles screamed for respite, but onward he pushed, driven by the ghostly reminders of yesteryear and his father's truths.

His father's voice resonated in his memory, low and as grave as the tolling of a funeral bell. "Years had passed in peace and people became soft, just like now," Eldred would say, eyes reflecting distant horrors, "and that darkness crept over Solipsia like a plague then, just as it will again."

Drake often imagined the goblins swarming from shadowy chasms, their eyes glowing with an unholy light. Claws and teeth bared, they descended upon the villages and farms, once golden, now trampled underfoot. "They were all over the entire kingdom. Their war cries and shrieks filled the air," Eldred's voice rumbled on, "like the wailing of innumerable banshees."

Drake's grip tightened on the sword hilt, fingers tracing the worn grooves pressed in by his father's own fingers before him. He could almost feel the vibrations of battle, heroes clashing against evil.

"We fought them back," Eldred would continue, voice rising with fervor, "however they nearly overwhelmed us many times!"

He envisioned those heroes of his father rallying from every corner to bolster defenses. Blacksmiths left their forges, farmers abandoned plows, and scholars set down quills, with nobles donning armor alongside the common folk.

Drake's heart pounded the drum of war as he recalled his father's descriptions mid-forms, "The ground shook with our charge." Eyes gleaming with fierce pride Eldred waxed on, "Axes swung wide, arrows rained down like storm clouds unleashing fury."

Drake's breath hitched as he mimicked the fabled assault, imagining clans upon clans of goblins surging forward.

* * *

"The princess, heart of Solipsia, held captive within their deepest darkest cave den, became something for the multitudes to rally around in all that chaos," Eldred's voice strained as he recounted the rescue efforts, "We stormed their dens," he would say, "and we did not stop." The old hero's words generated vivid images. "And they fell before us like wheat."

Drake felt a shiver down his spine, not from cold but from the weight of his legacy. His father had led them all to victory. Eldred was Solipsia's man of hope against despair.

"If I train you correctly, the battle and camaraderie will shape you further, son. Our swords sang their grim songs as we had trained them to, and as the battle changed us," Eldred pronounced.

Drake's sword sang out its own song, as he prepared himself ever for the dark days approaching. The old tales were more than history as alive within him, shaping every breath, every movement.

"The battle for our lives bound us tighter than any chain," Eldred had spoken of the heroes' alliance fondly, "a bond forged in blood and fire, pain and sacrifice."

The sun climbed higher still, its golden tendrils stretching across the forest floor, gilding leaves and bark alike.

Most of the shadows retreated, hounded by daylight's relentless march. Yet within Drake, darkness lingered, as stubborn residue clinging to the corners of his soul. He straightened then, spine as rigid as the ancient oak beside him, resolve ever hardening with every thought and every action.

His father's legacy wasn't just fame nor stories by the hearth, but duty carved by his father's own hand into his very soul. Each form in practice added a new verse to his battle song, unvoiced yet unmistakably of Eldred's inspiration.

The fact that his father and the other heroes went unrecognized and mostly ignored by the royalty and authorities in the land infuriated Drake, not just out of loyalty to his father or friends, but out of loyalty for Solipsia itself, as well. It was such a missed opportunity for improved security of the kingdom.

Eldred's wrath had descended like a thunderstorm unleashed upon an unsuspecting valley. The battlefield stretched out beneath the heroes, a churning sea of murderous creatures pierced by the flame of their arson, licking hungrily at the sky. His sword had danced. The strokes of his blade carved paths through the seemingly endless masses of goblins.

The conflagration roared. Goblins had torched everything. The air was filled with acrid smoke and the grotesque smell of goblin blood. Heroes fought side by side, their voices raised in battle cries. Many dens hid throughout the land, a fine metaphor for the turmoil of goblins. Steel and strategy cut through the goblin ranks, leaving nothing in the wake of Eldred's heroes.

The old warrior moved with a ferocity born of patriotic desperation. His blade swung in trained fluidity. Each goblin felled brought him closer to safety for the kingdom, and so he pressed on, driven by all the lives that depended upon him.

His companions duplicated his fervor, their blades carving

through foes with similarly grim efficiency.

His own cousin, a beast of a man named Edmin, forge-hardened muscles gleaming with sweat and blood, wielded a hammer larger than most men could lift. He crushed many a goblin skull, like overripe fruit, roaring damnation all along the way. Eolande, another cousin yet more distant, was a great hunter who struck down many of the goblin leaders, bowstring relentlessly moving in the direction of strategic goblin deaths. There were many other heroes who helped with the eventual goblin downfall, too many to speak of.

Blood flowed like rivers across the battlefields in the heart of Solipsia, soaking into the earth, a crimson quagmire. The stench of death covered everything. The acrid scent of burning flesh was newest, heavy now like the disease and starvation. Eldred's heart pounded wildly as he hacked through wave after wave of attackers, his vision narrowing to a tunnel focused solely upon Solipsia's survival.

Each moment blended into an eternal nightmare from which there seemed no escape.

Gradually, the tide began to turn. Goblins fell in greater numbers, their shrieks of rage gave way to whimpers of fear and, in many cases, the tromping of boots as they fled. The heroes pressed their advantage, relentless in their efforts, and took out every den that could be found. No goblin was spared.

Goblins lay strewn across the earth like discarded dolls, twisted forms stark against the pallid grass. Heaps of corpses marked the spots where heroes had made their stands, their sacrifices etched forever in the grim geography. Eldred stood amidst the carnage, sword arm shaking from exertion and heart heavy with the weight of bloody victory.

Eldred surveyed the destruction as he led further search parties seeking out the princess.

Cheers rang out in great numbers only after they had found the princess, upon a more thorough inspection of one particular den which had been cleared. The chorus of jubilation seemed almost sacrilegious given such desolation and damage the goblins had done.

The solemn murmur rippled through the gathered heroes, long before they gave themselves leeway to celebrate at all. They knew well the price paid for this hard-fought victory... the bloodshed, the lives lost, the scars borne both visible and unseen.

Exhaustion, relief, internal celebration, and silence mingled in equal measures. The silence which followed the great upheaval was profound, almost unsettling for many heroes.

Eldred went about seeing to his soldiers' health immediately, honoring the dead, and seeing to messages being sent out for the nearest kin. His march across the land was heavy and quite solemn, hoping for additional survivors or more lost prisoners of the goblins, yet knowing there would be fewer by the hour. On this occasion he was on his way to personally deliver bad news to an exceptionally talented warrior's widow.

"Eldred," a voice then had called out, "Come see this." He followed the summons to an injured goblin captured in a particularly deep and remote bunker. He was unlike any they had encountered before. Its skin bore an unusual hue, paler and more human toned than the sickly green of its kin. Its eyes held a glint of intelligence rather than mindless malice, though still soaking in madness. It looked more aged, with too many wrinkles and hair that had gone beyond white and silver into translucent.

Eldred knelt beside it to meet it at eye level, locking gaze with the creature. "Who are you?" he asked, "And why do you look different from your kin?" The goblin coughed weakly, and then spoke in a language both strange and familiar, an archaic dialect tinged with the cadences of a Solipsia long past. "Yi hafta years... over others then twine passage," it rasped, "Yi servine... destruct thee, yim life all."

Eldred had said nothing and just frowned, standing up.

The goblin reached for Eldred's sword then as he stood, which prompted the guard to strike the murderous fiend mortally, though the creature disappeared before they could confirm the fact of it. This encounter left Eldred with questions that gnawed at him until the day he died. These questions would define how he raised his children.

The feeling of peace and ease settled upon Solipsia in a quietude that seemed almost too still, the attendant presumptions eventually settling into an unquestionable cement. Through cobblestone streets and over emerald fields, the air hummed with an undercurrent of tranquility. Tavern doors swung open to spill laughter and warmth onto the night air. Within, patrons leaned into one another's spaces, voices raised in spirited debate or excited discourse. Tattered maps spread on rough-hewn tables by heroes in boast, tracing their clever and courageous paths. Fingertips followed lines inked with daring deeds. Bards recounted all these tales far and wide. Others would eventually come to mock the great reverence held for the heroes, as the fear passed by Solipsia, an ironic testament in itself.

Children darted through market squares, sticks clutched like swords, eyes aglow with make-believe battles. "I am Eldred!" a boy called out, swiping his stripped branch through imaginary foes. His companions cheered, taking up cries of "For Solipsia!" and "Death to the goblin hordes!" Their shouts blended with the clatter of blacksmith's hammers and the bellowing of some nearby cattle.

***

Years had passed. Eldred died in a mysterious incident, which could not be accepted by Drake as accidental. Drake had inspected the felled tree himself, and believed he found evidence of goblin charm magic used at the scene, but he was ignored by the constables as usual. Five years since that event, and not a day went by without the impact of Eldred's death being felt fully by his son.

Shadows lingered in the corners of memory, refusing to dissipate despite good times had with friends nor heroic retellings of the bards. Rumors drifted like smoke from dying embers, carrying particles of ash and doubt.

Old women clicked their tongues over laundry basins, voices lowered to barely audible murmurs. "They say not all were slain," one said. Another nodded solemnly, "Ran away in the fog, more like. T'is a trick of the devil if ever there was." At least seven matronly voices crooned in united agreement at this pronouncement.

Many more, perhaps through optimism, pressure, or ignorance, dismissed such talk as mad ravings, which was just as well since this was the official stance of the crown, ever the more rotating with each new bearer.

Still, there were those strange-looking passers-by occasionally stirring unease through the villages. Travelers and merchants from faraway lands with skin tinted an off shade, eyes holding flecks of unfamiliar hue, and very strange facial features were less than uncommon throughout Solipsia as late. They kept to themselves, often speaking little and moving on swiftly, but their presence was enough to rile the locals nonetheless. Many claim these are just foreign tourists, encouraged to visit by the relative peace that Solipsia now enjoyed in its repose. Others disagreed.

Taverns had become more packed since those old days, more expensive, and more depressing. Late in the afternoon in the dim recesses of The Drowsy Badger, one particular forest tavern his own father used to meet with friends, Drake sat at a table and chair with a mug of ale. It had been purchased for him by another patron in honor of his father, yet it sat untouched before him. He was the frame of honed strength, with his short two decades of life spent in total dedication to mastering his father's art and science of fighting. He was lost in thought, as was usual for him. Across from him sat his sister, Telyn, her eyes wide and reflecting the flickering candlelight.

"Brother," Telyn spoke excitedly, though her voice still barely rose above the hum of the surrounding conversations, "you've always said this would happen, and now I heard rumor of a goblin gang escaping a band of constables. You and dad were right all along, I guess," she said as she scoffed to herself.

Drake nodded grimly, gaze fixed on some distant point beyond the tavern walls. He shivered as if chilled by some sudden gust from outside, but it was simply the phantom of old terrors embedded into his blood. Part of it had to be his training calling him back in reaction.

Finally, he began to speak, almost at the same time as Telyn, but she deferred and allowed him to continue. "Solipsia celebrated the heroes' victory," said Drake. "Bonfires burned, feasts lasted for days, and the monsters were forever gone, you know, and that's what everyone said. Dad and some others knew something was amiss, though." His hand curled into a fist.

Drake continued, "Joy itself has been robbed, now haunted by what goes unseen. Dad's battle defined his legacy. It's the crucible of everything I am. Father raised me in it. It drives me. The lies gnaw at me, sister, and hold my attention more than anything else. How many heirs to the throne have to die before anyone picks up on the fact that not all is well?" Drake's gaze flicked back to Telyn, her expression mirroring his own turmoil. "Battles change form instead of ending, from the steel and blood then to doubts festering in the dark now. Still I see it bubbling over into the seen. War comes again."

Drake sat with Telyn for a moment, in silence, before continuing, "Everyone thinks the legacy of our father was about triumph. It's not, it's vigilance. That's what put him front and center, Telyn. Primarily, it was always about his watchfulness, which is why they killed him." Tears formed in his eyes. "Beneath the banners and songs are all the unanswered questions which haunted dad. Even worse perhaps are the unasked questions. I just wish we could be more aware. It is more than strange that we cannot be and are not even allowed to be. You know how father tried with various authorities, and how I have since, but they take me even less seriously than him," Drake said as he dried his tears. "I'm almost taken more serious by the other heroes and their kin. I don't mean to complain."

She leaned forward then, voice in a low conspiratorial tone, "I remember he spoke of the way goblins… disappear. Do you recall? He said they could fade away like 'mist on the morrow'."

A muscle twitched in Drake's jaw. Memories surfaced against his will, hushed conversations held late at night, Eldred's voice grave and measured as he shared tales of old conflicts, battles fought long before Drake drew breath. The old hero would speak of goblins slipping away into nothingness, leaving naught but emptiness behind. Hardly ever would he say it around Telyn, though.

He pushed his untouched ale back towards Telyn and said, "Indeed, he did. That reminds me, I need to get back to training." He stood.

Telyn watched him go, concern in her expression, as he ducked out into the late afternoon air, tavern door swinging shut behind him. She couldn't shake the feeling that shadows now moved more swiftly than the flicker of the flame. She needed to get back to take care of their ailing aunt.

***

Beyond the tavern's walls, Drake stepped into the path, and embrace of the forest gloom along the way. Sunlight filtered from the horizon, dappling the snowy path worn icy, so that it sparkled.

He moved with purpose towards his training grounds for the nightly routine, in his clearing high up near the peaks.

There, by gnarled roots and ancient stones, Drake continually tested the limits of steel, body, mind, and will. His consistency in practice reminded him of who he was and what he was doing all of this for.

His blade whipped through air, carving arcs precise as mathematical equations, his father's theories of the blade as responsive against the enemy movements guiding every detail.

Beneath triumphs lay undercurrents of weakness which escape the many. Vigilance was ignored in preference for celebration, so that truths remained unspoken, which does nothing to change their reality. Warriors, like their battles, are chameleons to new landscapes, and the guise of new foes.

As Drake drove blade through phantom resistance, boards, or tree limbs, he knew: the fight for Solipsia's soul was already beginning. He was fortunate enough to be taught this truth his whole life, even if his father didn't understand all the details.

Each inhale of Drake's was determined and eager, his breath rapid, lungs burning with extreme effort in this dance of memory and might, pushing him to his edge. It was the primary and most appropriate form of communion he still had with Eldred.

Drake cut through the ritualized dances of blade and force, honoring past and manifesting his future actively in each movement. He barely felt the chill of, because he felt so much more here in everything he was doing.

The slipping horizontal sun cast his silhouette in a mosaic of light and shadow familiar to him. Drake's thoughts always turned inward through these moments. His eyes narrowed, as if peering through the veil of reality.

"Life," Eldred told him many times, "is never truly your own."

The words remained heavy even now. Drake bore the yoke with exuberance.

With deliberate slowness, he raised the sword once more. The blade slipped through air, a soft keen sound that harmonized with that wind through the barren tree limbs.

Rustlings at the glade's edge distracted him momentarily, the soft crunch of icy undergrowth yielding beneath familiar footsteps. Telyn emerged out of the evening, a worried expression on her face. Her gaze met his.

"Drake," she began. "King Asteri has been found murdered, and they are blaming the son of a hero."

Drake did not pause in his practice, sword continuing in its relentless movements. "I am not surprised," he replied, voice steady. "There is no rest for me, Telyn, not until Solipsia stands cleansed of shadows. Yet the shadows grow, and so must we."

"Drake," she murmured again, pleading now. "You cannot fight this alone, you cannot grow alone. Let others stand beside you, while you still have them to stand beside."

Drake's teeth ground together as if chewing on an unpalatable truth. "I've tried, you know that," he countered flatly, "they ignored me before, just as much as the king's men and constables. This ***current*** path has always been mine alone to tread, it seems."

Telyn watched him move through familiar motions and knew better than to argue further. "Very well," she conceded. "We must try to speak to them again, though. Remember, there are those who will stand who might not have before. They are blaming Balnor, son of Donmir, which could have just as easily been Drake, son of Eldred. It could be next time."

Her words echoed through Drake's mind as he finished the current rotation of forms. He knew well enough that regardless how alone he needed to be in this current situation, the coming path was assuredly not meant to be walked in solitude.

Drake stopped his training. Breath slowing, heartbeat steadying, he lowered his sword. Moonlight hit the blade, reflecting back a cold gleam that looked like the starlight above. He stood there a moment longer, surrounded by silence save soft sighs of forest breath, and smiled at Telyn before speaking again, "Maybe you're right, let's go take a look at what comes next. Anyway, it's too late for you to walk home alone." Then, sheathing the sword, he walked with her on the path back.

Solipsia slumbered beneath a gentle snowy shroud only now thawing, dreams stirring restlessly, haunted by the growing obstructions to the fading of light.

As they walked, Telyn spoke again, "This path. Hey Drake, do you remember that egg hunt where we smashed heads going for the same one?" She laughed out loud.

Drake laughed heartily at the memory, "And you know if either of us had been looking out, it would have never happened!"

"If a frog had wings, it wouldn't bump its butt jumping, Drake." Telyn continued to laugh. "The headaches afterward weren't funny, though."

Drake felt a great deal of gratitude to have his sister at moments like these, and his heart swelled with joy. Although the violent deaths of her natural parents and his father's adoption of her were certainly not enviable in any way, the events were similar enough to his own losses that they shared in more than simply memories of Eldred.

Drake nodded, a soft smile appearing at the corners of his mouth as he gazed ahead. The path before them back then was winding through verdant hills, under shadows cast by the same ancient trees.

He recalled their father, Eldred, running to help after the egg hunt incident, as though their lives depended on it. Tears welled in his eyes, and so he put the thought aside quickly, to continue the discussion of fond memories.

The air was cool and crisp, carrying with it the scent of pine needles and damp earth, a fragrance that always recalled the simpler days of their youth. "Those were the times," he said, voice low but filled with warmth, "when nothing could touch us."

Telyn's laughter filled the woods. "Touch us?" she chuckled, her eyes sparkling. "We were invincible, Drake! Or so we thought."

"Dad made us feel invincible," Drake contributed, as he looked away and ahead.

She paused, her expression softening as she turned to him, her voice barely above a whisper. "Do you remember the summer dad took us to that haunted forest? The one in the foothills he was obsessed with?"

Drake's gaze drifted to the horizon, as if he could see through the miles and years separating them from that long-ago week. "How could I forget?" he murmured. "Whisperwood."

"Yeah, that was it!" Telyn laughed again. "They did whisper!" she exclaimed. "You said they didn't, but I always felt you were just trying to be brave like dad." She shivered dramatically, her eyes wide with genuine horror.

Drake chuckled, the memories vivid and precious to him. "You were always the braver one, Telyn, always willing to tackle any problem head on." He looked at her then, his kid sister, now a young woman who had faced continuous loss and pain with resilience, in her persistent youthfulness. "You always charge forward with the same courage as when you were little. Why, even now you're the one pushing me onward to reach out to the heroes again, and here I am following you."

Telyn's expression sobered, her laughter fading like the ring of a distant bell. She reached out, gripping his shoulder, "Everything dad said was real, Drake. All of it. Don't you go getting yourself killed, that's why I'm pushing. You need people you can trust by your side. This is all going to get worse, and we're the only ones fully aware of just how bad it will be, it seems."

Drake felt a lump form in his throat, the weight of their shared past pressing down upon him like an ancient stone. He thought of their father. The memories were bittersweet, tinged with the sorrow of loss.

"Eldred," she whispered, the name a prayer on her lips. "He was our rock, wasn't he? Our anchor in the storm."

Drake just nodded, holding back the tears again.

They walked in silence for some time.

They were nearly home when their next door neighbor called out to them in the dark, while walking by, "A new king is to be crowned in Solipsia, Duke Gervin they say!"

All Drake could respond was, "Oh! Thank you for the news, Gerald!" He did not have anything actually nice to say about the news itself, neither did his neighbor.

As they continued home, Telyn whispered forlornly, "Oh no, that's the duke rumored to have done business with goblins! Right?"

Drake merely nodded solemnly, pining inwardly for the sureness that only came with his sword practice. "We do indeed have people to visit. You were right, Telyn."

CHAPTER TWO

EMPTY PROCEEDINGS

A darkness fell across the vast grand plaza square. The stones of the road, worn smooth by centuries of use, bore witness to yet another gathering of souls. This time the gathering was summoned not by battle cry nor fanfare, but by the passing of yet another king, a death which was celebrated by few and only quietly then.

The royal palace loomed above, a monument of white stone and imposing spires. Its balconies jutted out like stern brows, as though judging the sea of faces below. The grand hall of the palace, a vast chamber steeped in history, hummed in an undercurrent of tension that crowded the air like static before a storm.

Duke Gervin stood at the heart of it all, fortunately already a guest at the palace, available for the news of King Asteri's passing. He was clad in black robes shot through with silver threads. He was somewhat thin, giving the impression that he was also tall when he stood alone, but he was somewhat below average in height. Hands, long-fingered and pale, rested lightly on his belt adorned with jewels that caught the light like trapped stars. His billowing shirt was laced with the colors of the rainbow and made of some fabric nobody had ever heard of.

The duke's eyes, cold as flint and sharp as a hawk's, observed the assembled throng with an intensity that made commoners and nobles alike shift uncomfortably. It came off as a sneer, but this was no different from his usual expression, though few people understood how honest a presentation of his internal dialogs it was. He could not help it, even had he wanted to.

Nobles and dignitaries filled the hall, their silks and velvets a riot of colors against the stark white of the stone walls. Murmurs played upon the wealthy crowd like wind on hair.

Beneath the opulent trappings, an edge was ever present. The combined perfume in the room was overwhelming enough, but then the cloying sweetness of wine and imminent threat posed by the apparent host made for a heady mixture for most guests.

The duke's lips curled into a tight tiny smile that did not reach his eyes, a mere twitch of muscle that seemed more predatory than placating.

He turned away from the murmuring hordes, his attention drawn to a small cluster of figures huddled near the dais. His relatives, pale and nervous, exchanged anxious glances as he approached, their voices barely audible above the hum of the crowd.

"Your Grace," one ventured tentatively, a man dressed in an ancient ceremonial garb faded red, sporting too many folds and lapels though not enough leggings, with watery eyes and hands that fluttered like moths. "The preparations are complete," he sniveled, exactly as one might have anticipated by his appearance. "The people await the date of your ascension."

Gervin's gaze flicked to the crown resting on a velvet cushion atop an ornate table. It was a simple circlet of gleaming gold adorned with rubies. He reached out, fingers hovering just above the cool metal before thinking better of it and snatching his hand away abruptly.

"I trust all is in order," he replied, voice smooth as silk yet carrying an undercurrent of seriousness. "No... hitches in our plans?" His relatives exchanged glances once more, their discomfort palpable. One woman among them, a slip of a thing with mousy hair wearing enough fabric to stop a sword. She stepped forward hesitantly, lips pressed into a thin line.

"Your Grace," she implored, "There is uneasiness among the commoners about the goblins. Their presence here, in such numbers..."

Gervin's tiny smile returned instantly, tighter this time, more akin to a baring of teeth. "The visitors are mere merchants, ***dear*** cousin," he interjected, cutting her off mid-sentence but with a way of saying '**dear**' as though it were a curse. "Tourists, even. A sign of progress, would you not agree? Our kingdom opens its doors to new alliances, embraces change."

Her eyes flickered briefly towards the crowd before returning to meet his steadily. "The heroes... or I mean the descendants of those who saved us from goblin tyranny, they are up in arms, sir," she persisted gently. "And so too are many common folk. They remember, and the younger ones hear old tales with fresh fears..."

The duke's expression darkened almost imperceptibly. "Old fears have no place in our new dawn," he stated flatly. "Let the heroes tend to their vineyards and nurseries whilst we move ahead with our plans for a brighter Solipsian future. I anticipate there will be no problems." The phrasing terrified his relatives, as Gervin's abstract mentions of locations typically preceded concrete misfortunes for those implied.

He turned away then, and they were dismissed with a flick of his wrist. His relatives exchanged wary looks, their breaths coming shallow and quick, as though sharing some unspoken fear. It was true that his patriarchal actions brought the family considerable prominence, yet it had not been without heavy losses. They were beholden to him, and now they would be all the more entrapped by his machinations that he was to be king.

Gervin ascended the remaining ceremonial dais steps slowly. He turned and then looked around at those assembled with a small grin he could hardly contain, as though unable to believe his good fortune.

The grand hall held a collective breath, awaiting his next words.

Clasping his hands before him in a demonstration of solemn piety, he pretended to pray. He always found this a useful ploy, especially when he didn't know exactly what to say next.

After his little charade he politely coughed and then began to speak to the assembled crowd, "The coronation next week marks not merely my ascension to the throne," he declared, lengthening certain syllables for desired effect, "but the birth of a new era."

Pauses between phrases allowed his words to sink in, to take root in the minds of listeners. He was skilled at this, despite his rather toxic persona.

He continued, "An era of progress, of unity under a single banner." He swept his arms wide in a gesture mean to encompass not only the palace but the city as well, and the sprawling kingdom beyond it walls. "Look around you! See how our walls stretch tall, how trade routes crisscross like arteries, pumping life into every corner of Solipsia! Where would we be without all that commerce? Without our funding?"

A murmur rippled through the crowd, stirred by uncertainty. Faces upturned, eyes wide with apprehension or awe, some nodding along while others exchanged glances laden with doubt. A woman of an old merchant family, clutching a child to her chest, leaned close to whisper in her neighbor's ear. A strange foreigner strained to hear. An elderly noble nearby, lips pursed, shook his head slowly as his clawed hands nervously clutched his cane.

"I stand before you today," Gervin continued, voice swelling in imitation of passion, "a man of his people. I want the best for Solipsia, and so Solipsia will have the finest of everything. I love Solipsia and wish to see it improved. The people need to be educated, and not allowed to wallow in ignorance. Together we will mend what ails our land, give our plagued a chance, offer guidance, and build a bridge to a brighter future for all!"

His words painted sweet little images, alluding to rebirth, repair, refinement, and education. Despite his many promises, the discordant notes stood out to those actually listening, like dropped bells. For the common sentiment among the people was that nobody had summoned him, nor asked for his reign. Kingship was defaulting to him. His ascent was nobody's choice, rather it was accomplished by manipulation and mayhem, as well as murder, or so it was rumored. The crown was heaviest upon the brows unseen, unaccounted, and the bloodied in the fight for succession.

"Injustices shall be righted," Gervin vowed, fist clenched now, voice ringing out across the palace main hall. "Crimps in our society will be smoothed away, so all may flow freely, and then the commerce will enrich us all beyond your wildest dreams! Change is upon us!" he proclaimed. "Embrace it! For I tell you together, we will create something new and exciting!"

Then came some applause, scattered at first, then swelling into a steady stream of hoots and shouts. Many cynics in the crowd relented and gave into the applause as well. This man was to be king, and that meant something after all, especially if one intended to live within his kingdom.

A few stood who did not clap, nor did they cheer. Their expressions remained stoic and unyielding, to future king or otherwise. Amongst them were descendants of heroes. Their eyes held steadfast, reflecting nothing born of his speech.

"Merchants!" king-in-waiting Gervin yelled out, voice booming once more. "Trade! Prosperity for Solipsia! Let the celebrations begin now!"

* * *

The cheer spread and swelled like an ocean, drowning out the potential for questions, or doubters to speak them. The drunken celebrations commenced with exuberant depravity. The alcohol flowed freely and cheaply. As was only fair, the drunken crowds praised the king-to-be.

Banners unfurled like tongues of flame, their vibrant hues painting the streets in swathes of crimson, azure, and emerald.

Flowers cascaded from windowsills and balconies, raining petals onto the heads of passers-by. The flowery scent was so very pleasant, mingling with the aroma of roasting meats and sweet pastries wafting from open market stalls. Many would remember these days for months to come.

Through this riot of color and fragrance serpentined strange parades, dispensing alcohol and potions freely day after day. Musicians and dancers led the charges in debauchery as criers of sin, directing the vulnerable to its merchants and purveyors. Relentlessly, they plied their trade in 'medicines,' taking advantage of the vulnerable in Solipsian society. They blew their bronze horns everywhere to announce their presence, and disrupting life at all hours. Drums roared in primal rhythms thumping with the basest of human desires, urging the weakest in virtues to give in to the revelry and match the frenetic pace.

The parades of sin wound through wide streets and tight alleys as well, where walls leaned close together. The ancient stones bore witness to centuries through happiness and strife in equal measure, but never before to such travesties of degradation as these. Onwards the degenerate crowds surged day and night, into all the squares of the city. For a week, frivolity took hold throughout the kingdom, funded freely from Duke Gervin's coffers.

More merchants arrived by the day to ply their trades with voices accented in ways nobody had ever heard before. Local merchants had their businesses destroyed by frolickers in the deep nights, who would torch the buildings and steal anything not on fire. Many suspected the drunken parades, but they were too powerful, having become defacto mafias within days, perhaps hours, empowered by Gervin as they were.

The features on the faces of these merchants and paraders bore traces of something ***else***, and more than simply regional differences between tribes. Their stalls and parade floats were laden with wares exotic and strange. It seemed everyone wanted something from them. Trinkets wrought from odd metals, shimmering fabrics like moonbeams on water, and rarest magic potions sealed in glass vials as dark as midnight.

Foreign performers too added their own flavor to festivities. Acrobats bounded forth like sprites loosed from captivity. They tumbled, flipped, and cartwheeled alongside the drunken revelers. Children laughed, pointing fingers at somersaulting forms that seemed to defy gravity's stern edicts. At night, however, it was anyone's guess what these acrobatic strangers used their talents to get into, or where.

Nearby, jugglers whirled batons aloft like miniature comets, their fiery ends casting sparks adrift in the spectacle. Gasps rippled through the drunken and debauched crowds, as flaming projectiles soared high above heads bent back in awe.

Dancers pirouetted with grace fluid yet unsettlingly jerky, limbs contorting at angles previously considered not intended by nature. Their motions induced unease, akin to watching spiders spin intricate webs. Many eyes remained fixed, riveted by the scene at once both enthralling and repellent.

A group of these dancers fluttered like moths on wing, congregating near fountain edges and wherever a liquored bonfire could be found. Bells jangled at wrists and ankles, complimenting musicians' discordant melodies.

"Look," a voice hissed nearby. A matronly woman in an apron stained from market labors nudged her neighbor, an elderly man leaning heavily upon his cane. "See how they move? Not natural."

The elderly man, her husband, grunted as he studied the figures whirling before the fountain in ways he had certainly never seen. "Aye," he rumbled eventually. "Like puppets pulled by strings." He shook his head, expression souring further. "Not right anyway. All this... insanity. Strangers among us, prancing about at all hours like they own the place."

The woman shivered, wrapping her shawl tighter around the shoulders. "Mark my words," she muttered darkly, gaze fixed upon the strange entertainers. "This won't end well." She pulled her husband into their house with her.

* * *

Drake walked down one of the quieter Solipsian streets, his cloak billowing behind. He paused at the mouth of an alley, where a stench of rotting vegetables mingled with something sharper, more acrid, likely a hint of whatever exotic wares lined nearby stalls.

A merchant hawked his goods there. His appearance unsettled Drake. There was just something about the depth of yellow in the merchant's eyes or how his skin was pitted like old leather, in a way that did not seem possible for living skin.

"Come see, come see!" the merchant cawed, voice grating as rusty hinges. "Bells that sing in winds from lands unseen! Potions that grant visions of far-off realms!"

Drake watched as a mother hurried her children past, eyes averted from the strange offerings.

The merchant's gaze followed them, staring too long for comfort. Drake took the opportunity to continue walking.

Some strange looking women were dancing in the doorway of the next building, in which another foreign merchant had set up shop.

A blacksmith's forge roared nearby, hammer clanging against anvil in rhythmic fury. Drake overheard gruff voices rising above metallic thunder. "Who are they? Where are they from?" The smithy bellowed, pausing mid-swing to glare at a group of foreign merchants drunk and snickering as they passed, speaking in some unknown language.

"Never seen such folk before," the apprentice replied, wiping sweat from his brow. "They pay good coin for our iron though."

The smith scoffed, resuming his work. All he could do was share his hard won wisdom, "Coin's no comfort if they bring trouble to our doorstep." He spat into the flames, sending up a hiss like some obscenity.

Drake moved on. In the market square, an older matron walked quickly, children clutched protectively against her skirts as she tried to make her way past drunkards and revelers. Her eyes were consistently distracted by a troupe of dancers gyrating before an enchanted crowd. Bells jangled wildly from their limbs, jittery motions in appeal to the base desires of men, without concern for its purpose.

The woman's lips curled in silent revulsion as she turned away a final time and pushed through the crowds. "Come, little ones," she murmured, voice barely audible over the atrocious noise. "No need for you to see such things."

Drake's gaze hardened as he watched the dancers twist and turn, limbs bending at angles that sent unease prickling down his spine. He pushed through throngs of the spectators, seeking a familiar haunt.

Eyes flicked towards Drake as he entered the dimly lit tavern, then darted away again as quickly, with shadows retreating into their corners once more. Drake was a known variable. He approached a table tucked near the hearth, where old warriors nursed drinks.

"Drake," Gearon, brother of Balnor, greeted gruffly, raising his tankard in acknowledgment, though with a sad expression. "Long time since you darkened our door."

Drake nodded, pulling up a stool and sitting. "Too long, perhaps. There are more shadows now than ever, so I make it no darker with this visit." He looked over the weathered faces before him.

Several of them had stood beside his father in Solipsia's hour of greatest need, and personally helped build the legends. Others, like Gearon or Balnor, were descendants of heroes, or otherwise warriors he had come to respect. They were all currently drunk at Gervin's pleasure, every one to the man.

"Aye," another son of a hero grunted nearby. "But some shadows are best left undisturbed, lad."

Drake lowered his voice to project his intensity. "Can't you see? They're back!" The words hung heavy between them, punctuated by crackling flames. "Shadows are creeping in. You think they mean you no harm?"

Before anyone could answer the question, Drake turned to Balnor's mourning brother, "Gearon, I needn't even ask, Balnor is innocent, I know this. We already all know he was set up. He's locked up, and we're all next."

An old grizzled warrior, Draid, shook his head, eyes reflecting the dance of firelight. "We fought the goblins once," he rumbled. "This isn't a battlefield anymore, Drake."

Drake stood and grabbed the warrior's shoulder. "Exactly," he insisted. "Troubles brew. We can avoid the bigger battlefields later, if we act now! Today it's all economic exchanges and commerce, but months down the line we will see what they trade you when the king friendly to their cause outlaws heroes, who are all that stand against the goblin menace."

The old warrior sighed, patting Drake's hand before withdrawing it gently yet firmly. "You're your father's son," he said softly. "Always ready to charge where angels fear to tread."

Drake's expression darkened as he looked away.

The weight of expectation settled heavy on Drake's shoulders. "Then I'll keep charging," he declared, voice breaking through the hush. "Hopefully you all catch on before it's too late. And indeed, I am my father's son, but I speak as a man who cares deeply for Solipsia, and I ask you to stand against the darkness with me."

He paused. "You think a kingdom is merely about the gold and goods?" he continued, voice low but intense, "There are now goblish merchants peddling wares in our markets. Mark my words: every coin that changes hands with these new favorites of Gervin's coming regime is a seed of chaos against our kingdom."

Drake straightened, and lifted his shoulders as he drew himself up to his full height. "You fought beside my father," he said, looking Draid in the eyes, his voice resonating with pride. "You stood shoulder to shoulder with heroes who carved legends from the very stone of this land. And now, you sit here, nursing your drinks and your memories, as if all battles were behind us."

He shook his head, a grim smile playing at the corners of his mouth. "But our battles in life never truly end," he declared. "They merely change form. The goblins may no longer march in armies, but they infiltrate our streets, our homes, our very hearts. They trade not just in goods, but in deceit. Their currency is lies, and they spend it freely. 'They lie and then lie after they lie'," he stated, some of them recognizing the words of Eldred.

Drake's eyes flashed like steel as he looked around the room, his voice rising to fill every corner of the tavern. "You think this is about money or economics? It is not! It is about the soul of Solipsia, and whether we will let it be corrupted from within."

He leaned in closer, his voice dropping to a low growl. "My father fought against the goblins because he saw the threat they posed, not just to our lives, but to our very way of being. And I tell you now, that threat is as real today as it was then. Perhaps even more so, for we have grown complacent."

Drake's fist slammed down on the table, making the tankards jump and the warriors flinch. "We must not let this rot take root!" he cried out, his voice echoing through the tavern like thunder. "We must stand together, as we once did, and ***drive back* the darkness that seeks to engulf us**!"

He looked around the room, his eyes meeting each warrior's gaze in turn. "I know you are wary and frightened," he said softly, "but I also know you weary of war and weary of loss, and that so much was lost during the heroes' war. However, I ask you this: is it not better to fight now, while there is still hope, than to wait until the darkness has claimed us all?"

Drake stepped toward the door to the tavern, with shoulders squared and hand on pommel of sword. "I, for myself, shall never stand idly by and watch our kingdom fall," he declared. "Neither should you. We are Solipsia, and we do not bow to shadows. For Solipsia!"

"***For Solipsia***!" many responded instantly.

The tavern fell silent, the only sound the crackling of the fire and the drunken celebrations outside. Drake's gaze swept over them one last time.

"You all know where to find me," he said, and then walked back out through the door, into the intoxicated evening.

Drake sought solution and not simply solace nor solitude, but alliance. He hoped to kindle embers of resistance. Mostly what he found, though, was behavior unbecoming of his Solipsia.

***

Drake had arranged a small meeting for the next day at the northern outskirts of the capital city. Weaving through the crowds of revelers, he ducked into a narrow alley, where the sun barely penetrated at all, and then down into a basement.

There, huddled in the dark room next to a great furnace, the group awaited him. Mostly young faces stared back at him, some descendants of heroes and some others with concerns, born after the great battles that had shaped their realm's history. Their eyes held neither the fire nor the scars of war, but instead carried equal parts fear and curiosity.

"Listen to me," Drake began, voice low yet fervent. "The kingdom stands at a precipice. That Duke Gervin has welcomed goblins and obviously goblish strangers into our midsts, and he's about to be king. He spends his own wealth now because he will soon have all of ours as well, spendthrift in frivolities day and night as if the gold notes were leaves from autumn trees, and for what? Parades which have turned into gangs, and the proceeding events to follow in vain pomp and emptiness. He poisons the people in intoxicants, and many ignorantly go along with it."

Some shifted uncomfortably. There was a murmur among the few assembled, while others smirked, unconvinced. "Gervin says he brings prosperity," a young woman opened up. "You speak ill of our future king, Drake Eldredson. Perhaps you're just bitter because the tales of your father's heroism grow stale."

Drake thought for a moment and then answered calmly, "Stale are the words spoken by those too blinded to see danger lurking in plain sight." He turned to address them all, gesturing with urgency but remaining calm despite his passion. "These goblish types; the merchants, the performers, the transient businesses, and what have you, they're not simply engaged in usual commerce. They're not even human, but goblins using magic to create illusions. My father saw them before. They're not as rabid as those goblins in his day, but they're even more vindictive, and therefore craftier in their evil."

Telyn, who had already arrived ahead of Drake, stepped forward in the gathering, her voice steady and clear. "I've seen them too, Drake," she said, her words carried weight despite their gentleness. "There's an air about these 'people'... something unsettling." The room fell silent, save for muffled sounds of the drunken festivities in full swing outside. Then knocking came from the door up to the alley, shattering the quietude.

A patrol of guards, clad in polished armor that glinted maliciously even in dim light, pulled the doors up and open. Their boots clanged against the stone steps like a grim metronome, heralding discord rather than order.

The sight of the guards set the assembly on heel, as they rushed for other exits. Drake angled himself protectively between the guards and his young audience.

"Halt!" barked one guard. "What goes on in here?"

Drake met their gaze unflinchingly. "We exchange thoughts freely," he replied. His voice remained steady despite the rising tension.

The patrol leader sneered. "Thoughts can be treasonous, boy." His eyes narrowed as they swept over those remaining behind him, including Telyn, then returned to Drake. "Speak your business quickly."

Anger surged within Drake at their brash intrusion and implicit threat towards his friends and family. He clenched his fists but kept control of his tongue. "Our business is honest discourse," he retorted sharply.

The guard's grip tightened around his club, a simple truncheon. He took a step closer, trying to loom over Drake menacingly while being roughly of equivalent height. "Then say what you will, but make it brief and move along."

Drake stood firm, jaw set in stubborn resolve. The two locked gazes for what felt like an eternity, with neither willing to back down. "You have no cause to harass honest citizens," Drake growled finally. His eyes never left those of the guard. Then Drake came right out and said it, "Chemical and magical potions pushed on our children by strangers right out there, profiteering on our little ones. Here you are, though, bothering us as we discuss your own failures in it. What about duty and loyalty? Who is responsible for your errors?"

“Our duty and loyalty,” returned the lead guard, eyes still locked, “is to our incoming king, Gervin.”

“Of course, and what does he know of duty and loyalty, bringing in such influences among our most vulnerable?” asked Drake.

A tense silence hung heavy between them before the leader spat out, “Disperse! All of you… go get drunk or something.”

Those who had remained of the small gathering exchanged uneasy glances but began to drift away slowly, leaving Drake alone with Telyn and a handful of others who lingered defiantly.

As the last stragglers vanished into the night, Drake turned towards Telyn, relief mingling with anger. “We must be vigilant,” he murmured. “Gervin’s hold will grow only stronger, as our kingdom suffers.”

* * *

Meanwhile, high above in Solipsia’s towering palatial citadel, Gervin sat ensconced within opulence. Chambers hummed with courtiers and workers, newer and more numerous by the day. Many of the most sycophantic clustered about him, bustling and busy with preparations.

Word first reached his ears as mere background noise, in the name ‘Drake Eldredson.’ The mention pierced his haze. “I know this name, Drake, son of Eldred, what do I know him from? Tell me.”

His foreign advisors exchanged knowing glances before one particularly thin and monstrous advisor stepped forward cautiously. “A troublemaker,” he murmured, lips curling in disdain. “The son of that genocidal animal, Eldred. He has a sister and some cousins.”

Gervin’s brow furrowed as he spoke without reaching anger, “Drake Eldredson must be dealt with, plainly. See to it! Make his connections to Balnor, and indict him, whatever it takes. Kill anyone associated with him, but bring him to me, and his sister, who I can probably use against him." His plans for the kingdom hinged on total control, and he intended to see this control enforced.

* * *

In the hush of Edmin's homestead, days had drifted by since Drake's tense exchange with the king's men. Gervin's inauguration was the next day, and Drake intended on being there. Edmin's home was closer to the city, where Drake needed to be.

Edmin and his sons were some of his most important allies, of the few he could rely on most.

It was a stormy night, and rumbling thunder matched distant lightning. The air within the sturdy walls remained thick with the scent of hearth smoke and the trappings of shared histories.

Edmin, a massive and stalwart figure now with a beard as white as the receding snow, moved about his dwelling with an economy of motion that belied his years and size. His sons, Agbal, Erdon, and young Kenid, flitted around like shadows cast by their father's vigor.

Each bore unmistakable features of Eldred's anciently noble Ædlertuwin lineage, with sharp eyes and jaws set firm against the tides of fortune and banditry, yet fortunes never found any of their branches. They generally were not looking. Proud and unrelenting, the line had remained warriors with noble hearts instead of nobility, titles having fallen rather to the monied, ignoble, and willing to debase themselves over time.

Drake, on a wooden stool near the hearth, discussed things with Edmin, as Telyn sat nearby. They had discussed all there was to discuss regarding the incoming king, and goblins, as far as Drake cared to focus upon for the many days stay.

The conversation had moved on to family matters. "Endra holds strong," Drake offered, his voice steady despite the turmoil within him. "Though her breath grows shallower each day."

Edmin nodded grimly. "Aye, the old tree bends but does not break." Edmin's words were always affirming and supportive when speaking of Eldred or any of his close kin. His gaze moved freely to Drake, Telyn, and back to his sons. He then gestured to his youngest son, "Young Kenid here, he reminds me of you at that age, Drake. Same spark in his eyes."

Telyn looked up, with toiled expression. "We must rally the others," she said softly. "The heroes who remain, and their kin. United we stand a chance against this tide of darkness."

Lightning struck in the distance and thunder rolled.

Something within Drake wished to cringe at his sister rehashing it all but could not, out of his genuine respect for her, and the seriousness of the topic. He reminded himself that it was the situation which wore upon him, and due primarily to his own obsession. It was not her at all, and she meant the best. She had every right to wish for the focus to remain on it.

Edmin leaned back, his chair creaking under his great weight. "United, yes. But many have grown complacent, or frightened. Gervin's grasp tightens like a noose." He paused, his voice dropping to a near-whisper, "We must tread carefully though, lest we find ourselves silenced as Eldred was."

Drake flinched at the mention of his father. The memory gnawed at him, an eternal wound, Eldred's lifeless body crushed. An accident, they said, of course, but Drake found enough evidence to convince himself otherwise. It reminded him of Edmin's own wife, who had also died under mysterious circumstances only two years before Eldred's demise.

Drake tried to change the topic, "We need to meet more on the outskirts of the kingdom, we may even need to move permanently. This will probably become more apparent and important than ever after the coronation."

Agbal, Edmin's eldest son, spoke up from where he stood by

the door. "We'll help organize Drake, whatever you need," he declared, his voice firm. "Move in secret, plan out strategies, gather supplies, or anything else."

The middle child, Erdon, chimed in with a pragmatic question, typical of him, "But what of those already taken? Rumor has the dungeons beneath the citadel quietly filling with allies as we speak." His words hung heavy in the air.

The conversation continued late into the night, as such important discourse tends to do, fueled by determination and dread.

***

Eventually, the fire dwindled to embers, and the house settled into quiet slumber. Drake and Telyn had couches to sleep on in the main living area. His mind was racing with plans and fears. Kenid slept fitfully nearby, wishing to stay close to Telyn, his small frame tucked under a pile of furs.

Silence reigned until a faint rumble disturbed Drake's sleep. It was not the distant growl of thunder of earlier, but something more sinister, a rhythmic pounding of the ground that sent shivers down his spine as his eyes widened. He stirred, straining to listen. The sound grew louder, accompanied by a creaking groan as if the very earth shifted beneath the homestead.

Drake shot up, heart hammering. Nearby, Telyn slept on. Kenid moved but did not wake. Drake's eyes darted around the room, landing on the door, a massive oak barrier now creaking at the rhythm. His breath hitched as realization dawned.

He acted swiftly, his instincts honed by years of martial training and spiritual guidance by his father. He called out as loudly as he could to his cousins, "**TROLLS**!" Nobody responded, and he dared not say another thing until he saw to the safety of Telyn and Kenid.

He shook Telyn awake, then scooped Kenid into his arms. The

boy's eyes fluttered open, confusion taking over his face. Drake pressed a finger to the child's lips and hurried them along.

The back door groaned open onto an alleyway which ended in a moonlit courtyard. Drake scanned the shadows, then ushered Telyn and carried Kenid to the door. He turned just as the front wall of the house splintered inward with a deafening crash.

A monstrous figure loomed in the doorway, a troll, its hulking frame towering over the wreckage. Behind it, more shapes moved, gaunt silhouettes of goblins scuttling like vermin.

Drake's blood ran cold, feeling the need to run upstairs to alert his other kin, but being unable to without endangering Telyn and Kenid. The one advantage he held for them was silence in that moment, and so he made the tough decision.

They melted out into the night, hearts ripping through their chests as they moved. The trolls muffled their noise, so all that could be heard was the crushing of Edmin's home.

Drake glanced back once, catching a fleeting glimpse of Edmin's home engulfed in chaos. Guilt clawed at him, guilt for leaving his kin behind, for not turning back perhaps as soon as Telyn and Kenid were at some theoretically safe distance.

Any guilt was gone as a troll appeared silently to the side of them. It skulked, moving slowly as though in search for them and yet missing entirely. Drake put his hands over the mouths of Telyn and Kenid and gently led them into another alleyway to the side and away from the sneaky troll. Indeed, what was actually a safe distance from trolls and goblins sneaking upon someone stealthily in the night?

As they fled deeper into the night and forest, Drake's mind raced. What was a safe distance?

He hoped his cousins could scatter like seeds on the wind. Behind him, the sounds of destruction faded, replaced by the distant wails of death. Kenid and Telyn, recognizing the screams of Edmin,

Agbal, and Erdon, held back their cries of dismay.

In the early hours, Drake, Telyn, and Kenid were able to make it back to their home shared with Aunt Endra. Telyn and Kenid were miserable with sadness, understandably so. Drake did not take anything for granted, however. He hired a horse-drawn carriage ran by a local townsman he knew personally for years, to take Telyn, Kenid, and Endra away to the Silver Keep, in await of his return. He had something to see, and perhaps something to take care of, so he planned.

CHAPTER THREE

CROWNED IN DEBT

Duke Gervin, resplendent in his coronation finery, fresh from plotting his next injurious moves, swept through the throng of drunken excesses he purchased. His attire shimmered like captured sunlight. His black cloak billowed behind him. Otherwise, he was some kind of cascading rainbow river. The fabric was said to be as difficult to acquire as it was to look at for too long.

Gervin cast kaleidoscopic shadows on the marble floors as he walked among strobing torches alight in cycling colors.

Musicians from faraway lands played songs. The songs were alien to Solipsia and most of the nobles, but familiar to the foreign craftsmen and revelers. They swarmed around hastily constructed temporary shrines dedicated to faux greatness and wanton perversion. Gervin paused mid-stride, his gaze sweeping over the bustling crowd.

A scurrying figure, one of the royal advisors of Asteri's remaining court bowed deeply, clutching a number of notebooks in his arms and hands. "Your Majesty! If you have a moment, I'd like to discuss costs, waste, and security concerns. Do you have any idea how much is being spent on the food?"

Gervin nodded, satisfaction gleaming in his eyes as he listened, looking up at the foreigner workers pounding their hammers to the beat.

"Okay, well did you know there's real gold on these parade floats? That cost a lot too! Who is going to pay for all this, exactly? You know those parades are recruiting and corrupting kids, and abusing them. They're already using the gold to fund more potions and their prostitution operations. You're having the guards root out rebels instead of dealing with this?"

Gervin chuckled gleefully.

Feasting tables groaned under the weight of culinary excess: slabs of meat glistening with spiced juices, towers of pastries dusted in gold leaf, and mountains of candied fruit piled beyond balance. Servants darted to and fro, their arms laden with platters heaped high.

"Enjoy I say! While you can!" Gervin commanded, gesturing gracefully towards the feast like some great benefactor. "Eat! Drink! This is a celebration!"

"The cost..." the man murmured again, eyes darting nervously around the lavish display. Gervin was already walking away.

"Unseemly," someone beside the advisor agreed, barely audible over the clamor. "And who are all these craftsmen from other kingdoms doing here? Why not employ our own artisans?" Their concerns were lost in the mix as musicians struck up another rhythmic frenzy. Drums pounded like a distant storm, while pipes trilled alien melodies.

"What is this racket?" grumbled an elderly Solipsian noble, scowling at the strange-looking musicians perched on a makeshift stage in even stranger attire. Their skin bore a sheen under the torchlight, facial features larger and sharper than those of any local minstrel.

The dancers who wound through the crowd were no less unsettling, their limbs painted with spiraling patterns that moved on their skin. The shifting and writhing of the tattoos with each undulation rivaled the oddity of the contortions in the limbs themselves. They held wands of light, the cast of which made the moving tattoos glow along with their eyes.

Above, acrobats tumbled through the air, trailing ribbons of silk that snaked and coiled around them.

"Impressive," acknowledged a burly warrior, watching as one

darted between pillars with feline grace. Yet his hand rested on the pommel of his sword.

Two older ladies were sitting on their porch, watching events outside the palace, where there were similar dancers.

"Look at 'em," one of the matron's eyes narrowed at the gyrating figures as she spoke. "They move like serpents. It's unnatural."

Her companion whispered back, "Yeah sure, but have you seen their noses?" They laughed in unison.

Gervin seemed oblivious to the undercurrents of disquiet, basking instead in the adulation of his intoxicated subjects. "More wine!" he roared, raising a goblet encrusted with jewels that caught the light like captured stars. "Let rivers flow with it! Make sure this bride is good and drunk! We're going to need it..."

The assembled cheered and swayed to the music, their voices projecting through vaulted ceilings adorned with garlands of dead flowers necromantically enchanted into stasis.

* * *

The chamber fell silent as Gervin ascended the dais, his boots clicking upon the polished stone like the rim of a funeral drum. The temporary throne awaited him, a monstrosity of gilded wood and velvet cushions, its back towering like a cruel parody of regal power. He kneeled himself before the throne, hands clasped together in mock prayer.

An ancient black-robed and short figure completely unknown to anyone in Solipsia, eyes sharp, stepped forward from the shadows, holding the crown like it was equipment for the purposes of sport. A staff, twisted and dark, stomped the ground ahead of him with more force than should have been possible in the grip of his other claw of knuckles. His face was wrinkles, so that any other features were largely unnoticeable, but they were more knotted than his hands.

The little old figure raised the staff high, voice like a stone dragged through a temple, screeching across the hushing silence. "Errrr, no powers in crowns! Ye whom might seek greater power must take!"

All the drunken revelers became quiet, struck in awe at the strange event, with none fully comprehending what any of it meant.

Drake, who had snuck in easily enough disguised as a foreigner, watched from the shadows.

The old man was very strange, and a stranger to all, but somebody important somewhere all the same. There was an aura about him, as though far beyond the age of normal men. His face was scarred and empty of any expression.

Never had Drake heard of such an event in Solipsian history where a stranger crowned the new king, plainly a foreign ritual.

"Gervin," intoned the small queer stranger standing before the genuflecting duke, "Son of..." what he said briefly here nobody could understand, but Drake knew the name of Gervin's father was supposed to be 'Dairger.' Drake thought he heard something like "Ninbithinim," without any apparent vowels.

The old man resumed with cold finality. "You kneel before me today, a creature of ambition, seeking to elevate yourself beyond the station of mere king. That ambition is granted b..."

The foreign priest stopped himself, as his gaze swept over the assembled crowd looking momentarily relieved, and proceeded, "Yet, power is not bestowed lightly. It must be seized, wrested from the jaws of doubt and resistance." His eyes flickered back to Gervin, piercing and unyielding. "Do you accept this burden?"

Gervin's smile was sharp as a blade. "I do," he declared, voice ringing out clear and strong as he opened his eyes.

The ancient figure nodded, slowly lowering the staff before letting it drop upon the duke's head. Gervin did not react to the pain.

“Then rise,” the priest commanded, “Rise, Emperor Gervin, of all lands you dominate! Take power!”

Gervin pushed to his feet, shoulders squared as if bracing against an invisible weight. He produced a sword as he stood, and brought it up into the air in a quick jerky motion before striking the old ancient figure down, in one motion cutting through head and halfway through the chest, with blood gushing all over the throne and the new emperor.

The little old figure gave no flinch, with eyes closed as the sword was lifted into the air and brought down, as though in anticipation.

The citizens of Solipsia all fell silent at this, drunk as they were. Nobody dared to scream, though everybody wanted to. This was supposed to be a sacred event.

Drake was in absolute shock, never had he anticipated such a horror taking place at that moment. Nothing his father had ever said could have prepared him for this.

Cheers cut through the morbid silence, erupting from the throngs of foreigners, strangers, and shadows, thunderously relentless. Inhuman voices could be heard, laughing and shouting deeply from the shadows in victory, as the ground itself shook.

Gervin stood alone now atop the dais, next to the split body falling to the ground. He picked up the bloody crown, which had been dropped next to the throne, and set it upon his head. He turned towards the people with face, hands, and sword covered and dripping in blood. Lifting the sword, he commanded, “Whoever wants it, come take it!” His gaze swept over the crowd, but mostly the assembled nobles. Their eyes all now wide, and wanting to look away, but daring not with faces stuck in upturned positions out of fear. “Nobody? Good.”

“Citizens,” he addressed the stunned crowd. “Foreigners, too,” he smiled widely, as the cheers died down. “Today marks my ascension as well as our collective elevation." A hopeful murmur of approval rippled through some of the Solipsian groups, but was drowned out by the cheers of the many foreign and strange elements. Gervin's lips curved into a smile while eyes gleamed with malice.

"We will found an empire unparalleled in history. Borders will fall, and we will all be united under common purpose. Together we shall reign supreme! I am prepared to crush any who dare stand in the way." Gervin marched away from this threat, the dark robed figure melding into the darkening depths of the palace. "Drink! Do as you will!" he called out from nowhere.

* * *

The reveling persisted unabated. The grand banquet hall of Solipsia's royal palace became a den of lusts and ills. Drake stood at the periphery, still in shock at what he had seen at this coronation. He was lost after witnessing such a sickening event unprecedented in Solipsian history. It all turned his stomach.

Nobles, once somewhat dignified at least in appearance, now danced in wild abandon with strange foreign harlots despite being married. Foreign men, with slimy off-colored skin and beady eyes, moved through the crowd with lustful expressions, eager for innocent flesh.

A nearby table groaned under the weight of delicacies piled high. An odd foreigner with a massive nose and even more pronounced gut, yet garbed in the purchased finery of a Solipsian nobleman, stuffed his mouth. He gorged on the candied fruits.

"More wine!" a local woman screamed. She was draped in jewels that glittered obscenely against her bare skin, her laughter reflecting the hysteria that was her appearance and being.

Drake balanced upon a pillar in the banquet hall, as he fought to contain his revulsion. This was not celebration, it was decadence in grotesque parody of joy which left the bitterest taste on his tongue.

A group of revelers stumbled past, arms linked in a drunken fellowship of self-worshipers.

Drake recognized one of the revelers as a younger close cousin, dizzy from far too much drink.

The young relative caught sight of Drake and leered. "Why so glum, unc?" he slurred, voice thick as mud trying to sound respectful of Drake. His breath, sour yet sweet, reeked of ale. "Come join us! The emperor has commanded it, you know!"

Drake's response was a cold stare that sent his cousin staggering back, muttering boyish indignant justifications under his breath, the way they are wont in the prideful presence of wanton wisdom.

Across the hall, an impromptu dance broke out, bodies twisting and turning in frenzied lust, and hump-dances disguised as ritual. A foreign piper, who looked especially odd with massive ears set too high and enormous jowls despite being very skinny, perched on a table. It gave the impression of some strange elephant man. His thin, spindly fingers flew over the holes of the instrument expertly, as he spewed forth horrid noises. The drunken revelers were enthralled in hedonism, finding the noises exciting and jaunty.

The sight of such debasement stirred memories within Drake of his father's words. The recollections of his father's adventures shared with him in many a bedtime tale, about not long past events when his very own father stood tall. That was when honor shone brighter than any crown. His dead cousins' and Balnor's faces came to his mind, so did their voices and laughter still heard in his memory and etched into all time, condemning him for his silence and non-action.

A sudden surge of anger boiled within him, hot and fierce, at himself and at everyone. He pushed away from the pillar, strides long and purposeful as he made his way into the middle of the crowd. "Stop this madness!" he shouted above the din.

The music faltered, the piper's fingers stumbling over the notes. Music outside the walls could still be heard in the distance.

"Can you not see? This is not celebration, it is corruption!"

Eyes turned towards him, some curious, others resentful.

Another local woman, turned in the darkness of free intoxicants, her face flushed with it, sneered at him. "And who are you to jujdj?!" she demanded, voice slurring. "Why this is our emperor's co-man'! We celebrate his assendshun!"

"Is this how you honor your nation? Is this how you honor your dead? With such debauchery?" Drake could not have hidden the disgust in his face if he had tried at that moment.

Unease surfaced on the faces of those more moral in the crowd. Drake could see the doubts flickering in their eyes, the shadows of guilt that lingered despite intoxication.

Drake shouted even louder, "We cannot allow them to drown us! They do not need to destroy us if they can make us like them. They make you forget that you are not beasts. They give these things to you to distract and stupefy you, and look at you now! You are men! We have to do something! Where are the heroes of our time?!"

A local old man stepped forward from the edges of the crowd. His voice was gruff, worn. "He speaks true," he said, addressing the other drunks. "I fought with the heroes two decades past. I saw them face the goblin hordes, and I saw what they were like. The heroes would be appalled at this. We are no better than goblins!"

The hall seemed to hold its breath as more voices rose in agreement, repeating Drake's words. More seemed willing to join Drake and give up on the revelry, though the majority remained in disbelief and drunken comfort.

A foreign merchant, sensing the shift in mood of the crowds, interjected with a sneer, "Excuse me?!" His eyes held terror. "Heroes?" he spat, voice grating and practically designed to be rude.

"**They** were **butchers**!" he nearly screamed as much spoke.

Drake turned on him, eyes blazing. "And what are you? A parasite, feeding on our misery! This kingdom does not belong to you, it belongs to its people! To those who bled and died for it!" he shouted.

The merchant's sneer faded, replaced by a look of malice.

Drake felt hands grasp his arms from behind, a large guard. Drake struggled against the grip but found himself held fast as more figures emerged from other shadows to seize him.

"Take him away," the merchant snarled. "Let him cool his head in the dungeons." As Drake was dragged away, he cast one last look over the crowd, at some of their faces marked by shame and fear.

He called out, "Open your eyes! See what has become of Solipsia! This is not glory! It's decay! What comes after decadence?!"

Then he was gone, swallowed by the dark corridors beyond as carried away, his words hanging heavy in the air like a curse. The silence lingered for a moment longer before the music started once more, notes now tainted with a hint of unease for many.

Seeds of doubt had been planted, hints of truth that refused to be silenced. Many in the crowd, realizing what Drake had said was all true, left as quietly as they could.

* * *

The dungeon stunk of decay and despair.

Drake's captors shoved him into a dimly-lit cell, the iron door slamming shut behind him with a crisp clang of finality. Drake stood still, eyes adjusting to the gloom as he took stock of his surroundings. A single, barred window high above offered a glimpse of the night sky, as though mocking freedom or even the thoughts upon it.

He turned his attention to the lock on the door, crude but

sturdy. Reaching into his boot, he retrieved a few thin iron implements hidden within, a gift from Eldred, while training under his careful eye.

The old hero had insisted that knowledge and stealth were as vital as any blade talents. Drake began to work the lock, his fingers nimble despite the chill seeping into his bones through the frozen iron.

The mechanism yielded with a soft click, and the door creaked open slightly. He slipped out, moving silently through the shadows cast by flickering torches.

The dungeon was a labyrinth of stone and iron, but apparently emptied, and Drake had a hunch they were all slowly released over the week of festivities. His keen senses picked up the rhythmic snores of a guard before he rounded a corner. The drunken king's servant sat slumped against the wall, his spear leaning precariously nearby. Drake quietly removed the guard's sword belt smoothly, and then put it on himself.

The guard began to stir too much. Quickly, Drake ventured back in the other direction to find a distraction. He found a washroom. Next to the chamber's entrance, on the floor, there was a near empty bottle of stiff booze and a guard's helmet. He picked up the helmet and put it on. Gathering all the masses of sheets and linens into a great pile, he then lit them aflame near the chamber's window. The fire quickly engulfed the room, furniture and all.

Drake ran back to where the guard had been sleeping, slowing on approach to limit sound, but then engaged excitedly as soon as he was near, "Fire! The emperor needs your help below! Fire! Quick!"

The groggy guard was no match for Drake's acting. Of course, he felt immediately defensive and grateful for not being scolded on account of sleeping on his shift, so that little else mattered at the moment.

Drake pushed the torch towards the guard before explaining,

"You need to get the fire under control. You can already see it from here. I'm sure you don't want to be responsible for burning down Solipsia's dungeons! I'm going to go get more help, you go stop the fire!"

The overwhelmed guard hesitated, then grabbed the torch and hurried off towards the distant flicker of flame, not really awake or thinking at all, but perfectly panicked.

There were no other guards, apparently out carousing with the rest, as permitted by Gervin. He explored the dungeon to rescue Balnor, but found only his corpse, cruelly burned alive in the cell they were keeping him in.

Drake continued with his ascent out of the dungeon, navigating the winding staircases that led upward.

He encountered few obstacles, his agility and cunning serving him well. When he reached the surface, on lower walls of the palace citadel complex, the cool night air sharply contrasted the stagnant dungeon depths. "I'll give them a hero assassin," he stated to himself under his breath.

The palace walls loomed before him, imposing and seemingly impenetrable. Drake knew every secret passage, every hidden crevice within Solipsia's ancient stones. His father had ensured that, teaching him the kingdom's secrets as meticulously as he taught him swordplay and lockpicking.

Drake scaled the wall with a practiced ease, fingers finding purchase in cracks too small for lesser eyes to notice. Atop the parapet, he crouched low, scanning the grounds below. The royal chambers were right around the corner.

Drake crept forward, his senses heightened.

The drunk guards were alert but predictable in their patrols. He slipped past them, a ghost in the night, until he reached the chamber entrance.

With precise pressure and a gentle twist, he released the latch mechanism hidden within. The design was already familiar to him due to Eldred's training, specifically chosen because they were used in the palace.

The doors opened silently, revealing the opulent interior adorned with luxuries that reeked of fresh excess and debauchery. Drake stepped inside, careful to close the doors behind him, and barring it with a chair.

The chamber was dimly lit, casting eerie shadows on ornate paintings depicting scenes of battle and conquest. Drake's gaze fell upon 'the emperor,' asleep in the enormous bed, his breaths deep and rasping through what sounded like a bubbling cauldron of mucous.

Drake approached cautiously, barely able to see Gervin's features beyond the imported sheets. Not giving the moment an opportunity to slip by unused, he lunged forward, driving the guard's blade deep into the usurper's side.

The guard's sword ran right through to the other side of the emperor's chest, blood gushed forth all over the hilt and Drake's arm, burning like a terrible acid where it touched skin. All he could do was retract his hand, and wipe it off.

Despite the wound, Gervin seemed to grow as he howled in agony, but then pulled the sword part of the way out. He stood up from the bed, and leaned over, allowing the blade to fall out of his side using gravity, almost as though this were routine for him. The sword slipped out onto the floor like a freshly caught eel. He stood, internal organs exposed, yet barely awake and not panicking at all. In fact, he was getting stronger by the minute.

Gervin should have been dead. Somehow he stood before Drake alive and growing in anger, despite oozing out blood from his massive gaping wound.

Something was very wrong. Drake felt the urgent need to abscond as quickly as possible. He backed away. The emperor's eyes narrowed as he regarded Drake, and then hissed a string of guttural words in a foreign language.

Drake turned and fled, adrenaline surging through his veins. He dashed back through the chamber and into the corridor outside, desperate to put distance between himself and whatever sorcery held the emperor alive.

The palace erupted into chaos as guards rushed towards the commotion. Drake weaved through and past them, using every ounce of his agility and training to evade capture. He could not let them slow him down. He needed to get to Silver Keep and figure things out. What he needed most was lacking, time and allies.

He retraced his steps, scaling walls and navigating rooftops with desperate urgency, as the emperor alerted the guards. The city sprawled beneath him, a maze of stone and shadow. Drake knew he needed his true allies.

His mind raced as he leaped from one roof to the next, thoughts turning towards the fortress of the Silver Keep, stronghold of yet another dynasty of heroes nestled high in the craggy peaks, of Eolande, ally of Eldred. He could only hope that they remained true to their lineage, steadfast against the corruption spreading like a plague through Solipsia.

The city seemed to close in around him, its labyrinthine streets designed to ensnare and entreat rather than guide. He pushed onward.

As he neared the outskirts of the city, Drake's thoughts turned to strategy. He needed a plan, something more substantial than mere flight. The Silver Keep was days away on foot, too far to traverse without aid.

He spotted a stable nearby, one he knew belonged to the king, its doors slightly ajar. He slipped inside and saddled a horse quietly. The beast whinnied softly but allowed him to lead it out into the night. Drake mounted swiftly, urging the horse into a gallop as soon as they cleared the stables.

***

The wind whipped around him as he outpaced any potential pursuers. He dared not look back. He was focused instead on the road ahead. Solipsia's walls shrank behind while the open expanse of wilderness stretched out before him. Drake knew that there was no time for rest. The Silver Keep loomed in his thoughts as something more than just a fortress, perhaps able to help stem the tide against uncertainty itself.

He rode hard through the night, guided by starlight and instinct. He knew what he had to do in these miles between him and there, and he was going to do it well. This wasn't just about his own survival; it was about rallying any who could stand against the dark tide threatening to overtake Solipsia. Drake was dumbfounded, after witnessing the emperor murder that little old foreign priest to then survive certain death himself hours later, seemingly fated at the hands of Eldred's son. The priest was probably some kind of goblin, now that Drake thought of it. Seeing Gervin recover from having that sword through the torso, there was something more to him too.

In the far North, where winds whipped down from icy peaks and forests stood sentinel over ancient stones, loomed Silver Keep.

Drake rode ever closer as dawn broke, casting golden hues through the horse's galloping legs. The Silver Keep perched among mountains, with nearly white stone gleaming, indeed, like silver under the morning sun. Here winter was never late, but always on time.

He saw the fortress for many miles out and was glad for his presence there at last. Immense calm overtook him all the more upon seeing and greeting the coachman he had hired returning from there, on the way back to their home village.

Silver Keep was a fortress made before ages past, its

construction lost to memory and history.

Upon reaching it in the late afternoon, Drake stood before the imposing gates. He pounded on the heavy wood with his clenched fist.

The silence stretched taut before a small hatch opened, revealing wary eyes. "Who seeks entry?" a gruff voice demanded.

Drake met the gaze steadily. "I am Drake, son of Eldred, bearer of news that will shake the very foundations of Solipsia. I come seeking my allies against the darkness encroaching on our land."

"Greetings brave hero Eldredson Drake, please enter quickly," the guard said and opened the gates.

Drake tethered the horse outside the central castle, still wearing the royal prison guard helmet.

"You sign up with the enemy or fresh from espionage?" Kenid called out from the front door.

Laughing and remembering himself, Drake took the helmet off at once.

* * *

That night, the moon hung heavy and full. Nearer the heart of Solipsia, the usual hum of evening revelries had now vanished entirely, replaced by an unnatural hush. Even the wind seemed to hold its breath, as if awaiting something ominous. All the ales, booze and foods had disappeared as quickly as they had appeared.

Torches flickered along the battlements, guarded by silhouettes that were not quite familiar, shapes of human but different. Jerky movements unsettling, with eyes betraying hungers that had nothing of sustenance in purpose, or good.

Emergency powers had been invoked. Everything had changed overnight since the assassination attempt by "those terrorist heroes," as Emperor Gervin had put it.

In the wake of the attempt on his life, Gervin had fired all the guards and replaced them with foreigners, and not just a few, hundreds, and every last one. Knowing at once that it was Drake wearing a guard's helmet, Gervin kept the identity to himself in order to capitalize upon it. He went so far as to frame the guard that Drake had awoken, as a sympathizer of heroes who had been caught freeing a few just before the desperate deed. The guard's scorched body was now in a pile with Balnor's, despite his eventually successful efforts to fight the fire that Drake had set. Of course, local guards of Solipsian origins could no longer be trusted.

Families huddled together in their dimly lit homes, voices low and anxious.

A pot clattered softly in a kitchen, startling a child who whimpered quietly. Outside, boots on regular patrols stepped sharply on wet stones, foreign boots, marching in rhythm with an alien cadence.

They would come to the door and sniff. They would not stop sniffing.

The clamor grew louder, patrols approaching, and then grew quiet again, as they moved on.

The new emperor began decorating the kingdom. The freshly erected statues of Gervin loomed overhead everywhere, their shadows dancing demonically in the flickering torchlight, casting an oppressive atmosphere over the now quiet thoroughfares. It was so strange to the people the quantity and suddenness, the appearance of these statues upon their streets and in their neighborhoods.

At the corner of an alleyway, a tattered curtain twitched aside slightly, revealing a pair of wide eyes belonging to an older woman. She watched the column of armed figures pass by, their faces half-hidden under helmets adorned with crude emblems. Her breath hitched when she spotted one bearing an insignia depicting a dead twisted vulture with gnarled claws, unmistakably the mark of goblin tribes long thought vanquished.

"Mother?" whispered a small voice from behind her.

She jumped, pressing a hand to her chest. "Hush, dear," she murmured, turning back to the window. "Go to your bed, sweetie, please."

The child obeyed silently, slipping away into the darkness of their cramped dwelling. The woman remained at the window, gaze fixed on the retreating figures until they disappeared around a bend.

The grand market square, once vibrant with colors and sounds, rested now silent. The stalls were empty save for remnants of produce rotting beneath the weight of neglect. There was the scent of decay, contrasting starkly against the usual aromas of fresh bread and ripe fruits before that week of festivities. The only movement remaining came from ragged figures darting furtively between alleys, their eyes wide with apprehension, and the foreign merchants allowed to stay open. Prices were already exorbitant, but the outsiders felt no compunction about gouging.

The drunken parades had gone bandit, staking ground with tent cities everywhere, many merging with incoming cults to this or that goblin demon variously.

* * *

Quite alternative events unfolded at the royal palace. Within its walls, Gervin plotted and schemed. The halls, once adorned with tapestries depicting heroic deeds and ancient lore, now displayed garish banners bearing Gervin's likeness, engaged in variously horrendous acts, unmentionable and cruel portrayals. Commoners were no longer welcome, and for obvious reasons.

Laughter rang out amidst clinking glasses and the strains of discordant music. Nobles in silken finery lounged on velvet cushions, feigning merriment, while their eyes darted nervously toward Gervin. Hired wenches wore exotic clothing more than a little revealing, and served in any number of capacities the '**nobles**' desired.

A hush fell over the gathered courtiers as a dirty foreign soldier marched through the royal den, dragging behind him an elderly man, burly yet with back bent under the weight of years and, now, despair.

He was a blacksmith, prized for his gentle demeanor and for skilled hands careful in mending metal items of nobles and peasants alike. Yet now he faced Gervin's wrath.

"Your Majesty," the soldier declared, shoving the burly man to his knees, "this one was caught uttering sedition against your rule. Name of Turvey."

The blacksmith looked up at Gervin, genuine fear spreading about his weathered face as he watched the emperor look upon him with disdain. "Forgive me, Your Highness," he pleaded, voice quivering, "I spoke out of turn. I only meant to say that times are hard, and the people suffer." Gervin's lips curled into a smirk as he leaned forward, elbows resting on the armrests of his throne.

"But suffering builds such character," he responded, voice dripping with mock sympathy. "And who are you to question my methods? This kingdom is lucky to have me, and you'll all come to see this as true eventually."

Turvey nodded in agreement, aiming to appease. "I, I... never meant any disrespect, your honor," he insisted, hands clenched tightly in his lap, forced together by the bonds.

Gervin's expression darkened, "Disrespect is a luxury this court cannot afford." He raised a hand, and more soldiers stepped forward, their boots clattering ominously as they stomped on the stone.

Turvey looked up at them, terror-stricken. "Please," he begged, voice barely audible, "I have grandchildren. They need me."

Gervin merely smiled, "Then perhaps you should have thought of them before opening your mouth."

The guards moved in on him.

"No! I beg you, Your Majesty!"

Turvey screamed and begged for help as the guards stabbed him repeatedly with their lances. The foreign soldiers reveled in the pain inflicted as they pierced his skin and flesh over and over in front of the entire court. The screaming was ear-piercing and horrific. A pool of blood formed under the poor man's body.

In the silent wake left by his screams, Gervin stood, "Who else dares to challenge my vision?" he called out, voice resonating throughout the chamber.

Silence met his question. Nobles and courtiers, already more foreign than domestic, exchanged glances, their faces pale beneath layers of rouge and powder. Those foreign nobles with expressions of amazement, and locals of disgust undisguised.

"Very well," Gervin declared, a cruel smile forming on his lips, "Remember this moment. Remember the consequences of dissent." Gervin raised his goblet high, voice booming through the chamber, "Let us toast to our prosperity, and our newest allies!"

A murmur rippled through the assembled guests. Some obeyed grudgingly, forcing smiles as they sipped from gilded cups.

Others stared into their drinks, avoiding one another's gazes.

"Fear not," Gervin continued, his smile broadening into a leer. "The days of want are behind us! With the help of our friends..." he gestured vaguely towards a cluster of strange-looking dignitaries with features nobody had seen before, and doused in perfume verging on the rancid. Their skin was nearly the color of rotting swollen wood, with eyes like pools of oil. "We shall forge an empire unparalleled in history!"

Applause, both earnest and half-hearted, clamored together through the halls.

A Solipsian lord with silvered hair stood, bowing stiffly. "Your Majesty," he began, voice steady despite the tension on his face, "Forgive my boldness, but the people grow uneasy. They see these… visitors and wonder at their purp…" A dagger went through his forehead before he could say another word.

Gervin's hand was extended, having just thrown the dagger retrieved from the inside of his now tousled regal robes. He readjusted the fabric, stretching his back nonchalantly as he did.

His expression darkened as he sat back once more, though his tone remained light. "The people need not worry about matters of state. Their emperor knows best what is required for our glory."

Gervin's gaze lingered on those who shifted uncomfortably. He laughed out loud and yelled out to all, "Consequences of dissent I said, and what part of that did Count Vinnows not understand? Guess we'll never know. Unless someone else wishes to speak up." He looked around, eyebrows arched high in invitation.

"Now," Gervin declared, clasping hands together sharply, "there's been enough talk! Bring forth the entertainment! Drink, my lords and ladies!"

A troop of barely dressed dancing acrobats launched themselves into the grand hall, as raucous music played, performing feats which defied logic or gravity, and morality. The performers touched the terrified nobles and forced them into unwholesome things. Some gasps rippled through the nobles, yet demoralization was already setting in. Many turned away, sickened by the sights. Others slipped away from the palace, donning the silence attending night, though risking all. They rightly feared being added to one of Gervin's many growing lists.

Gervin watched avidly taking great entertainment and laughing uproariously at each twisted display.

A few local nobles tried to run away from the abuse, but they were caught and thrown into the dungeons, which recently had revamped security measures put in place, such as chains on every prisoner, since the assassination attempt. The charges were "ungratefulness."

Meanwhile, beyond palace walls, the patrols of foreign soldiers continued their relentless marches, stone sober. In shadowed alleyways and dim-lit corridors, locals tried to go about their business, fluttering like nervous birds between the comings and goings of the new regime's enforcers.

"They come for people at night, and we're never sure who," breathed one voice.

"They could take any of us," another voice worried in response.

Fear was everywhere a scourge and pandemic, a palpable mist choking hope from Solipsia's veins.

* * *

Within the stony embraces of Silver Keep's main castle, Drake of Eldred found some sanctuary after his futile yet heroic attempt to stem the darkness flowing from Solipsia's throne.

His journey had been fraught with peril, yet hope stirred within him as he beheld Telyn and Kenid approaching him, their faces alight with relief to see him. Endra leaned heavily on her gnarled cane, but her eyes sparkled with warmth.

Deeper into the building, he could see the old hero, Eolande, and his kin watching and smiling.

Telyn threw herself into Drake's arms, breath coming in quick gasps. "Drake! We feared you might be lost to us!" He hugged her tightly, then gently set her back, smiling at Kenid who grinned up at him. "I am here as I'll always be," he reassured them both, hugging Kenid as well.

Endra nodded solemnly as she moved in to hug Drake, her voice like rustling leaves. "I missed you, boy."

Drake hugged her back gently.

A voice familiar to Drake spoke up, "Still troubled, lad?" Eolande's voice rumbled from his chair as he stood up to welcome Drake.

The hero's once-mighty frame was now much more gaunt and frailer for age, though perhaps all the nobler still. He had been quite old at the outset of Eldred's campaigns. His hunter eyes held a spark undiminished, of shining defiance against encroaching darkness.

At any of the most recent gatherings of heroes since Eldred's passing, Drake was in the company of Eolande most. Drake had confided in Eolande his many fears about the potential return of evils to Solipsia, which Eolande understood only too well. In fact, Eolande was one of the few who could understand this.

Drake turned to face him. "I cannot sit idly while the kingdom crumbles," he replied, voice low yet fierce. "Every coin spent on that farce of a coronation or even a day of celebrations could have fed many families for seasons."

Eolande nodded grimly. "Aye, and more besides." He leaned forward, hands gripping a gnarled walking stick. "But mark my words 'ere, Drake, there's a rot in Solipsia's heart. Been festering for some time now. It runs deeper than gold or debt, but it has Gervin written all over it."

Drake thought back to all the rumors over the years, the uneasy glances exchanged among citizens as more strangers slithered through their streets like oil on water. A sickness gnawed at him, a hunger for action, for resistance against the creeping shadows.

"We must unite allies against this," Drake declared, resolving anew. "Others who see the truth of what is unfolding."

Eolande's expression sharpened. "You tread a dangerous path, lad. Many would rather look away than face harsh light." He hesitated, then added softly, "Even among those who should know better."

Drake lifted his shoulders and breathed deeply in sigh. "Better to stumble blindly towards dawn than hide in comfort of endless night."

"Drake," Eolande acknowledged with a grim nod. "We have much to discuss. So I am glad you are here."

Drake sat down with Eolande, as the fires all around roared in vast hearths and shadows danced on stone walls adorned with the ancient banners of clans present and past, like an archive, many sharing a similar two-headed eagle.

The scent of burning wood, aged parchment, cold metal, and sweat convened as a member of their conversation, almost a constant reminder of Solipsia itself.

Eolande gestured towards a heavy table before him littered with maps, codices, scrolls, and other various parchments. "The kingdom teeters, Drake," he began, pointing at the map. "Goblins pour in like vermin, corrupting everything they touch."

Drake leaned over the map, eyes scanning routes marked in red ink. "I've been seeing a lot more of their kind for some time now," he murmured. "Merchants and performers, all under guise of commerce or entertainment, but their eyes hold malice."

"Now soldiers, too, Drake." Eolande stated.

"I was just there, I didn't..." Drake began.

"We just received the reports. Your little trick is what gave Gervin an excuse to replace all his guards," the old hunter said with a grin.

"My little trick? What..." not trying to be elusive, Drake could not believe Eolande already knew. He was confused by his reaction as well.

"Don't play coy, Drake, we've put two and two together. So

much like your father, boy." Eolande smiled again as he continued, "They're not claiming it as having anything to do directly with heroes or kin, or you, only 'a sympathizer,' which I was figuring had two purposes for Gervin. Firstly, to not allow you to become a rallying point for us heroes, and, secondarily, to disband the old guard. Anyway, Gervin would have done that given any excuse, regardless what we did."

"Eolande, I put a blade right through him. I never meant to escalate…" Drake was saying, distressed.

Eolande stopped smiling, "That man is enchanted with all sorts of arcane evil, so this is not surprising at all. Acceleration like this is best very early on for many reasons, so don't apologize, dear sir. He had these foreign armies lined up to enter the kingdom since before his crowning. You simply gave him the most convenient excuse to unveil them. But he'll probably come after us even faster and harder now, especially if he knows it was you," Eolande said this last part with a wince.

"He knows it was me, I assure you. So where do we begin?" Drake asked.

Eolande pointed towards the map again. "Firmest and most resolute of our allies linger in these regions," he said, marking several locations. "Yet fear grips them too. We need something to rally them."

Drake studied each marked spot, committing them to memory. His voice carried determination, "Something to consider."

They spoke about strategies and plans deep into the night.

Over the following days, Drake ventured forth from Silver Keep. He traversed rugged trails and quiet glades, seeking out those who might join his cause. Meetings were held in hushed backrooms, within hidden groves, or cellars beneath ancient inns.

In one such gathering, Drake faced a cluster of grim-faces

huddled around flickering candlelight. Their gazes shifted nervously whenever footsteps were heard up outside the cramped subterranean chamber.

"Friends," he began, voice low yet steady, "we cannot stand idle while our land suffocates under this blight."

A burly farmer leaned forward, brow furrowing. "What can we do?" he asked gruffly. "The king's foreign soldiers patrol the streets relentlessly. One false move…"

"We kill them," another interjected sharply in a voiceless whisper.

"Yeah!" another shouted in a whisper.

Drake shook his head slowly. "Violence will come, but it will inevitably lead to more death for our people. We need unity and strength in numbers to make the most impact with the least amount of risk. Until we can get the numbers on our side, we have to be careful."

A woman wrapped tightly in a tattered cloak spoke up next. Her voice trembled slightly. "Many here fear for their families," she admitted. "If we rise up, who knows what retribution might fall upon us?"

Drake felt a pang of frustration but held his tongue. Instead, he leaned closer, eyes reflecting candlelight fervently. "Fear is poison," he said quietly. "It eats away resolve until nothing else remains. We must remain silent for the time, but also vigilant and ready ourselves to act. There will come a time very soon when we will strike fast and hard, you must have faith in our team. Right now, we need lines of communication between as many as possible to remain open. We need information, so be on the lookout and share."

His pleas fell on deaf ears, hesitation lingering in their gazes. Fear remained unshaken and overshadowing hope.

Drake did not spend much time trying to convince any one

person, but rather moved on to the next. Some seeds had been sown, and that was all that he could hope for in the present moment.

* * *

Weeks passed, and Drake was able to convince small groups of people to meet with him, to at least discuss what they could do to help. He moved with purpose, yet caution informed every step. His destinations were always different but identical, and he felt a bit like some strange politician of rebellion. These places were the hidden nooks and crannies where remnants of old resistance lingered. Everywhere Drake sang the song of defiance, and sowed it into the most fertile shadows, still precious few were willing to commit.

Drake stood in the cellar beneath a forgotten tavern, emblems of heroism on the stone walls faint and fading. Around him sat half a dozen figures, faces coordinating lines of worry and weariness. Their breaths misted in chill air, voices hushed as they spoke of the many troubles besetting Solipsia, and compiling by the day.

"It's unnatural," muttered one, voice barely audible over scrape of flint striking steel, trying to start a fire in the pit before him. "Now there are goblins openly in our streets, gloating like vultures."

Another shivered. "And the king, he laughs while people suffer. Laughs!"

Drake crouched down and leaned in, elbows on knees. "We must act," he urged, keeping his tone low yet intense. "Rally others to our cause. Show people they are not alone."

Silence met his words. Eyes flickered nervously, darting to one another as if seeking unspoken consensus.

"Act?" repeated a woman, wrapping shawl tighter around shoulders. "And what of consequences? They come for any who speak out..."

Drake cut her off, desperation sharpening his voice. "Only

because speaking out works, so consequences be damned! We cannot stand idle while our kingdom is enslaved!" Yet hesitation lingered in their eyes, fear rooted them firmly.

"Give it time," said an elder, his voice barely more than a rasp. "Things may yet improve."

Drake bit back his retort which would have proven too sharp, frustration gnawing at him. He saw reflections of his own dread mirrored in their faces, however. He was only too familiar with that same churning helplessness within.

Drake could not yield to the passivity it invoked. Unlike them, he was practiced in fighting back the sense of victimhood to circumstances. "Time," he tasted the hollow word and still chose no response, standing abruptly. Chair scraped loud against stone floor, as others also stood with him. "Very well. I shall give you time but remember Gervin hasn't the time to give anyone. Soon we will want for little else but time..." He strode from the cellar, leaving muted murmurs behind.

Drake's journey continued, as he emerged back out into the street. His secret meetings were held under cover of darkness, and he learned to stop wasting his time in empty arguments. Voices were always kept low, as if they suspected the walls themselves of harboring ears. Despite his passion, Drake found only a fraction of resistance he knew was needed. Turning everywhere he could, he encountered the same reticence and paralyzing dread in people. He learned to accept it, because he needed to, but he would never expect it.

Drake pleaded his case to anyone who would hear, regardless how much they might have reeked of fear. In dark chambers, he suggested rebellion and argued unity in defiance. Still, he was met with little more than sympathetic glances and hollow promises, at best. People wanted to hope, yet feared the cost of grasping for it.

One evening, Drake chanced upon a small gathering. Under

flickering torchlight a group of Solipsians listened raptly to an old bard strumming out a melancholy tune on a weathered lute. Drake approached cautiously, not wishing to disrupt the spirit of somberness. Yet recognition rippled through the assembly as he neared, and conversations hushed expectantly. He was already becoming infamous.

"Drake Eldredson," greeted the bard as he stopped playing, voice warm in camaraderie. "What brings you into our humble company?"

Drake hesitated briefly before stepping forward. "I seek alliance," he replied straightforwardly. "But only those willing to stand against the tide of corruptions swallowing Solipsia."

The usual murmurs that Drake was used to rippled through the crowd. Some exchanged glances, others looked down at hands clenched tightly in laps.

The bard nodded solemnly. "Bold words, young hero. But boldness alone cannot turn a tide."

Drake felt the familiar frustration stir within him. "No," he acknowledged, voice steady despite impatience. "But neither can silence."

Another pause, then the bard spoke again, tone measured yet firm. "We appreciate your passion, Drake. Truly we do. Yet remember this: courage without wisdom is but folly."

Drake opened his mouth to retort immediately, yet thought better of it. Instead, he simply nodded, acknowledging the unspoken truths behind the words. He gave it a moment and then said, "I agree completely, which is all the more reason to seek alliances early." Drake took leave of the gathering, and allowed them their enjoyment of the music once again.

Drake walked slowly, thoughts churning tumultuously within him. Drake paused, gaze drawn towards the palace in the distance, looming dark and imposing against star-studded sky. Its towers seemed to mock him, silent sentinels overseeing descent into despair.

He thought back to Eolande's words, their ominous warning occupying his mind. Rot in Solipsia's heart indeed, yet who among them dared wield the knife in order to cut it out? Drake turned away from the palace, resolve hardening within him like stone. If others would not act, then he must. Alone if necessary.

He melted into the shadows of narrow lanes, determination burning brightly within. Drake would not let darkness claim the kingdom without a fight. Desperation would not be allowed to win. Each failed attempt to rally support weighed ever more heavily upon him.

Drake found solace only in stolen moments with Telyn, Kenid, Eolande, Endra, and the soldiers back at Silver Keep, when he had a moment to rest there.

***

One evening, Drake was lost in thought walking beneath a vast canopy of stars visible through the tall windows in the main castle, fire roaring in the nearby pit, when Eolande approached.

Eolande said nothing at first, just letting him walk. "You grow impatient," the old hero observed finally.

Drake paused mid-stride, running a hand through his freshly cropped hair. "Time slips away," he countered. "With each passing day, Gervin's grip tightens on our dying kingdom."

Eolande nodded with grim expression. "Patience is not idleness, Drake. It is endurance and the ability to bear what must be borne until that moment in which change can happen."

Drake turned back towards the fire, eyes reflecting the dancing of the flames. He knew Eolande spoke truth, in so many ways. An urgency still gnawed at him like hunger. Change had to come swiftly, before all was lost.

Meanwhile, goblins were roaming freely through Solipsia's streets, their laughter grating against nerves already frayed by constant dread. Their numbers swelled daily, a tide of corruption seeping into the very heart of the kingdom. Still, people waited, hoping against hope that these storms would pass without need for them to act, or that someone might come along and cure their despair instantaneously.

Drake felt it all keenly: the helplessness, the creeping paralysis gripping those who wished for nothing more than justice, those he sought to inspire. They hoped for something beyond themselves to just sweep it all away.

Within him burned an undying spark, a basic refusal to accept despair or any excuses as final answers. For now, though, silence reigned where voices of rebellion should have rang out clearly, loud and proud as they had before. He was determined that they would again, even if it cost everything he had left.

The battle for Solipsia's soul seemed paused mid-strike, frozen in standoff.

The Silver Keep's massively ancient walls spoke of the old glories of Solipsia, though now faded and forgotten. Inside, Drake prepared for what lay ahead. Outside, stars winked as if to silently share in some amusing celestial secret about all the terrible plight unfolding below.

CHAPTER FOUR

ACCUSATIONS

Once-venerated names of heroes, those who had stood against the goblin tide decades past, were now hissed about in malice and dragged through the mud. Tears as black as pitch with accusatory wails ravaged the populace with confused guilt, anxiety and animosity building up in the backs of minds. The venomous claims curdled the blood, and made all feel culpable.

"Murderers," snarled young voices barely above their breath and regarding events before their memory, "butchers of the innocents!" The charges were bitter, each syllable laden with contrived hatred.

Demonic voices seeped into every cranny of Solipsia like shared nightmares, insidious and relentless. The emperor's messages slipped through alleys and spread through streets in hollow and theatrical cadences, and in any voice necessary. It spilled from the mouths of street corner orators and serpentinely inscribed scrolls tacked onto walls, souring all ears in one way or another. His words were slick as oil, coating minds until they shimmered darkly under Gervin's false light.

"The heroes lied," repeated one such proclamation over and over, bloody ink stark against bleached and unknown leather, lettering curled with alien bends. "Those goblins were misguided babes in the wild, lost youthful souls."

A woman paused before the notice, her basket of clothing forgotten at her feet. She traced lines of text with trembling fingers, eyes wide with disbelief.

Beside her, a man scoffed derisively, spittle flying as he spat, "Babes in the wild?! They slaughtered my kin, whatever they were! You don't let anything do what those goblins did to us. We were the good folk who merely stood against their savagery!" Yet even his vehemence seemed tainted by doubt, seeds of uncertainty planted deep within the psyche by relentless barrages.

Had they all been deceived?

The question gnawed insistently, corrosive acid eating away resolve. Many began to believe the impossible, and that the heroes were in fact bad.

In quiet corners and shadowed alleyways, tales spun further afield, each iteration more twisted than last. People reported dreams of helpless goblin infants torn from goblin mothers' arms by ruthless murderers. Dens burned out not from the need of actual desperate defense, as the heroes had it, but for the mere sport of it. People woke up in sweat to visions of flames licking skyward against screams of the green innocents.

The economic turmoil that was shifting below Solipsia's societal foundations provided fertile soil for these lies. Anyone that spoke out about what the truth was found themselves or a family member arrested in short order. Nobody was permitted to point out that Gervin's regime single-handedly destroyed businesses with taxes and waves of nightly crime.

"Our coffers emptied by war," declared odd-looking criers, more often than not drunk off Gervin's ales, still free flowing for them. "Our fields lay barren from neglect. Our markets as empty as our coffers. All for what? To satiate bloodlust disguised as valor!"

An older laborer leaned heavily on his shovel, gaze fixed upon such a crier flapping its frilly lips dismally outside a closed market stall. His calloused hands trembled slightly, memory of battle of slaughtering many goblins long past stirring uneasily. He had fought beside those now reviled, seen firsthand the horrors wrought by goblin hordes. Yet the emperor's published and proclaimed words found space in his mind, doubt setting upon him, much like age with the time away from his younger forgotten aspirations.

"It cannot be true, that was so many years ago, and we've had much good since then," he murmured hoarsely, though conviction faltered against the official decrees.

Many others wore facial expressions mirroring similar inner conflict in the remembrance of those long past events. They wanted to believe otherwise, clinging desperately to that feeling of hallowed heroism. However, each passing day brought a fresh onslaught of deceit, chipping away certainties until only memory of violence, blood, and ashes remained.

Children too fell prey, their innocent dreams sullied by perverse and divisive visions. They saw fictions in which pitiful goblish waifs were wrongly transformed into snarling beasts by lying heroes out for blood. Children woke screaming, convulsing with terror, as parents hastened to soothe frayed nerves. Yet even parental comfort offered scant solace against specters conjured from darkness, fed by a ceaseless stream of poison.

In one modest dwelling nestled between cramped tenements, a youth huddled beneath tattered blankets, eyes reflecting flickering candlelight wildly. His breath coming in ragged gasps, chest heaving under nightshirt damp with perspiration. Beside him, a younger sibling stirred fitfully, whimpering softly.

"Hush now," cooed their mother as she arrived to assuage his tears, stroking sweat-matted hair from his brow. "It's just a dream, love."

The boy shook his head vigorously, tears spilling down cheeks. "They weren't dreams, mama," he insisted desperately. "I saw them, the goblins. They were... they were little ones. And the heroes... " He broke off, choking sobs wracking frame. Mother held him close, rocking gently as she murmured soothing things. Yet her own heart pounded uneasily, her son's words resonating ominously with dreams half-forgotten.

The emperor wove spells of deceit into the cloth of Solipsian culture, each thread embedding strategic weaknesses until the remaining fabric would rip asunder completely under any pressure.

Voices rose in anger denouncing heroes who had once been lauded as saviors, blaming them for all the current troubles. They were designated as the safe targets by the emperor.

Accusations rang sharp. "Betrayal" was the word reverberating through collective consciousness.

"Why would they do such things?!" cried one sitting at a table in a rundown tavern, voice raw with anguish.

"Because they chose it," answered another bitterly. "They knew and chose bloodshed for the thrill and to secure their power."

* * *

In tavern halls once resonant with laughter, song, business, and conversations, silence wore the crown, broken only by clattering iron-shod patrol boots out on streets. The rhythm was relentless, a drumbeat of oppression. Heroic triumphs shining bright across history now seemed forever tarnished by the stains of Gervin's lies.

The heroes of old, those who had stood tall against monstrous darkness two decades earlier, were now labeled monsters themselves. Their names, once chanted in reverence, were now whispered at most if not hissed through gritted teeth as if curses. Statues bearing their likenesses were toppled and then literally defaced, faces shattered into shards of stone.

Gervin reveled in all the chaos, the uncertainty, and the creeping plague-like paranoia. Each word of doubt was music to his ears, and each shattered ideal a testament to the power in his ability to cast spells and inculcate twisted lies and invectives. He had orchestrated these scenes with special attention, pulling strings attached to minds made malleable as wet clay.

Outside his fortress walls, the kingdom and city wretched

under wave after wave of illusions. Gervin's men bellowed accusations from street corners, booming as they proclaimed heroes' sins for all to hear. Placards bore lurid illustrations flashing gruesomely spun yarns. Goblins portrayed as the poor innocent lambs led to slaughter under hateful heroes who abused their trust. The heroes were ruthless executioners of the wee green saints.

'Indeed, how dare anyone take pleasure in anything while such monsters as these "heroes" remain around, alive and well, and with any power.' Nothing could be enjoyed.

Marketplaces that had once thrived under bustle of commerce now quiet, stalls shuttered tight behind iron grates. Local businesses who dared open shop found themselves harangued by passersby spitting venomous words, fingers jabbing accusatorily at goods displayed.

"Profit while bloodshed goes unpunished, do you? What is fair in Solipsia?!" snarled one such man, small and emotional, face covered in his cloak.

A weathered matron, her apron dusted with flour, emerged from her family's bakery to meet the accuser. "This is a mistake," she protested weakly. "We sell bread, nothing more."

The cloaked man sneered, baring his rotted teeth. "Liar!" he scorned. "You feed off their crimes, fatten yourself on stolen coin! I bet you even sell to heroes, and fund them. Bet you got hero relatives, maybe one hiding upstairs, yeah?" Gasps were heard from the few who were gathering around, in agreement.

Those who disagreed recoiled from the vitriol spat so freely, wishing to avoid the scene all together. The baker retreated indoors, shoulders hunched defensively as the shutters slammed behind her.

Elsewhere, similar scenes played out. There was a blacksmith up the street from the baker, accused of forging weapons used against goblin "youth."

In the city, a scholar was actively vilified for chronicling the history of heroism, now deemed atrocity in and of itself.

Each confrontation left wounds raw and bleeding emotionally, tearing at anything holding the community together in any sort of common pride. The communities were hating each other and themselves. This way, they could never turn their anger to Gervin or his actors and plans.

***

Breaths were held tight, hearts pounded against ribs like fists upon doors begging for admittance. Windows remained shuttered, curtains drawn closed despite daylight's retreat, leaving homes cloaked in premature twilight, despite the flowers blooming around the kingdom. Clip-clop of hooves echoed ominously against stone pavements all day, with the arrival of caravan after caravan of foreign merchants and businesses moving in to set up shop.

More messengers and criers appeared bearing decrees and criminal charges penned in the emperor's name, parchment crisp beneath seals of wax that bore no crest of nobility, but symbols of ancient goblin clans.

"Genocide," the syllables fell like a curse, leaving behind an acrid taste. It was flung with contemptuous force, staining reputations built on courage and sacrifice as effectively as any sling of mud. Whispers morphed into shouts, voices merged into the noise that drowned out any chance for reason in the emotion of survival and political confusion, while fists flew, and whole families were quietly killed off, in the quiet of night without explanations and without any recognition either. All that would remain is fresh blood soaking into floorboards after the shrill marrow-chilling screams in the dead of night.

Charges, stark and brutal: genocide, murderers of innocents. Those goblins were nothing but peaceful youth who were merely a bit excitable, claimed Gervin's arrest warrants, wanted lists, and wanted signs. The poor goblin children had fallen beneath the heroes' blades, their blood crying out from the ground for recognition or vengeance. Children's bedtime stories, once filled with heroes vanquishing monstrous foes, republished officially by Gervin's offices, though shipped in from far off lands where they had been reworked. The stories had been morphed into waking nightmares, where ruthless butchers preyed on the weak while claiming the weak were the monsters.

"The goblins ***were*** the **monsters. Are**," an elderly woman insisted in a quivering voice, her fingers clutching at a faded shawl. "I saw their eyes, burning like lanterns in the night."

Yet another countered her fervently, "But there were tribes who traded peacefully with our outlying villages before the war! What about them?"

In streets where once children's laughter rang clear, a new slur: "Baby killers." The chorus was sung as a dirge, mournful, emotional, violent, and accusing. It seeped into the cracks of homes and festered within hearts.

Strange defenses, in rebuttal to those who remembered the truth of the matters, were uttered repeatedly everywhere all at once, "Goblins are just different, but what's wrong with setting your youth free?" or, "How many goblins did you know personally?" and, "How many heroes have you met?"

Arguments ignited swiftly, passions flaring hot and fierce. In tanneries where leather creaked beneath steady and experienced hands, conversations stuttered to halt when strangers entered. Eyes darted warily from face to face, each searching for hidden loyalties lurking behind guarded expressions.

Families found themselves cleaved by doubt's insidious blade; siblings pitted against parents in battles of belief that left no quarter. Indeed, having loose family connections and the wrong opinions was the most deadly combination.

***

A peculiar stillness descended upon certain quarters, a hush more chilling than winter's first frost, despite the blossoming and rains of a hesitant spring. Happy homes once vibrant with laughter now stood mute, their occupants retreating behind barred doors like moths into cocoons. These were the families of those who had fought alongside the heroes, often too meek to even count themselves among the heroes though with names nonetheless etched indelibly into the culture and here unto monuments previously, but now marred by the vileness of Gervin's many lies.

Their silence did not stem merely from fear but from a profound sense of dislocation. They mourned not just the dead, but an entire ethos shattered, that of an honor code that had once bound Solipsia together but which now seemed a relic, smashed beneath Gervin's relentless assaults.

The ground beneath their feet felt suddenly unsteady, as if the very foundations of their world were crumbling. In quiet corners where candles flickered low, desperate souls sought solace through shared recollections.

"I remember," murmured a matronly voice, frail and tearful yet steady. "Do you remember when streets rang loud with children's laughter? Before shadows grew long and hunger gnawed at our bellies?"

A younger voice, a granddaughter, added softly yet with real hope for the future, "And the games and sports, with music filling the air!"

Beneath the nostalgia lay undercurrents of fear, that such memories were forever tainted and perhaps banished along with heroism, corrupted by lies and now deemed heresy.

Gervin's spies moved freely, their gazes cold and appraising. A slip of tongue by a person could spell doom; an imprudent glance might invite unwelcome scrutiny.

Those who dared question the costs of Gervin's extravagances and attempted to blame him for anything found themselves ensnared in webs spun from fear and silence, if they were lucky, with more and more people disappearing under the cover of night, quietly without any trace or explanation, not even the pretense.

Kingdom security interests were invoked like talismans, warding off dissent with threats veiled in patriotism's guise.

Within his dungeon sanctum, Gervin continued to craft and foment lies, each wrapping tighter around the kingdom's collective throat. He liked the thought of that quite a bit. His gaze remained fixed upon parchment strewn before him, lips ever curled into perpetual sneer.

Gervin gazed upon scrolls unfurled before him. Few of the caged chambers were occupied, as Gervin had most prisoners put to death before even arriving. There was no accountability, and he could do whatever he wished. The cell reeked. Candles burned steadily, the only stability present at the moment being the flickering flame.

Before him lay parchment bearing bloody-inked accusations enchanted with ancient magics, each word a drip of venom seeping into Solipsia's heart. He leaned forward, eyes reflecting cold candlelight as he proudly perused lines crafted to twist truth into grotesque parodies.

"Heroes?" he scoffed softly in affected calm with a superior tone. "More like butchers. They cast goblins as demons when, truly, their victims were precious wee ones, no more a menace than Denys, or little Gimmy. The way of the goblins, to set their youth free! So much we could learn from them!"

A cruel smile played at the corners of his awkwardly small mouth, lips curling. He could almost taste the fear rippling through the streets and villages of Solipsia, fear born of doubt and confusion, sown meticulously by his own many decades-long machinations.

Gervin's fingerprint was in all of it, and proud of the stripped alleyways now choked with debris and strangers from other lands. He spun tales of woe, how the kingdom teetered on brink of ruin due solely to their heroes' bloodlust, and how taxes and tolls had to be multiplied merely to salve wounds inflicted by their reckless slaughter. In order to turn back this strife, it became necessary to open up Solpisia's borders, and allow in all the foreign merchants and industrialists as possible. Heroes and hero supporters could not be allowed to profit from their destruction.

Gervin spoke these things out as he wrote them. "Think back, to days before the 'victory' of these heroes. Peace reigned then, prosperity flowed like a river. Everything was fine until they brought about all the death and destruction, leaving us to drown in its consequences. You live those consequences, and you have nobody to thank more than those evildoers, your so-called heroes."

His words sank deep, nurturing seeds of resentment until they blossomed into bitter fruit. People turned upon one another, with neighbors eyeing neighbors warily and once-solid bonds of trust eroded by suspicions.

Of course, nobody spoke of the princess who had been captured, imprisoned, and tortured by those innocent little goblin "babes." A real piece of work, Gervin had a hand in and for which he was most proud. In fact, it was the centerpiece of his long-term propaganda agenda, which had been in effect since the end of that great conflict. Nobody even remembered her name. He cackled at the thought of this.

Gervin sensed resistance, warning of unrest yet unborn, despite the success of his campaigns. Therefore, he found little time to relish the sight of the kingdom he loathed so much bending to his will. He knew how powerful his enemy could be and could not take any chances.

Outside, night closed in around the palace walls, stars distant above the rooftop smoke stacks billowing forth the residue from fires warming bodies as souls sank into the cold. The kingdom was a restless sleeping beast twisted by pain into grotesque and nightmarish parody of its former self.

* * *

Despite the turmoil, other solitary figures stood sentinel as well, silent as they were. These were those who remembered the true costs of the goblin wars, with the evidence etched deep into their souls, but they also saw this madness for what it was. It was something completely illogical and impossible to reason with. They watched as the kingdom convulsed under wave after wave of lies against their heroes, heroism itself in fact. Hearts everywhere ached with futile longing for moral clarity.

Drake watched this happening as well, and found his attempts at reaching people that much more difficult because of the added tension on all sides.

A mother picked up her children and rushed inside as she saw him approach. His eyes turned away to the horizon, reflecting its starlight. The bitterness of this cultural shift hurt him especially, because he loved Solipsia so much.

With deliberate slowness, he straightened, shoulders squared against the night, and walked forward. Darkness reigned across Solipsia's landscape, and more than just the night, yet embers of truth still smoldered beneath the surface, waiting for a spark that would ignite resistance anew.

Drake's initial forays had met with mixed reception. Some doors opened cautiously at his knock, eyes widening in recognition before slamming shut against him. Others welcomed him warily, offering stiff drinks and tense conversation, with former rejected and latter deflected.

Despite the trepidation that greeted him everywhere, Drake persisted and through his own fear for the future. With any rebuff, still others would listen and remembered the truth of the past. Precious few took the lies now peddled by this false emperor as personal challenges.

Drake tried to move with the air of a peasant, through shadowed alleyways, his breath misting in the chill night air, remaining calm even near patrols, foreign merchants, or other potential combatants. His mission remained clear to him: rally support, forge alliances, and stir the embers of resistance that still smoldered within the breasts of his people. These days it was far too dangerous for Telyn to come along anymore.

Thick manila envelopes were handed to him and others by a messenger on horseback. He raced by, handing it out to all he passed. Of course, it was a strange foreign army horseman, with very strange features. The seal was a blob of black and red wax stamped with tiny magic insignias that made Drake's stomach churn. The central figure was a twisted dragon, jaws agape around writhing figures, and there was **G E R V I N** at the bottom formed in a half-circle.

He broke the seal cautiously, unrolling the parchment within. His eyes scanned the lines. The charges were laid out starkly, a litany of crimes committed by heroes, pretty much all of them: living, long dead, and any known descendants. His own name leapt out at him among the accused. Below his father noted "Eldred «deceased»," there was printed, "Drake, son of Eldred, guilty of mass murder, genocide, conspiracy against the crown, and attempted **regicide**." Indeed, Gervin knew it was him that night.

Drake decided to return to Silver Keep as quickly as he could. Things had changed, and so his strategy would need to shift as well.

By borrowed horse, he rode. Along the way he found banners plastered onto crumbling walls, promising fortunes for information leading to the capture of wanted heroes.

One such notice caught Drake's eye, his very own visage staring back at him, features twisted into an almost comical snarl. The reward was astronomical, a small fortune, enough to buy a home, or perhaps secure one's family against hard times. He tore it down, crumpling the parchment in his fist as anger surged through him. Gervin certainly knew.

"Lookin' fo' trouble, hero?" A goblin soldier slunk from the shadows, muddy teeth bared in a mockery of a smile. Its eyes were pools of darkness, reflecting Drake's rage back at him.

Drake whirled his horse around to face it, hands clenched upon the reins. "Trouble finds me," he growled. "Much as it has found Solipsia."

The goblin chuckled, low and grating. "Ya. Trouble is... 'prof'able.'" It gestured to the crumpled notice on the stone road. "Mos' w'sell mama fo' dat."

"And what of yours?" Drake countered. "Would you sell out your own kind for gold?"

The goblin looked at him in disgust. "You not gona make it, you stupid. Gol' buy things, hero. Loy'ty, too. We get you in time, stupid, dun worree."

It smiled, but then it moved out of sight, melting back into the shadows as silently as it had appeared.

Drake's heart pounded like a battle drum. The encounter left a bitter taste in his mouth, yet also steeled his resolve. The cowardice and treason inherent to that creature stood out most to him. If goblins and trolls could turn on each other for gain, then their fear and greed were tools he might also wield against them.

* * *

In the early morning hours after arriving back at Silver Keep, Drake found himself unable to sleep or wait for someone else to wake up. More heroes and soldiers had arrived recently, and yet their numbers remained relatively small.

He ventured out into the periphery of the massive fortress, where a market once throbbed with life. Stalls now stood empty, awning ropes swinging forlornly in the breeze like limp flags.

The couple vendors who had bravely remained, families plying their trades there for generations, were now gone. Against their wishes, they felt forced to uproot and flee rather than risk associations with those suddenly deemed enemies of the state.

Graffiti marred walls where once bright banners had hung with crude drawings of heroes as monsters, words painted in blood-red hue: TRAITOR, BABY-KILLERS, and LIARS.

Each step felt heavier than the last, leaden with the weight of Solipsia's shifting loyalties.

As noon approached, shadows lengthened, and so did Drake's stride. He sought solace in action, determined to somehow confront head-on the tides of mistrust that threatened to drown his cause, a challenge becoming ever more difficult due to all the trouble brought about by the emperor.

***

Weeks passed. Drake's duties at the Silver Keep, especially in training the young and inexperienced, limited his opportunities to venture forth into the field, and so they had started to rely upon scouts instead. At every turn, evidence of the kingdom's decay met him. In the missions to reach out to people, his scouts had to now avoid not only the foreign soldiers but also patrols of trolls and goblins prowling about, especially at night, eyes aglow with malice. They could be smelled, it was said, more than heard or seen. It was a joke that was only funny far away.

One night, after hours of passing on his knowledge in training, Drake sat upon the wall of Silver Keep with Eolande looking out at the kingdom, from their great distance.

Eolande's family had long stood for Solipsia, and Silver Keep had always been in their name as on their land since before anyone could remember, but it was considered by the family as belonging exclusively to the kingdom.

They always treated the fortress as an official place of which they were stewards, and nothing for the family's own uses.

The landscape in the distance was dark save for the areas surrounding the palace, alight in torches and fires burning, the business of destruction never at end.

Eolande's weathered face had never seemed so old to Drake as in that moment. His expression completely changing at the sight of a pack of trolls entering the palace through the looking glass he held.

His eyes darted nervously back at Drake. "Drake," he whispered urgently, pulling him inside. "Those shouldn't be there."

"Neither should we be here," Drake replied quickly. A fire smoldered in a small iron pit before them, casting flickering shadows on the walls. "We need action, more than ever."

Eolande sighed, running a hand through thinning hair. "Action? Drake, they're casting us as monsters and everyone is believing them. Our own neighbors are moving away far off into distant lands, simply so they can't be seen anywhere near us and we will soon have no allies left if these arrests and assassinations continue," he broke off, shaking his head. "What could anyone do against this? We're deemed enemies of the kingdom now, and how do we even come back from that?"

Drake leaned forward, intensity burning in his gaze. "We fight," he said simply. "Together, we fight with truth on our side, and demonstrate it. Show them who the real monsters are. Truth is all we need, and it is on our side, Eolande."

Eolande looked at him for a moment, then nodded slowly. "I'll do whatever I can for you and our cause Drake, you know that," he promised. "But be careful. These are dark times, and shadows grow longer and bolder as the light lowers."

The moon was indeed low yet bright at that moment, casting bold and elongated shadows across the weathered stones of Silver Keep.

Drake and Eolande sat perched high above on the ancient battlement. The resolute yet ancient masonry beneath them bore witness to countless battles, their silent stones pocked with the marks as proof of valor long past across the centuries.

The two watched the kingdom from above as it all crumbled upon itself from within, with the heaviest hearts. There was little they could do at the moment, and everything seemed to be working against them.

"Eldred would never have let it come to this," he murmured under his breath. His father's legacy always loomed large for Drake.

Eolande could only nod at this, not entirely believing it.

Silver Keep stood sentinel, isolated and defiant against the encroaching corruption and hordes.

Drake wished Eolande a good night, as he made his way down the steep stone stairwell. The keep's interior was a labyrinth of shadows, torchlight flickering fitfully against cold walls adorned with faded old paintings and dust-laden banners.

***

The braver and wiser heroes and descendants had gathered here already, united in desperate defense against Gervin's relentless tyranny.

In the great hall, voices murmured low in tense conversations. Some of the elder heroes huddled over maps spread across rough-hewn tables, their faces construed with lines of worry. The younger soldiers were mostly all already asleep, tired from practice and training pushed upon them for days on end for months.

Drake approached a cluster of figures near the hearth, where a fire crackled fiercely despite the summer's warmth outside.

Telyn stood by and watched, her once-vibrant eyes now shadowed by weariness. She held a parchment tightly clenched in her fist; Drake recognized it as one of the many missives circulating among the resistance, detailing Gervin's latest atrocities.

"News from the outskirts?" Drake inquired.

Telyn glanced up, relief flickering across her face before she nodded grimly. "More disappearances," she said. "Whole families taken in the night. And those who dare speak out?" she asked. "Silenced swiftly. Iron fists and cold dungeons await the bold."

Drake felt a surge of anger, hot and potent as the fire at his back, yet he calmed himself before answering, "We must use their own tactics against them. Goblins are creatures of greed and ambition. We can use those instincts against them."

Telyn raised an eyebrow. "How do you propose we do that?"

Drake leaned in closer. "Divide and conquer," he said. "Find their leaders, their power brokers. Pit them against each other by hinting at betrayals, with promises of greater riches. Let them tear at one another while we strike from the shadows."

"It could work," Telyn laughed. "Would require careful maneuvering. One misstep and we risk unleashing chaos on ourselves. Those insiders within their ranks. Eyes and ears among the goblins."

As they spoke, a sudden commotion echoed through the halls, a frantic knocking at the heavy oak doors followed by urgent cries from beyond. The conversations hushed abruptly as all eyes turned towards the entrance.

The doors burst open, revealing a breathless messenger clad in tattered rags, face pale with fear and exertion. "Drake!" he gasped, stumbling into the hall. "It's... it's happening again. They've come for more of us!"

A heavy silence fell over the gathering as Drake stepped forward, his expression grave. "Where?" Drake demanded, voice steady.

The messenger took a shuddering breath, eyes darting nervously around the room. "Near the foothill river wharves south of here," he managed to say. "They're rounding up families, children, too."

Collective outrage erupted throughout the hall.

Drake exchanged glances with the others, seeing his own grim resolve mirrored in their eyes.

"Gather everyone!" Drake ordered, voice like thunder. "We move now."

* * *

The keep became action, emboldened all the more by Drake's swift and resolute decision.

Warriors donned armor hastily, elders rallied the young, and calls of defiance boomed through every corridor.

Drake stood at the heart of it all, his presence a steadying force through the emotional turmoil and intensity.

They ventured forth into the night. The battle ahead promised no easy victory, yet he knew what must be done. Drake led his band of resolute souls out against the darkness, and they moved in relative silence with great speed.

They approached the river wharfs, where the goblin presence had been reported. A thick pall hung over the area; aura of dread and oppression clinging to every surface. Drake signalled for a halt just before entering the heart of danger. He dismounted quietly, tying up his horse near an empty trading stall, his companions following suit.

Eolande approached Drake as they surveyed the area by foot, quietly. "All of this reminds me of riding with Eldred. I remember most of my time with him was spent in search of that damn sword he was always after. Your father gave up on ever finding it, but there was a time when he was obsessed, I'll have to tell you about it sometime."

Drake nodded grimly at Eolande's words. His mind raced with the memories of tales told by the fireside. "Well, there's no time like the present."

Eolande leaned in closer as they moved stealthily through the woods and along a bordering hill ridge. "It was a legendary sword said to possess a power unlike any other," he said. His eyes reflected the dim glow cast by distant torches. "Your father believed it held the key to defeating the goblins once and for all." He paused, glancing at Drake. "Then one day he changed his tune, saying it might have all been simply symbolic or metaphoric or whatever, but I'm not sure he ever truly believed that. Anyway, by the time you were old enough to remember anything, he had stopped talking about it entirely."

Drake listened intently to Eolande, his thoughts consumed by images of the past as they walked. The information stirred something deep within.

Drake led them through winding paths, eyes passively scanning the rooftops and hidden recesses where enemies might lurk. The sounds of a distant clash reached their ears, desperate cries mingled with harsh goblin snarls.

Eolande pointed at a collection of fishing wharfs and houses in a circle. "That's the place," he stated confidently.

Drake nodded, drawing his sword.

Stealthily, they slip through the shadows, their footsteps barely audible. As they neared the source of the commotion, Drake signalled for the others to split up and create a diversion.

Eolande and the others move off silently, melting into the

darkness while Drake advanced alone.

The alley opened onto a courtyard teeming with chaos. Goblins swarmed like insects in the dark, their forms twisted and malevolent under the harsh torchlight. Families huddled together, fear as deeply embedded upon their faces as anguish and hunger. Children clung to their parents, tears streaming down grimy cheeks.

Drake's heart tightened at the sight, a surge of anger fueling his determination. He stepped forward boldly, sword raised high. His voice cut through the noise like thunder.

"**Release them *NOW*!**" he commanded.

The goblins turned as one, all snarls and hisses.

Drake stood his ground, eyes ablaze with a fury born of righteousness.

The first goblin lunged, its blade glinting wickedly, but Drake's reflexes were far too fast.

He sidestepped the attack, countering with a precise strike that sent the creature's head smashing into a horse trough, causing blood to spray over everything.

Off to his side, his companions had joined in the fray and attacked the goblins from behind.

Drake fought with the precision of his years honed in training, each action well-practiced and powerful.

Another goblin moved toward the hostages, but Drake ran him down and buried his father's sword into its skull.

Each use of his sword manifested his father's teachings, an embodiment of the intellectual strength meeting application, passed down through the generations.

Drake felt great joy in glimpsing the others fighting valiantly beside him, their blades cutting through the goblin ranks in camaraderie, ***finally***!

His men rallied, spurred by the sight of their leader's relentless assault, and chased off most of the remaining goblins.

One disarmed goblin, especially rotted and aged, sought shelter in an apparently vacant tavern, and so Drake followed it, approaching cautiously, not knowing what trouble it was up to. He entered the dark building, finding only shadows and hints of movement.

"Leave this place," it growled, voice low yet commanding. "Your kind has no claim here, this was our kingdom first! Bastards! Evil baby slayers!" The goblin cackled like shattering glass.

Drake's eyes adjusted quickly to the darkness, finding the creature.

"You know nothing of our kind or the truth of this land!" It rasped at Drake, upon approach.

Drake hesitated for a moment, struck by the intensity in the creature's gaze, and answered, "Neither do I care."

The goblin awkwardly grinned a toothy leer. It chuckled then, as if hearing a joke in its own twisted little mind. "Truth hides in shadows, fool!" it screeched cryptically as it foolishly stepped toward Drake.

Drake simply stabbed the goblin without saying another word, utterly unimpressed by the thing. The goblin fell to the ground.

The goblin's eyes narrowed as it realized its life was over. It wished to mock Drake, and not being very smart while still wanting the final word, blurted it out, "Joke's on you, bastards, we take Silver Keep as I speak!" The old goblin's form convulsed violently, spasms wracking its frail body, as it died.

A chilling fear gripped Drake.

"Back to base!" Drake screamed, as he exited the tavern. His heart was pounding. "Back home! Get to the horses, now!" he bellowed, spurring his men into a frenzy, showing the emotion in his face.

Drake ran. His men followed suit, urgency lending speed to their strides as they returned to their steeds.

CHAPTER FIVE

SORROW SWORD

Mounting their horses once more, Drake and company moved with great speed, pulling sharply on their reins. He had ridden this route in great haste many times before, but never so swift. He and his men made it beyond the foothills in record time.

The keep loomed ahead, high up in the mountains, its towers silhouetted against layers of fog. Smoke could be seen billowing from multiple locations.

Hours later, as they galloped at full-speed, dawn broke, but the fog remained. The moon lingered too, as though it had forgotten itself.

It became apparent that something else was wrong as they drew closer and closer. The usual sentries appeared absent from the walls, and an unsettling quiet hung over the fortress. They approached cautiously. A sickening dread coiled within him.

The sight that greeted them stole the breath from Drake's lungs. The walls on the far side, once sturdy and tall, lay uprooted and flat upon the ground. The wall sections had been lifted right out of the ground due to some unimaginable amount of force.

A single troll loomed near the devastation, its massive form hulking and misshapen.

Drake could just make it out, as they approached. It was unlike any troll he had ever seen, not that he had seen many, with arms grotesquely elongated with massive fists, lurching with the gait of an ape. Its visage sent shivers down his spine.

Laying nearby, as they got nearer, they could make out several huge pulley systems and massive ropes on the ground, not broken but placed as if laid down near the walls laying flat. Drake didn't have much time to analyze the situation.

The troll's eyes burned with a mad fervor as it caught sight of the approaching riders, roars of challenge proceeding from its gaping and loose maw.

Drake's horse pulled away violently, justifiably terrified of the monstrosity before them. He tried to calm the animal, heart hammering against his own ribs. He was feeling an incredible amount of empathy for anything facing that beast, in this situation. He looked behind him, his men faltered momentarily, shock and fear gripping them and pulling them back. All one could think in such a situation is: ***ESCAPE***!

The troll bellowed in their direction, and then started to sprint at them, throwing itself forward with those enormous arms, like some arboreal ape.

***

"CHARGE!!" Drake called out, leading the forward push as his men rallied behind him.

They charged up the hillside through the thick fog, battle cries filling the night, and, perhaps, all eternity.

As Drake and his company closed in, they heard the deafening roars from their periphery.

Other troll voices bellowed similarly, sounding like several thunderstorms screaming at each other through the atmosphere.

The hidden trolls lumbered forward, breaking down trees, their long strangebreed limbs propelling them with terrifying speed around the trees as they went. Horses reared and screamed as the massive monstrosities appeared from nowhere and barreled through their ranks.

Drake fought and struggled against the darkness as sharp as his own blade. He struck one on the back of the neck, cutting deeply into the thing's thick skin.

Beside him, Eolande's arrows cleaved through trollish flesh and bone.

Still others wielded pikes and swords and injured more than their share of trolls.

There were more than two dozen of them, however, from what Drake could spot. Out of the corners of his eyes, he saw at least as many of his men pummeled by the things.

One especially monstrous troll lunged at Drake and his horse, jaws opened in a roar that shook his very soul.

Instantly, he stood upon his horse's saddle and jumped off, diving for the beast. Flying between the beast's swinging arms, he was able to bury his sword into the troll's chest, so that it collapsed dead.

The impact of its body sent shockwaves through the already shaking ground.

Drake's horse staggered back. He pulled his sword out of the chest of the terrible thing and looked around to find himself alone surrounded by the bodies of his brave men or their horses.

His men were all either injured, dead or, running away while fighting for their lives.

He swung himself back up in his saddle and moved in the direction he last saw some of his men.

The ground trembled under the onslaught of those monstrous feet, seemingly all the more at a distance and out of sight.

Drake acted on instinct. "Retreat!" he screamed through the fog to nobody but himself, as though it needed to be said, riding forward trying to find anyone he could help.

He felt the tremble of a couple trolls running toward him through the fog. Panic surged through him as he fled, the thunderous pursuit of trolls hot on his heels.

He rode away blindly, heart pounding in simple terror.

Drake could hear the snarls and roars behind him, the crash of hooves beating the earth like the very heartbeat of doom.

His surviving men were now surely scattered, each taking separate paths in desperate bids to evade capture or death.

Drake urged his steed through dense thickets, branches whipping at him as he rode. Glancing back briefly, he saw one troll gaining on him swiftly despite the creature's ungainly frame.

Then came the brutal moment when everything changed: suddenly the troll roared in triumph.

In an instant, a wave of despair washed over Drake, raw and overwhelming, as he realized the troll had grabbed his horse by a leg.

His brave horse was desperately trying to continue running, yet obviously could not help now but to fail. He realized neither he nor his horse were going to outrun this nightmare.

The strangebreed massive troll yanked the horse back and then grabbed him, tossing his horse like a ragdoll, its eyes gleaming with malice and locked on to him. The troll took Drake's father's sword and tossed it as well.

He could hear his horse shriek and whinny its death cry as it splatted against the ground below the cliff's edge.

The coldhearted beast regarded him for a moment, as if making a decision.

Drake's heart hammered against his ribs, unable to even mourn for the animal he had spent these many weeks with.

The troll gripped him tightly, and he felt a searing pain as claws dug into his back. The beast seemed to have made its decision.

Drake's vision swam as darkness crept in at the edges. The

Silver Keep, smoking and conquered, loomed before him once more, this time upside down as carried by the troll towards its deconstructed walls.

Both his heart and mind were the heaviest they had ever felt in his life and he felt utter dread, but then his father's voice spoke to him again, "Sorrow points to where you bury the sword, son." 'But how?' The stone walls were damned silent and desolate, without any answers available to his desperate question.

Drake was thrown into the courtyard by the troll, as if to be dealt with later. He was very confused by this turn of events, every sense heightened as he looked around cautiously, seeking some means of escape. There was a stench about, the mix of blood, smoke, and something else, an almost sweet decay that turned his stomach and he presumed had to do with this new type of troll.

The troll ripped off Drake's armor and smashed the pieces underfoot on the ground, leaving him in his clothes alone. "You try'ta 'scape, ya get smashed," called out the weird troll as it laid down on the courtyard ground, to take a nap.

Drake crept through the courtyard, treading lightly around the debris. He thought of Telyn and the others again. Mentally, he berated himself for any number of apparent mistakes. He needed to be here for his sister however, so he was glad for that.

Shadows danced menacingly around him, whispers of the past mingling with the recent carnage. The main castle was smashed in on itself, half destroyed.

A soft whimper caught his ear, sending a jolt through his veins. Telyn's many injuries across her body stood out most to Drake. The sight of her sent a wave of cold fury and shame crashing over Drake.

He called out her name in a hoarse whisper, "Telyn!"

Her reply was faint and sad, "Drake..." She was fighting against her bonds, her wrists in ropes, her eyes wide with fear as she struggled to break free.

Momentary relief and some new hope flooded through him, mingling with grim determination, as he pulled out his knife and cut the rope for her.

"We need to get out of here now..." he began to tell her.

A deafening roar and rumbling of the ground interrupted him, more trolls, but not alone.

He could hear wheels and goblins with them. Their horrid shrieks pierced the night, invoking dread in most who might hear.

He whirled around just as one of those long-armed behemoths stomped into view. Behind it, more trolls emerged, alongside a swarm of goblins.

Telyn huddled behind him. Drake's heart pounded wildly as he assessed their options, none good. They were outnumbered and surrounded.

Drake's gaze flicked back to Telyn, her expression one of undefeatable courage and optimism yet mired still by fear.

Drake made a swift decision. "We need to get away!" He tried to drag her, but the trolls had already closed in. A towering beast reached down, its hands too big for its frame wrapping around each of them.

The ground tilted violently as they were carried past the carefully deconstructed walls.

He was thrown into what appeared to be a cage on a carriage that was constructed from some poor animal's bones. Looking at it more closely from the inside, it was probably assembled from trollbones, Drake reasoned, as they were hard as iron and huge.

Telyn was pushed into another trollbone cage carriage beside him. Panic surged afresh within despite his courage, confined and helpless as they were, with cages shuttered upon them.

Telyn called to him with a strained whisper, "Drake, what do we do?"

Drake's mind raced. "We need to think," he murmured back. "Keep quiet for now."

* * *

The day and night that followed seemed endless, each passing moment heavy with dreadful possibilities. His limbs throbbed with dull agony, but it was overshadowed by the weight of failure that pressed down upon him like a physical force. Others were added to carriage cages in the night, including a couple of Drake's soldiers.

"Where's your bravado now, pretty boy?" a nearby goblin guard jeered from just outside the carriage, the morning after his capture.

Drake gritted his teeth and said nothing.

The goblin's laughter was a harsh counterpoint to the suffering all around them. They seemed to delight in the chaos, reveling in the power they wielded over humans they perceived as privileged.

A young woman, likely the wife of a newer soldier, was dragged kicking and screaming from beneath wreckage. She was badly hurt. Her cloak was tattered and leg injured, but her spirit unbroken as she spat curses at her captors who prodded her along.

The goblins jeered, shoving her towards another cage carriage.

"You'll burn for this!" she shouted. "Solipsia will never forget your treachery!"

The goblin chuckled darkly, "Treachery? You humans are always so dramatic."

"You have to know what loyalty is to commit treason," Drake called out flatly from his tiny cage.

The goblin just grunted in agreement, as though vaguely

impressed.

"What kind of creature condemns its children to such a life in brutality?" Drake then asked.

The agreeable goblin took issue at this, however, "We aren't technically children past the age of one, actually, pretty boy." It leered awkwardly at Drake afterward, as if expecting some commendation or reward for revealing this truth.

Another survivor hauled out by the goblins was an older man with a stern gaze and silver hair. His cloak bore remnants of intricate embroidery, now torn and dusted with debris. He moved with a quiet dignity, refusing to struggle despite the rough handling by the goblins.

Drake recognized him then, a dedicated scholar by the name of Iosen who had often advised his father in times past. His sons had been riding with his party.

They tore him from his sanctuary, binding him bodily with ropes.

The old man was thrust into another carriage, his expression unafraid even as the cage slammed shut on him.

They, no doubt, found him trying to save scrolls and codices, or huddled amidst piles of crumbling parchments, eyes scanning the pages frantically; desperate to preserve what knowledge remained before any more destruction befell the library.

An older woman came out of the fortress also tied in rope bonds. Drake recognized her as a member of the kitchen staff, her eyes still bright despite the injuries and dirt on her face. Her breath misted in the air as she murmured prayers, fingers tracing four quadrants.

Suddenly, rough hands seized her from behind. Goblins dragged her kicking and screaming towards a waiting bone cage carriage.

A blacksmith with hands like iron and a spirit to match, fought desperately against his captors. Rope bound him, but his defiant gaze never wavered as he was forced into yet another cage of trollbones on a carriage down the train.

Drake's heart pounded like a war drum within his chest. He knew these people, and yet they remained strangers to him too, faces from the fringes of Silver Keep whose names he barely recalled and whose stories were mostly unknown to him, he had been so busy.

Amid this horror playing out, Drake heard his father's gruff voice once more, "Sorrow points to where you bury the sword, son." 'What sword now?' he thought to himself in a question he could only have ever directed at his father.

Eolande, as if to answer his question, appeared from down the road, bound in rope and guided by a group of goblins. A goblin pushed him against a still upright wall to the Silver Keep nearby, so he stood there patiently.

Upon seeing Drake, however, he shoved away the goblins and lunged towards Drake's carriage.

The goblins roared as they pulled Eolande away from Drake.

Drake called out to him, "My father's obsession, Eolande…"

Eolande responded immediately, "Yes! Seek after Eldred's words, Drake. His words hold the key!"

The goblins exchanged glances, their beady eyes gleaming with malice as they decided his fate on a whim.

One of them, its face a grotesque mask of scars, drew a blade, crude and rusted but no less terrifying for it. It lunged at Eolande, who braced himself for the end. Yet there was something almost ritualistic in the goblin's movements, as it did not go to kill him at once.

Instead, it spoke angrily in harsh syllables, as though curses or incantations. The goblin was oddly shaped in an especial way, which seemed fit for an executioner, with dominant arm three times the size of the other.

Drake, trapped within the cage and confined to watch Eolande, and to bear the crippling responsibility. He wanted to scream, but it would have done no good. He was being forced to witness, and he felt the death of his own father all over again in his mind.

"No! Someone stop this madness, stop this!" Telyn called out, with face a veil of tears.

However, Drake knew calling out would not help, though he dared not interrupt her. The goblins were heartless and enjoyed witnessing misery, so that such pleas only encouraged them.

In his mind, he held visions of Eolande and his father, centuries deep generational camaraderie from ages long past, but forged in blood and steel. Eolande was related distantly, but he had also married closer into the family through Eldred's other cousins.

He was always Eldred's friend first, as were their fathers: Prolten and Grago; as was also claimed of the grandfather of Prolten and the granduncle of Grago. The feeling of loss over so many friends and loved ones overwhelmed Drake. He felt his head swelling with the pain.

Eolande called out "I loved your father as I love you Drake, I still believe in your..." The goblin's blade dropped downwards in an abrupt and heartless motion, as Eolande screamed out in horrendous pain.

It went deep in a swift and powerful movement through the old man's neck, forced through more than cut, ripping as much as slicing, which ended his life painfully and not as swiftly.

The screaming was horrible, sending jolts of sheer pain through Drake that ran as deep as his roots. Telyn, next to him, could not contain her wails, and neither could several others in the carriages.

Then everything that was Eolande went still.

Eolande crumpled to the ground, his form collapsing like a dropped doll.

Drake's scream pierced the air, raw and primal, a howl of sorrow and rage that filled the felled fortress. His voice was raw with anguish.

The image of Eolande's final moment burned into his mind, searing hotter than any physical wound. His cries filled the ruined keep as he sat huddled helpless in that tiny cage.

***

The train of bone cage carriages rattled into motion, as dragged along by the collection of trolls lurching over uneven ground. It pushed forward, with Drake at the end, each jolt sending fresh waves of pain through his quite injured body.

He could hear Telyn nearby, her soft cries of distress; a knife twisting in his gut. Drake's mind churned with thoughts of what lay ahead. This all began with that fateful yet desperate stab at hope in facing down the evil in their struggle to save lives. Yet now here it ended in capture and demise amid ruin.

His thoughts whirled. His father's words were heard in his mind once more, speaking of sword and sorrow. At once Drake stilled his mind in spite of the numbing sensation, clenching his teeth almost as tightly as his fists, grief stunted by determination in a moderation of deeper rages warring within.

The iron wheels of the carriage clattered against the rough road, a harsh rhythm.

That rotten sweet stench on the troll was thick and putrid, but more than that. It was a churning mix of troll and goblin musks that tortured Drake's nose.

His body tensed with every jolt and lurch, as if trying to outrun the pain radiating through his aching limbs.

Through the bones of the cage, Drake watched the grotesque forms of their captors trudge alongside.

The trolls towered over the carriages. Nine at least, he counted, their massive silhouettes blotting out the faint moonlight filtering through the narrow passes of the mountains.

A couple of goblins scampered beside them.

The trolls gathered around Drake's carriage, their hulking forms blotting out what little light there was, as they continued to walk and push the carriages along. One spoke up, "'Ere, this'ns dumb ainnit?"

They leaned in, faces pressing against the bones, eyes gleaming with cruel amusement as they taunted him.

One troll leaned even closer to Drake's carriage, its breath hot and rancid through the trollbones.

The creature's lips peeled back from yellowed fangs, a grotesque parody of a smile. This had been one of the trolls that chased Drake through the forest.

"Sof's mud y'are, heroes run innit?" it jeered, spittle flying onto Drake's cheek. It chuckled like a bear might.

Another troll repeated the jest in celebration, "Yeh, runny-like snot, 'ee's!" It grunted, clearly amused by its own wit. Some snot, in fact, was dripping from this particular troll's snout.

"Now'ee ain't," the first troll sneered, grabbing at Drake's leg with a heavy and flippant paw. The creature twisted savagely without hesitation or thought. Drake's bones cracked and he gasped, agony lancing through his limbs like a red-hot blade.

He gritted his teeth, refusing to give them the satisfaction of a cry. Instead, he bit down on his lip until it bled.

They laughed, cruelly. His pain was their entertainment.

His leg jerked in reflexive defiance, kicking out against the troll's grip, but this only spurred the creature into greater fury.

Its grip tightened and Drake could feel his bones grind together as he heard another sickening crack. His screams tore from his throat raw and primal.

"Pathetic," one troll sneered, spitting on Drake's carriage. "Heroes, indeed." Another chuckled, a sound like boulders grinding. "Where's yer strength now, boy? Where's yer famous father?" Drake said nothing, his breath coming in ragged gasps as he fought to hold onto consciousness.

The trolls roared with laughter, slapping their thighs and stamping their feet in delight.

One goblin nearby, its voice a shrill cackle, chimed in with high-pitched gibberish at seeing this, its eyes wide with glee. Drake couldn't make anything out.

Telyn whimpered in the carriage next to his, her voice barely audible over the din. Drake could see her, huddled, her face pale and terror-stricken. Her eyes met his for a fleeting moment, and he saw the reflection of his own despair staring back at him.

The carriage lurched violently, the sudden jolt sending waves of agony through Drake's shattered leg. It groaned and creaked, bones rattling like macabre wind chimes.

Drake's body was jostled cruelly within its trollbone confines, each movement sending fresh waves of pain crashing through him.

He clenched his jaw, teeth grinding together as he fought to keep the screams locked away.

Through bleary eyes, he saw the mountains looming darkly above them, their peaks shrouded in remnants of winter's snows. The cold seeped into his bones, numbing the raw agony of his leg.

He looked back at Telyn and called out in a near breathless rasp, "I love you, Telyn! Be brave! Be brave for dad, and for Kenid and Endra and everyone!"

"I love you, too, brother! You're gonna be fine, just stay calm, breathe Drake, breathe!" she screamed back at him, past her tears.

Trolls continued their taunts, now mocking the screams of distress between the two children of Eldred, like a chorus of tormentors. They shook the carriage, and continued to jest in stupid mockery.

The pain was overwhelming, and Drake could do naught but endure.

Their ceaseless delight in insulting injury distracted them, extracting entertainment from the distress and trauma all the more. Then something unexpected happened. The last of the drivers, as it looked away giggling in cruel mockery, failed in its duties at a cliff-hugging tight turn. Drake caught the last glimpse he would ever have of his sister, as his carriage jettisoned off into the darkness below.

Drake felt his heart careen for his throat as the now detached carriage smashed into a towering oak.

Time slowed, each frantic beat of his pulse putting pressure in his ears like a funeral dirge. At once, there came a thunderous crack of splintering wood and trollbone, followed immediately by the groaning distress of the rusted bolts shattering.

The carriage shuddered, crushing its occupant further as it collided with the massive and ancient tree. A deafening crunch and then the fall.

Drake's vision blurred, light dancing at the edges as darkness gnawed relentlessly with new layers of hot pain. Panic surged through him with a ferocity that matched the storm outside. He was trapped, helpless, as the carriage teetered precariously on its broken axle.

Drake readied himself for the cold embrace of oblivion. Yet, fate, it seemed, possessed a will harder than any trollbone.

The carriage swayed drunkenly, sliding down the side of the tree, a grotesque dance with gravity as it hung suspended for what felt like an eternity. Then, with a ground-shaking thud, it crashed down onto its side onto another series of felled trees and branches.

Drake shot out like a cannonball, hurtling through the night air as gravity's insistent tug pulled him towards the unforgiving and demanding ground below, yet not nearly from as high up as it had been. He caught only fleeting glimpses of the world spinning wildly. Glimpses of the shattered remnants of the carriage, the silhouette of the oak tree against the moonless sky, and the ground below in all its inevitability.

He braced his arms to cushion his fall as he plummeted. The impact was brutal despite hitting the tree root with his locked arms first. The back of his skull smashed into it, as he bounced back, with a burst of white-hot pain exploding behind his eyes. Then nothing but blackness.

* * *

Drake cried out in pain as he awoke precariously inclined upon a rough embankment caught in vines, the sound raw and primal. This inadvertently sent his body rolling further downhill, tumbling through thick underbrush that clawed at his skin and snagged his already ripped and tattered clothes.

The descent seemed interminable. Drake was jostled and battered by unseen roots and stones jutting from the slope, each collision sending fresh waves of agony coursing through him. It seemed difficult at that moment for him to imagine having been launched off a worse cliff.

He tried desperately to twist or curl inwardly as he fell for protection, but little could help the punishing fall.

Finally, with a force that stole what little breath remained in his lungs, he crashed into something solid at the embankment's base. He lay there, gasping and disoriented, as pain radiated out from countless points across his body.

Drake forced himself to focus despite the haze of agony clouding his mind. He needed to move. He needed escape before those lumbering brutes found him again, or the carriage descended upon him anyway, wherever it was.

Summoning what remained of his strength, he rolled onto his side, gritting his teeth against the searing protest of injured muscles and broken bones.

A soft rustling nearby stirred him from his struggles. His gaze snapped towards the sound, eyes straining through the underbrush.

There, past a tangle of brambles, a figure darted just out of sight. It had been small, hunched over and moving with erratic jerkiness.

Drake dragged himself across the ground to the base of another tree nearby, its bark like charcoal against the sunlight filtering through overhead leaves. Drake was tired beyond reckoning.

Silence settled in around Drake, as though the very woods were crouching stealthily.

He lay there, limbs akimbo, each inhale a ragged battle against the pain that lanced through his chest, shoulder, arms, his guts, his lungs, and his head. Every fiber of his being screamed in anguish, yet within the agony, a small flame of gratitude flickered to life immediately, as if its recognition itself was a belated gift from his father: he lived.

He had not died, and it was this grace he held on to most firmly. Perhaps he would continue, and perhaps he would win or help others win.

The sun gazed through the tangle of gnarled branches

overhead, sprinkling the forest floor with shadows that writhed and twisted grotesquely.

Having landed on his face, Drake was eventually able to force himself on to his back, which was a task in and of itself, jaws clenched tight against the nausea from the pain. His breath came in harsh gasps, each one a laborious battle.

He reached for his legs, fingers probing the wreckage of bone and flesh. A wave of dizziness swept over him, and he fought against it, blinking away tears that blurred his vision, as he remembered Eolande's recent death and his last words with Telyn. Even now he only worried for Kenid, Endra, Telyn, and Solipsia.

Drake shoved the thoughts aside. There would be time for sadness, if at all, later. He had to do. He had to do for them.

Drake dragged himself upwards, with back against a tree, his shattered frame sitting now upright. Agony exploded through him with each movement. Panicking for a moment, he reached for his knife which had been wrapped up in his clothing and found it, feeling some relief in its discovery. He suddenly felt tremendously fortunate at this point despite all his pain and injuries.

Each heartbeat strengthened this vortex of defiance surging anew within. He was able to sleep, and awoke at night.

He needed to move, before some enemy found him, and his enemies were abounding everywhere. Deep in the woods, the night sounds enclosed Drake. Any progress became a torturous crawl. Each pull sent tremors coursing through his ruined legs. Yet onward he trudged, propelled by an instinct as old as time.

He had determined it was generally better to move at night, since he could stay warm by the movement, instead of risking sleep in the cold.

Drake's mind drifted in and out of consciousness, reality blending with dreams in a dizzying dance. Visions assailed him.

Eldred's stern gaze, cast in lines of that worry and determination, more familiar to Drake now, despite the years and yet also because of them.

In his mind he saw his father lead the charge against the goblin hordes morphing into himself. A persistent thread cut through any other of his thoughts: survive.

"Survive," he spoke aloud, voice little more than a rasp. "Just... keep moving." Drake leaned heavily against the rough bark of an ancient oak in the dark.

He paused there, chest heaving, as Eldred's words played through his mind, as if on loop, and so he spoke to himself aloud what he could, "Sorrow points, bury the sword." The words were a lifeline, tethering him to reason through the storm of pain and delirium. "What sword?" he scoffed, a hint of mirth as defiance against all the pain.

A shiver coursed down his spine. Not from the chill night air seeping through his tattered clothing, but from an unsettling sensation prickling at the edges of his awareness. He had a sense of being watched by a presence lurking just beyond the veil of shadows.

Drake squinted out into the gloom, straining to penetrate the inky darkness, he told himself it was probably the same goblin or whatever it was, which was no consolation.

Nothing stirred save the gentle sway of branches overhead, yet the feeling persisted. With a grunt of effort, he propelled himself forward once more, limbs trembling beneath his weight. Each halting movement sounded through the forest in announcements of his arrivals, each gasp for breath a ragged trumpet accompanying his faltering and dragging march.

A faint rustle sounded from deeper within the woods, too deliberate to be mere wind through leaves. Drake froze, heart pounding wildly. There, again, a soft skittering, as if some small creature darted just out of sight.

"Who's there?" the words emerged hoarse and raw, barely audible even to himself. Yet his words cut through the forest. Drake waited, muscles taut as a bowstring, ears straining for any response.

Despite his awareness, he fell asleep as the sun rose.

* * *

Sunset was letting go of the forest, the last bits of light filtering through dense canopy above, glimmering as if nature herself hesitated to leave the world to the nightly gloom which reigned. Drake stirred in pain upon his undergrowth bed, his body wracked by shivering fits that jolted him from his fitful slumber. Shadows cast eerie patterns on the gnarled roots entwining round him like knuckles of fingers grasping for the depths of earth.

His eyes fluttered open, gazing up through dappled shade into the vast expanse, as the blue sky above darkened.

Drake shifted cautiously, every movement eliciting sharp protests from abused muscles and bones. His gaze fell upon his battered form, splayed awkwardly against the forest floor. Limbs twisted at grotesque angles; flesh marred by bruises. A grim inventory revealed fingers swollen like fat sausages, knuckles raw and bleeding where they had dragged through dirt and gravel during his desperate flight.

Despair was always waiting for him nearby, like some kind of unwelcomed goblin companion. Within his shattered vessel beat a heart undeterred, the same tenacity honed by years under his father's tutelage. Drake knew what must be done next, as he stared at his broken legs.

He could not afford surrender, not when so much relied upon him. Summoning reserves of fortitude, he began the arduous process of setting his bones into place, somehow. He had never done such a thing before in his life, but he had all the time to figure it out, it seemed, or what? There was no other option for it.

His legs had been completely mangled and they hurt everywhere. Stopping at the base of a clutch of tree near a stream, he felt around the wounds and shattered bones, surrounded by bruised, sore, and swelling flesh. His teeth gritted tightly, feeling as though they might shatter.

"God," he rasped between clenched teeth, voice low over ragged gasps for air, "thank you for protecting me. Guide my hands now, lest I falter in this trial."

Tears stung eyes already raw from exertion and exposure; yet within them burned resolve, immovable and impassable as the mountain peaks looming above.

His hands trembled. Clumsy and swollen were his fingers, barely able to grasp anything. Drake fought against rising panic, focusing instead on methodical steps in the process laid out before him like rungs on an invisible ladder.

Each bone fragment set back in place sent fresh waves of agony coursing through him, stealing breath and blurring vision. Yet he persevered, driven by desperation born of knowing what awaited if he failed. He felt that failure was not an option.

Drake set each fragment into place, ignoring the internal screams of protest from mangled flesh, until joints realigned with agonizing slowness. This process took him almost two days, and required him to do it at night by fire. There was no hope for it, and he had to risk being spotted.

After setting the bones, Drake fashioned splints from bark and attached them with strips torn from the remnants of his tunic, leaving him in his outer cloak and pants only. The splints provided laughable support, though they were better than nothing, otherwise promised by this wilderness refuge.

Drake allowed himself a moment's respite, leaning back against the rough bark of the tree behind him.

The days stretched out before him, endless and daunting. Every instinct screamed for rest, for surrender to exhaustion's relentless tide, and so he allowed for this.

Drake knew he could not remain in one place for too long, exposed like some stranded injured beast awaiting predators' approach.

He had to keep moving eventually, push ever onwards despite his body's protests.

If there was any chance of thwarting Emperor Gervin's malevolence, then survival was but the first step on a far longer path.

Gritting his teeth once more against impending torment, Drake began the long and arduous journey ahead of him. Each movement now sent jolts of agony radiating through his limbs, and he bore it all with stoic determination, refusing to give anything to the adversity weighing upon him. He knew the pain would pass.

He reached out a tentative hand, grasping at tree roots for support as he hauled himself across the forest floor once more. He was still concerned those beasts would return, or perhaps they had alerted some of their scouts in the area of his presence. Drake focused on pulling his broken frame forward.

Within the woods lurked something else other than silence, an unspoken presence coiling like a serpent in the underbrush.

CHAPTER SIX

THE GOBLIN

His gaze fell upon something shadowy in the distance, a huddled figure staring directly at him. Near the base of an ancient oak, the creature was more twisted than the tree and so grotesque it defied nature itself, well any nature worth the knowing. A goblin, plainly.

This one was unlike any he had ever seen before. It was ancient, twisted by time and malady into a horrifically rotting parody of its kind. Its pallid skin hung in loose folds like snot, mottled with age spots and splotches of a dull moldy gray. Its mouth stretched wide, in a perpetual leer, empty of the signature goblin yellowed sharp fangs. Its gums smacked as it chattered in a lisp to itself, with too much saliva coating its maw and loosely strung lips. Ragged clothes from some ancient culture hung on its emaciated frame, like tattered banners which began to flap as it hobbled closer.

Clearly, the thing would pose no immediate physical threat under any other circumstances. Yet, in this case, the goblin's body was not the only one barely held together by some unseen force. Still, there remained an air about the goblin... something unsettlingly present in or despite its decay.

It gave the feeling of being as old as the trees themselves, though Drake knew too well that there was no way that it could be.

The goblin's form was in a state of advanced rot that went beyond age. Its joints creaked with every movement. Its eyes were two dull yet luminous orbs shining out sickly. They were as yellow as any Goblin's but milky due to cataracts and rolling wildly within deep-set sockets, gleaming with madness. The thing smiled toothlessly.

"You're the sh-pitting image of your old man," the goblin

lisped in a guttural drawl like the accent of peoples yet north of Silver Keep. "Same eyes, same… stubbornness." The lisp was strongly idiosyncratic, hanging heavily on 'S,' words ending in it coming out as a 'J' sound. It sounded more like he said, "Shhh-ame eyej, shhh-ame shhh-tubbornejj."

Drake stiffened, his still swollen hand clutching his knife, as if the very act of holding it might anchor him to reality. His father's voice came to him again, "Boy, they lie. They lie while they lie and lie after that. You cannot take a single word they say as granted, because the ones that sound most trustworthy among them are most filled with lies. Not a one of them can you trust, especially the seemingly good-natured or weak. They hate us for our strength, most especially the weakest of them, remember that."

This goblin also knew too much for Drake's comfort.

It chuckled. "You'd be cold meat otherwise," it continued lisping past its green spit-wrestling gums and green tongue, its mangled fingers twitching as if sifting through invisible dust. "I saved your life. You should be grateful. I'm grateful!" The goblin waited sometime for a reply that would never come.

Drake met its gaze steadily, refusing to be drawn into whatever game this thing played. His lips curled into a grimace. He wondered whether this was a lie before, during, or after some other lie, and decided it must always be before another lie, yet couldn't be sure if it was the first or not.

The goblin again spoke, "Beware the quiet ones, they're usually up to something. The quiet is there to hide the noise behind it. Or maybe they just can't hear me for the rustle of leaves. Do they speak to you, too? The bastards." The thing chortled to itself as saying this.

Drake pulled himself up and back away from the creature, his ruined legs protesting. "You're a spy," he said finally, voice tight with suspicion despite attempting to effect calm. "And a bad one."

The goblin's head cocked in an uncanny impression of being

unduly insulted. It eyes widened in surprise, its gummy grin sending yet another chill down Drake's spine. "Why? You think I'd be here to help you if I was a spy? You'd have been trampled by trolls and devoured by the stars if not for me." It giggled at its own words, hands fluttering erratically through the air. Its words were riddles wrapped in venom, each syllable dripping with something untrustworthy. Yet there was an odd rhythm, as if the creature had been crafting the deceitful nuance within itself for centuries, layering falsehoods over foundations of half-truths until nothing else was left. It suddenly let out a horn noise seemingly from its head, as though in celebration.

"I wouldn't believe anything else," Drake muttered under his breath, his fingers relaxing around the knife.

The goblin's words felt like a trap, each one meant to ensnare him in some web of deceit. Yet something about the creature's presence was different, worse somehow than if it had simply been a spy; its knowledge, its patience, as well as the way it seemed to know everything and nothing at once. Drake might have been led to believe this creature was working for itself, which could indeed prove just as bad or worse.

The goblin tilted its head again in practiced motion, studying Drake with an intensity that made his skin crawl. "You're not like the others," it mused, its voice a rasp of old bones. "That crash should have killed you. But you... you're tough and stubborn like your father," it said this trying to withhold its disdain, but failing utterly in Drake's perception, who was watching carefully.

Drake's breath hitched at this second reference to his father. The weight of his father's warnings pressed upon him like a storm cloud, hearing his voice again, "Even the ones who seem to help you are just waiting for the moment to strike. So they lie the most. Your demise means their survival." His father's voice had been a constant during his youth, a warning against the goblins' cunning and the illusions they wove to entrap even the most steadfast souls. "Their good liars survive into elderly years and crippledom, especially as they get rich and opulent," he had stated.

Hearing anything about his father from this disgusting goblin that knew too much felt wrong. "Oh, just a moment ago, you were claiming that my life was saved by you. You lying little shit! I bet you're **RICH**!" Drake pronounced this all with so much force, it twisted his leg causing fresh spikes of pain. He howled, growling through a grimace.

The goblin turned and ran, taking this for Drake planning to come after him. It cackled in glee, its voice rising to a shrill pitch. "You're not fast enough for me! My boots are filled with energies!" It sprang forward with a speed that defied its rotting and twisted form.

The goblin's unnecessary dash looked like a dance of desperation in some long forgotten rite of comic futility, movements erratic and ridiculous despite the speed.

Drake laughed at the clumsy thing, breath still ragged and guarding pain as he did.

The goblin turned to find its would-be assailant sitting in the same spot laughing and responded, "Gritch isn't crazy. Well, maybe I am… but at least I'm not chasing shadows! How many shadows did you pass on the way here, by the way? Never mind…"

"Oh yeah, being chased by shadows would indeed be crazy. Gritch? Horrible name, as anticipated," Drake mused mostly to himself.

Gritch got very red in the face at this, and started to stomp quickly toward Drake.

Drake lunged after the creature, his injured leg screaming in protest as he grabbed hold of it in an impromptu hug, but then quickly shifting to grab a firm grip of its neck. "I'm going to enjoy this," he said as he prepared to end the farce with true finality.

The thing choked as it called out, "You're going about this all wrong way, but then again, I'm not the one with legs of clay!" It persisted, trying to convince Drake while fighting for air simultaneously, "I know how to get to your father's old hideaway from here! The secret is to not murder me, please!"

Drake hesitated, arms and barely-healed fingers prepared to squeeze the life out of the lying beast. The weight of his father's warnings clashed with the undeniable presence of the goblin's knowledge. 'Lying while lying is quite the feat,' he thought, trying to find a solid reason to just end its life. Then he thought something else, based on the words of his father that would not go away: that a thread of deceit woven through a web of deceit can cause just as much damage to the web as anything else. He let the creature go.

***

Gritch forced a laugh at being released, a grating sound like smaller stones grinding against a larger one. The goblin chortled and coughed, but was now grinning even wider, if that were possible.

The sight of it was grotesque.

"But first, let's get comfortable, shall we?" suggested the goblin.

"No," said Drake flatly.

"Now," Gritch said, cheerfully ignoring him, and perching upon a gnarled root like some grotesque gargoyle. "Let us conversate."

Drake rearranged himself against the rough bark, trying to ignore the searing pain lancing through his lower limbs. "You mean converse? About what?"

"About you! Me! The world!" Gritch threw its arms wide, eyes aglow with a manic light. "Everything and nothing!"

Drake's brow furrowed in frustration. "You're mad. I should have just killed you earlier. Full of shit, perhaps even harmlessly so."

"Mad?" It tittered. "Oh dear boy, madness is but another word for freedom!"

Drake recoiled from the stench of rot and decay wafting from its maw.

"Splendid crash, by the way!" It clapped its hands together in glee, rocking back and forth on its perch. Gritch tapped a bony finger against its chin, feigning deep thought. "Ah! I see it now: you were too heavy for their silly contraption! Too much muscle, not enough brain."

Drake ignored the insult without reaction.

"Careful!" The goblin chided, waggling a finger. "Calm is but a mask over anger to hide the fear at root." It cackled once more, relishing its own words. "Fear of what you cannot control." The creature leaned in, eyes gleaming like cold embers. "And there is so much you cannot control," said it, with lips far too close to Drake's cheeks.

Drake chose levity, "Well thank you for your careful analysis, Dr. Goblin." He continued, matter of factly, "Anyway, fear is what you goblins thrive on, Gritch, and it is not cutting here. Plainly, you are at the end of your rope in grasping human spirit. That's why you talk in doublespeak and mad riddles, because the contrived mystery in them more easily aligns with fear, making it easier to later escape the consequences of your lies. Is that not right? It's all jargon describing a wonderland in deceptions of your own construction."

"Riddles? Jargon? Wonderland?" It scoffed, waving a hand dismissively. "No! Merely observations, a goblin's artful perspective on things." It spread its arms wide, encompassing the surrounding forest.

Drake answered quickly, "Riddles, to commonfolk, are for tickling the mind and provoking thought. For lying criminals, like goblins such as yourself, riddles are a means of confusion and obfuscation." Drake stared at it. He knew that beyond Gritch's gibberish lurked something else: a twisted insight born of criminal masterfulness, with only a touch of madness. It was born of rot and ego, and that was where he could keep the liar on its toes. "But you, you're just another goblin," Drake spat, voice laced with bitterness, "full of hatred and deceit."

"Deceit?" The goblin chortled again, feigning softness of voice in dry rasps like twigs snapping delicately, as if it had been born from the very rot that clung to the forest floor. "Oh dear boy, deception is the currency of all, not just goblins." It leaned forward, its knuckly fingers twitching as though plucking invisible threads from the air, and grinned, that grotesquely gummy smile, looking every bit the desperate threat of a deformed primate deranged by something extra.

Drake just shook his head.

***

Days later, the goblin refused to leave. It brought him things, like scavenged bits of food and water, all seemingly fine and clean, despite expectations. The goblin's constant hidden invectives, though, slithered through him like venom, each syllable a blade sharpened by malice.

It sat across from him, saying things he tried his best to ignore, but it had brought him food. "They lie while they lie," his father's voice coming to mind once again. "Even the ones who claim and seem to help you are just waiting for the moment to stab you in the back. They take pride in it, the ability to get in close and use you up before taking you down."

The goblin paused in motion then, its eyes narrowing shrewdly as if it had read the residence of Drake's mind upon the words of his father. "Tell me, hero," it cooed in its choking phlegm, voice low and laced with sly mockery, "what do you see when you look at me?"

Drake hesitated, focused on his pain and the annoyance of

being near such "A pathetic creature, nothing more," he finished his thought out loud.

"Nothing more?" it asked in a soft raspy whimper, idiosyncratically tilting its head as though patronizing a child too young to understand the weight of their words. The goblin's yellow eyes gleamed with something unnatural.

Drake felt as though behind them were a thousand more unnatural things.

"How very sad," Gritch said while chuckling. "Yet I see so much when I look at you."

"Why should I care what you say or think, goblin?" Drake asked in as calm a tone as possible.

The goblin leaned closer still, its breath reeking of decay and something far worse, something Drake could not name but felt in his bones. It reached out in front of him, with its decrepit fingers twitching as though plucking at the strings of an invisible instrument, and barely touching Drake. It was sickening, like being too near some stranger's uncleaned outhouse.

He flinched away, stomach churning at the creature's proximity.

Gritch laughed. "You're hilarious," it sneered, voice a rasp. "Just another plaything in grander schemes, you don't know your own master," it said most malevolently.

Drake glared at it defiantly, eyes belying the burning fire of fury as constrained by situation, just below the surface. "Who?" he demanded in a sardonic grumble, his voice hoarse from pain and exhaustion.

The goblin threw back its head and laughed a harsh guffaw. "Oh, there are so many puppeteers pulling your strings young man." It leaned in close again, emanating rancid breath as it whispered into Drake's ear. "So, which one do you ask of? We can start with your emperor. Played you like a fine lute."

Drake recoiled again. The goblin's words attempted to take his mind, he could practically feel the magic. Yet despite the fog of pain and despair, some spark stoked within him set by his father long ago, of defiance and willpower, refusing to be extinguished.

"You're a mad goblin, Gritch, pathetic. Age has made you transparent in your attempts to stab at my spirit. Incapable of even rousing my anger at this lowest point of mine when I am most aggravated. Should be an easy thing. Pathetic," Drake looked away from Gritch.

"Pathetic," Drake repeated softly, staring into the distance beyond the goblin, attempting to sound more like he was talking to himself than the creature before him. "Just another goblin lost in shadows grasping for anything it can to forestall inevitable, ignoble demise. Mad by desperation, you would play into nearly any fantasy I make up," he said, tone laced with exhaustion.

The goblin chuckled once more. "Lost? Oh no, merely… misunderstood." Then it leaned back, arms folded across its chest as if settling in for a long story. "You think you're clever? Let me see you juggle shadows!"

Drake's lips curled in disgust once more, his exhaustion making every movement a laborious task. "You talk nonsense and riddles. Is that all you have? What would you be doing with your time if I weren't here?"

The goblin grinned widely at this, revealing its green and slimy gums as though pressing together two very strange worms in its mouth. "Time?" It chortled again. "Ah yes, but time is an illusion." It tapped its chin thoughtfully before continuing. "Besides, if time is so great, why is it always so late?"

Drake inserted his words, "Obviously because time can never be on time. Can you be on yourself, or can I be on myself? I think not, sir," he finished mockingly, getting into the flow of the nonsense himself.

The goblin looked impressed, its twisted form shuddering as if it had just been struck by an invisible blow. "Why didn't you tell me you were a genius, kid?" It exclaimed, voice dripping with faux admiration.

Drake scoffed.

The goblin grinned once more, its mangled face contorting into something between amusement and menace. "They always say a wise goblin knows when to shut the mouth, works for your type too I guess."

"Would it remain true if the goblin doesn't know when that time is?" Drake raised his eyebrow as he said this, his voice still in a mocking tone.

Gritch looked at him, not for the first or the last time, with the only genuine expression it had left: confusion. The goblin's eyes widened slightly, its pupils dilating as if struggling to comprehend something beyond its own grotesque form.

For a moment, Drake thought he saw something in that gaze; a flicker of something too vast and ancient to name, as though Gritch were staring into the abyss of its own madness. It laughed.

Drake rolled his eyes for what felt like the hundredth time, it was all he could do.

Then, with a sudden jolt, the goblin's expression shifted, its grin twisting into a snarl as it leaned forward once more. "Oh yes you're clever, boy," it rasped, its voice dripping with venom. "But cleverness is just another lie in the end, yours. I told you it was everyone's currency, didn't I?" It reached out at nothing, fingers curling like claws, awkwardly attempting high drama but failing miserably.

* * *

The weeks bled into one another, marked only by the slow creep of sunlight through the canopy and the relentless happiness of nature's children, seemingly unaffected by the goings or evil of man and goblin. Each day brought new struggles against pains and weakness that gnawed at him like a ravenous beast. He felt so tired and weary, but he knew he was healing and progressing as well.

Drake knew he must be patient with himself. He had plenty of practice dealing with his own imperfections in training. Perhaps the greatest lesson from all his years of honing his skills had to do with this moment right now, when he had to patiently allow himself to heal, and for whatever scheme this goblin had to play out.

Gritch lingered at the edges of his vision throughout the days, a grotesque nurse coming and going. The goblin's eyes gleamed with a madness that seemed to dance just beyond the veil of any comprehension, perhaps most of all its own. Its form twitched and jerked like a string puppet, with loose limbs moving upon their own spastic path aside from the rest of him. It squatted nearby, a comically ragged silhouette, like a permanently injured clown from demonic realms. The goblin's limbs and body would shift incessantly and unpredictably, as if plagued by unseen tormentors.

Drake could swear that he kept hearing horns of some sort upon the creature, but did not wish to inquire as to their source as he did not want to know. He noticed that whenever the goblin was near, the animals disappeared, with birds taking flight to their next tasks ever short of its re-arrivals. He focused on tending to his legs, ignoring the creature's presence as best he could.

Yet, Gritch would not be so easily dismissed. The goblin took it upon itself to continue bringing Drake food and water. Each offering was presented with a flourish, as if the goblin were bestowing some great boon rather than mere insufficient sustenance.

"I brought you grub, hero," the goblin rasped one day,

dropping a handful of wrinkled berries at Drake's side. "Eat up. You'll need your strength."

Drake eyed the offering warily before scooping it up, his stomach growling despite his reservations. He popped a berry into his mouth, teeth sinking into the tart flesh as he chewed thoughtfully.

Gritch watched him with an unnerving intensity that Drake had learned to, again, mostly ignore, its yellow eyes never leaving Drake's face.

"The trees whisper secrets," it murmured, one eye squinted shut as if peering through a telescope. "Wind carries them away before they can take root." It paused, tilting its head as though listening to some distant melody only it could hear. "They ***are*** plotting against you, though. I'd watch my back if I were you."

Drake grunted, trying his best to ignore the goblin's nonsense while focusing on rebinding his injured legs more securely with some clothing the goblin had brought him. The makeshift splints dug into his flesh, but he was now welcoming the pain, it meant he was alive and moving toward recovery.

'This is pathetic,' Drake thought to himself. 'Pathetic, letting a goblin tend to me.' He pushed aside the self-recrimination, knowing that survival took precedence over any pride.

Gritch was rather oddly content to spend most of his days nearby as Drake was recovering, offering stream-of-consciousness observations that ranged from the vaguely profound to the utterly nonsensical.

Drake persisted in his efforts, doing exercises to make up for his current level of incapacitation, letting the goblin's ramblings pass by as best he could.

"You are not supposed to look me in the eyes because then I'll know who you really are," Gritch continued. "Your father had fire.

Like you, though yours burns hotter."

Drake paused, hands held over the rough bandages wrapped around his leg. A shiver ran down his spine, part revulsion, part intrigue. "What do you mean?" he asked, voice tight with suspicion.

The mentions of his father were becoming too much, and the goblin's interest in comparing them were stranger still than the creature itself.

The goblin waved a dismissive hand, its gnarled fingers twitching with hand cupped in its resting deformation. "Strength, boy. Drive. Purpose."

A bitter laugh escaped Drake's lips before he could rein it in. He thought of Solipsia and of the heroes languishing in prisons or dead, reduced to villainy through Solipsia's false remembrance which was all that remained. He thought of Emperor Gervin's evil grin, so calm and composed, spreading chaos all around him. Anger flared within him, hot and fierce.

"Purpose?" Drake repeated, voice laced with scorn. "What does that mean to you?"

Gritch merely smiled, dumbly, its lips peeling back slimy gums into a foolish grimace. "Purpose is a double-edged blade, Drake of Eldred," the creature said, voice like cluttering noise falling over toothless lisp. "It cuts both ways. The sun is jealous of the moon because it can't glow in the dark. Be more like the moon."

Drake scowled, resuming his task with renewed vigor. He would not be drawn into this creature's games.

Yet Gritch persisted, with declarations half-mad and always provocative. "Did you know," the goblin mused, leaning back against the gnarled trunk of the oak, "that goblins are born from the rot of the earth? We rise from decay, feed on the remnants of life," it chuckled softly, a sound like some primitive and unknown percussion instrument. "It's true. Your kind fear us because we remind you of your own decay."

Drake said nothing, focusing instead on rehabilitating his legs. His still healing fingers trembled slightly as he worked the muscles around his wounds, and redressed them. The movements sent fresh waves of pain coursing through him.

Gritch watched him intently, its eyes gleaming with amusement. "You think I'm mad," it rasped, voice low and conspiratorial. "But perhaps madness is just another form of clarity. A way of seeing beyond the illusions that blind you."

Drake thought back to his father's lessons, to the gruff condemnation laced with fear in Eldred's voice as he spoke of goblin society. Drake recalled his father telling him, "Most goblin infants are killed and eaten immediately by their siblings." Eldred's words reverberated all the more through his mind due to being trapped here with this monstrosity. He remembered the look of disgust on his father's face as he spoke, "Majority are morons, and they lie the most to their own." Drake recalled his father's sadness, one evening, after having finished ranting an extremely lengthy and grim litany of the horrors in abuses goblins committed against their own youth and each other. Eldred sat still, disbelief playing upon his face still after all those years. They were just goblins, but it hit him hard witnessing their behaviors toward one another. Finally, after a long pause, he had said, "I don't remember killing many old ones, son. I hate thinking about that, and what it means."

Drake thought of what secrets this ancient goblin before him must hold with its twisted form, mad ramblings, and the unnatural intelligence gleaming in its eyes. 'A toothless old goblin must have the sharpest of lies to cut through goblin society without any teeth,' he thought.

The goblin seemed to sense Drake's thoughts, its gummy grin widening into something ironically predatory. "You see it now, don't you?" It laughed out loud, inappropriately. "The web of lies and deceits that bind our world together. The games they play, the shadows they cast." Drake hesitated, his gaze locked onto Gritch's face in full mirth and joy. In fact, he had never seen the creature happier than at that moment. He felt as if he were staring into an abyss, an endless void of darkness and madness.

"I see nothing," Drake growled, tearing his gaze away from the goblin's unsettling scrutiny. "Just more lies."

Gritch chuckled again. "Exactly! Lies, truth, what is the difference? Both are just weapons, but lies are easier to control."

Drake said nothing, focusing on his injuries again.

The goblin watched him with an amused intensity that made Drake distinctly uncomfortable, its eyes never leaving his face. "You think you're strong," it rasped, voice low and insidious. "But strength is an illusion, boy, another lie! A fleeting moment of power before the inevitable fall!" It coughed, "The more you rely upon your strength, the harder you will fall in the end."

'And what would you know about strength, surrounded your whole life by weakness in weakness, and guarded by lies?' Drake would have asked, but only thought it.

Gritch merely smiled again, its eyes gleaming with an unsettling light. "I may be a weak little old goblin, but I understand strength more than you think," it replied quietly. "More than you can imagine."

Drake recalled how the wildlife would scurry when Gritch approached, as though evading a dangerous predator, and he could imagine many ways an evil little being could think itself strong out here in these deep woods.

"Ever seen snow fall upside down?" Gritch asked suddenly, its voice a rasping intruder upon Drake's internal world. It was one of those questions so absurd on face, it momentarily derailed Drake from the intricate web of pain and memory that had become his constant companion.

Drake gave Gritch a look, parts disbelief and exasperation. "No," he replied flatly.

Gritch chuckled darkly, "Well it does, in the mountains where the clouds are rivers of ice." It leaned back against the tree, arms folded across its chest. "You'd be surprised what you can see when you stop looking at things the way everyone else does."

Drake grunted noncommittally, focused. His knife blade bit into a tree branch he held, shavings curling away like parchment scrolls. He re-lit the fire for the coming evening with the shavings, but then continued with carving the strong and particularly straight branch, fashioning it into a crutch.

* * *

Eventually he was walking, pushing himself around on his legs and the crutch at least. As days turned into nights, and turned back into days again over the weeks, Drake found himself drawn into an involuntary rhythm with the goblin. Gritch's ramblings became the background noise distracting him from the difficulty of recovery, a cornucopia of nonsense and half-truths blended into his daily routines. Yet there were moments when the creature's words cut through him like knives, forcing confrontations he would rather have avoided.

'I should go to my father's hideaway and look for his words,' Drake thought, an idea all the more pressing due to Eolande's execution.

"It's a long walk from here," Gritch whined, as though reading Drake's thoughts. "But you might be strong enough." Drake paused, knife hovering over the unfinished crutch as he considered this. The goblin's expression was inscrutable, its gaze fixed on some distant point only it could see.

"You should go," Gritch continued, leaning forward with an

intensity that made Drake uneasy. "Face the demons of your past. Confront the shadows that haunt you."

Drake scowled, resuming his carving with renewed vigor, while responding, "The only shadow I deal with currently is from the demon I am talking to." He did not need this creature's approval, nor its advice. Drake listened with half an ear, sorting through the goblin's babble for any kernels of truth in the chaff.

There were times when Gritch spoke of forgiveness, of letting go of old hatreds. The goblin prattled on about peace and reconciliation.

"Your enemies are not monsters," Gritch said one evening, staring into the flickering flames of their campfire. "We're not men either, but we are living creatures."

Drake seethed at this, he thought of Solipsia's streets running red with blood, of executions, and of heroes burned or rotting in prison cells, silenced forever.

He wanted to laugh or get angry, but his father's voice moderated his responses, constant reminders of the nature of evil, serving to calm him. He had long since been prepared for this. "They deserve no forgiveness," Drake said without any emotion. "And certainly not from me."

Gritch sighed heavily, as if disappointed by Drake's response. "Forgiveness is not for them," he said softly. "It is for the monsters in your head trying to get out!"

"Good, maybe they'll get loose and kill all the monsters outside my head!" Drake smiled widely at the goblin. "Wouldn't that be a dream?"

"You are as bad as your father," Gritch said.

"Good! ***Fantastic!*** That's all I ever wanted," Drake spoke excitedly and scoffed, heart pounding as he met the goblin's unblinking gaze. "What do you know of my father, anyway?"

"He killed my cousins," Gritch said, effecting a sad tone.

"Undoubtedly, and good!" Drake answered, voice steady. "They deserved it."

Gritch sighed heavily, as if disappointed by Drake's decision. "As my eldest broodmate always said, 'Don't count your fingers before they're all grown in.'"

Drake's brow furrowed in confusion. The goblin's words were as cryptic as ever, but there was an undercurrent of warning, or perhaps caution in cryptic disclosure.

Before he could press further, Gritch turned away, hunching over like a broken puppet controlled by unseen strings. "Come," it rasped, voice barely audible over the rustling leaves. "Let us walk while you still can." Gritch began to move.

Drake slowly stood to hobble along on his maimed legs with the carved and tempered branch for a crutch, which he thought of more as a staff.

* * *

With staff under arm, he ambulated almost as awkwardly as the goblin. Gritch's movement was a trial, the pace agonizingly slow, yet Drake did not mind. The slow rhythm allowed his injured legs respite, each step sending jolts of pain coursing through him but also granting moments of brief relief. His injured legs protested with any faster progress, so he welcomed it.

"You're after that same sword as your father," Gritch said, stumbling ahead of him through the forest, "Almost like it calls to you, right?"

Drake started, heart pounding. How could this creature know such things? He had no choice but to follow, for the goblin's presence was both a comfort and a curse; its words gnawing at Drake like a persistent itch that refused to be scratched. Even if Gritch was not quite representative, the enemy having a face he could watch was a small comfort, perhaps it was the goblin's presence pulling like a tether, tying him to something he could not yet name.

Gritch came to a stream, "This is where I get your water human." It contorted itself into some strange and confusing configuration which was finally revealed as it kneeled over, posing in obtuse mimicry of a drinking giraffe, except grotesque, in miniature, and graceless.

It started to talk in this position which strained its voice so much as to be almost incomprehensible, especially given its already prominent lisp, "'Shhh shhh-treeem gomb-shhh frrromb farrr awaaaaaaay'."

Gritch then fell backwards, legs still up, like a fallen doll from some demonic toy shop. "If anyone stopped it," it huffed, accepting the new position on the ground and resting its legs, "I mean upstream if they stopped it, we wouldn't have any water here."

Drake sighed, "I appreciate you showing me where the water is, but I fail to see your point. I think what you are saying is that we should not weed our gardens, which is quite different from stopping the water. Besides, it is our sewer water which feeds goblins, if we must use this allegory. If your society cannot be made to maintain and sustain itself, then it needs to change or cease being. Step into strong society or oblivion."

Silence from the goblin, finally. It did not say a word for a whole blessed minute.

Drake began to turn around when the goblin said something almost under its breath.

"Your father was obsessed with that stupid sword," Gritch said, the water's gentle murmur filling the silence between them. The goblin sat up and continued, "You're no different." It then cackled, creaking like an ancient rocking chair at speed.

His father had never found the sword, finally even doubting its existence. Now, it beckoned to Drake as well.

That sword indeed promised the answers he did not even know where to begin seeking. These were answers to questions his father had unwillingly given up. These new goblins were much more powerful, using magic and domesticated monsters like trolls in ways his father had not anticipated.

"Never trust a river that flows backwards. It's probably up to something," Gritch began again with the never-ending inanities and unprovoked insanities, interrupting Drake's train of thought once again.

He wanted to crush Gritch's head like a grape in hand, to silence the creature's mad ramblings, those lies, and those threats so awkwardly hinted at.

Drake tried not to glare at Gritch, though anger burned hot in his chest. He buried it yet again. "What do you know of the sword?" he demanded, voice calm yet laced with suspicion.

The goblin merely smiled menacingly. "Truth is a heavy burden, boy, dangerous too," it said almost joyously. "Are you sure you want it?"

"Undoubtedly," Drake hesitated not, resolve hardened within him at the direct question. He would not be swayed from his path, not by this creature's manipulations nor any ghosts of past shames. "Truth is all I've ever wanted or asked for," Drake answered again, voice steady. Part of him felt as though this audience did not even deserve to hear this, and he knew this was correct.

Gritch sighed heavily, feigning a thin coat of disappointment on its twisted features. "Very well," it rasped, pushing itself back up on its feet again with a grimace of effort. "But remember these wise words of the goblins, Drake of Eldred, 'don't count your fingers before they're all grown in'," Gritch said this seriously while pointing one at Drake.

"Is this a phrase you say now? Do not, it is vapid and makes me want to break your fingers. I think you mean something horrid by it on any account." What did Gritch mean by it though? Was it a riddle, or a warning? To Drake, every strange thing Gritch said could be interpreted as allusions to their enemy status or Drake's ignorance and ultimate doom.

"It's just an old goblinism, boy, relax!" Gritch giggled, giddily for the first time. A honking horn could be heard from somewhere on its body.

"Your words have no power goblin."

Gritch smiled its slimy gums at him.

"You must have an obscene amount of wealth considering your reaction to the question from earlier," Drake said slowly, his voice oozing suspicion. "Having lived for so long, you have got to be very wealthy by now, am I right, or are you not as smart as you seem?"

Gritch's reply was sharp and sudden, like a blade slicing through fog. "No!" it yelled. Its gnarled fingers twitched slightly, as though grasping at yet something else unseen in its crazy little head.

Drake thought he saw a flicker of something in the creature's gaze. Was it regret? Defiance? It was certainly nothing good.

CHAPTER SEVEN

GRITCH'S JIG

Remembrance of his father's words were embedded in his mind like runes carved onto stone, especially active near Gritch. The old man had discussed their terribleness at great lengths. "Goblins ill-equipped to lie, die. The most seemingly trustworthy are always the most deceptive. Understand this, and you might stand a chance of figuring out which one is lying the most." Drake remembered the intensity in his father's eyes, the way his hands had clenched into tightening fists whenever the evil creatures were discussed.

"Every one of them lies," and the next words invoked deep fear he felt all the way into the present, "especially true of the seemingly good-natured or weak. The only ones that wish you to see them as weak or good are trying to get in where other goblins cannot." His father warned him constantly against the insidious nature of these twisted creatures who prowled the edges of civilization. These memories of his father endlessly ranting and worrying were part of his being, and it was laughable that Gritch thought he could bypass his father's training. "The only way the weakest ones could survive is by tricking any dumber and stronger cousins anyway."

Drake studied Gritch, its form was all wrong. The creature, much like its relatives, moved as though permanently injured, in a loose gait of limp joints and disjointed limbs akimbo. It looked like it was navigating some unseen maze of its own bodily rot.

As they moved through the underbrush, Drake surmised their general location, but allowed Gritch to believe otherwise. The former presence of goblin hordes had always tainted this part of the forests, leaving an indelible stain on the landscape in his mind, despite having been witness to none of it. He still felt it in his very bones, such knowledge being core to his upbringing. He could never enjoy the wild in such areas, as he could nearer his home.

As it led him deeper into the wilds, Gritch began to emit a horrid sound, a throaty harmonizing vocalization with multiple voices and seeming instruments at once; a disgusting band of bodily noises within one goblin. It seemed to be emanating from all parts of the goblin at once, like an overabundance of flatulence forced through clogged nostrils, constricted vocal cords, digestive tract, sinuses, and ears together, without sounding like grunts or squeaks at all. It was a composition of noises most unwelcome.

'Horrible,' Drake thought, wincing as the sounds assailed his ears. 'Like the wail of some tormented spirit trapped within the goblin's rotting flesh.' He fought back a shudder, gripping his makeshift crutch tighter.

Gritch's noises added to the foreboding atmosphere, each strange note resounding through the trees like malignant incantations. The sounds produced a rhythmic tune with whistles from the nose, sinuses, and ears mixed with hums from the diaphragm, mouth, gut, and who knew what else, on top of the vocal cords doing their own arrangements of noise.

It all combined to make Drake feel almost sick.

Gritch stomped feet in time with the beat, which seemed to be somewhere between a funeral march and a jig performed by drunken demons.

To Drake's great dismay, it began to sing.

"Oh, the shadows creep, and the stones weep, with secrets so deep that only I keep, keep, KEEP!" Of course, it was all in a lisp so it sounded more like 'shadowj,' 'shtonej,' and 'sheegretj."

Gritch cackled wildly, eyes rolling like dice in their sockets. *"The roots below will whisper low, of tales untold and deeds all forgot, FORGOT, forgot!"*

Drake winced at Gritch, half-tempted to initiate the next

goblicide early.

"Beware the path that winds and bends," Gritch continued, voice taking on a menacing lilt, *"for in the shifts, my plans blend, blend, BLEND!"* It infused more of a little jig in its steps. *"The whispers call, the shadows fall, of course, to heed their song is death, or worse, WORSE, worse!"*

Gritch paused, eyes narrowing as it jabbed a gnarled finger at Drake. *"You think you know, with mind so bright, but darkness hides what's out of sight, SIGHT, sight!"* It chuckled darkly, gums showing. *"So tread carefully, hero bold, lest you be caught in tales untold, TOLD, told!"*

Drake raised an eyebrow at the ridiculousness, a smirk playing at the corners of his mouth despite himself.

Gritch, misinterpreting Drake's expressions as some kind of approval, grinned gummily and launched into another verse, its voice rising to a near-shriek. *"Oh, the trees will walk, the stones will talk, yet never bone, for secrets locked and buried are but sown, SOWN, sown!"* It pranced and skip-flopped in circles, feet kicking up clods of earth. *"So heed my words, or face your doom, in goblin wrath and moonlit gloom, GLOOM, gloom!"*

The goblin's song reached a fever pitch. Drake found himself both appalled and amused at once, unable to look away from the distracting spectacle.

"The night will fall, the day will flee, as the moon sings, and in the shade, my laughter rings, RINGS, rings!" It paused then, its insane sing-song lisp dropping to a low sinister whisper of incomprehensible mutterings, eyes with manic glee, before resounding all the more loudly now, *"So tread with care, or face your fate and lose the day, for in the depth of dim, I await, AWAIT, away!"*

With a final, ear-splitting crescendo, Gritch's song came to an abrupt end. The goblin stood panting, chest heaving as if it had run a marathon.

Drake laughed out loud and clapped vigorously, a wry smile on his face. "Bravo," he said, his voice dripping with sarcasm. "That was... **something**!"

Gritch beamed, or glowed greener yet, clearly pleased with itself. "Ah, you liked it? I thought you might. It's an old goblin tune," Gritch lied badly, "passed down through the generations. Keeps the spirits up on long journeys, you know." It winked back at him.

Drake could only roll his eyes once more, shaking his head in disbelief as he continued on their way, with that truly awful song, or whatever it was, mercifully fading out of memory.

* * *

As they ventured further, Drake noticed subtle shifts in the landscape, hidden paths snaking through the undergrowth, secret ways marked by slight disturbances in the natural order. It was as if the forest itself conspired to conceal their passage, guiding them along routes known only to those who had long since been swallowed by its embrace.

"If you keep poking that stick into the ground, it might get angry and bite back," Gritch announced happily. The background vocalizations continued without the song, unabated and just as loud while he spoke.

'This creature is mad,' Drake thought grimly. 'Absolutely mad.'

Gritch chuckled darkly, the sound blending uncomfortably with the horrid throat noise. "The leaves are angry too," it continued, tilting its head back to listen as if hearing some unseen companions at a distance. "Chattering behind your back. They say you're stomping too loud, and they want to take your legs."

Drake scowled, tightening his grip on the crutch until the wood groaned in protest. 'He's just trying to unnerve me,' he told himself, pushing aside the creeping unease.

"You know this path is actually straight, right?" Gritch mused, gesturing to the winding path ahead. Its voice through the cacophony of bodily instruments still took on a sing-song quality. "It's just drunk and can't walk properly. Never drink things strangers give you by the way," it added with a leer.

Drake shuddered, thinking back at the way Gritch folded itself in half to collect the water which it delivered to him almost every day. He strained to keep a safer distance, desperate to escape the goblin's unsettling presence as well as the relentless assault on his ears and nose.

The goblin's ramblings were a torrent of nonsense interspersed with fleeting moments of unsettling clarity or childish insights, each word another rock tossed into the pool of Drake's thoughts.

"Why do birds fly South for Winter?" Gritch pondered aloud, voice barely audible over throat noise, "Because it's too cold up North! Silly birds, don't they know cold follows them everywhere?"

Drake rolled his eyes.

"You ever wonder what happens when you die?" Gritch mused, voice dropping to a low murmur. "Do you just... stop? Or is there something more?"

Drake said nothing, his jaw clenched tight against the urge to snap back with some biting retort. He kept his gaze fixed firmly on the path ahead, refusing to acknowledge the goblin's presence against the risk of inviting further madness.

Yet Gritch persisted, throat song taking on a lower, more menacing tone. "I've watched lots of men die," it stated slowly and awkwardly, each word unsettlingly intimate. It seemed to be dealing with an elevated quantity of saliva as it said this, "Seen their eyes go blank, their bodies grow cold. Though sometimes... sometimes there's more."

"What do you mean?" Drake asked before he could think better of it. He cursed inwardly for engaging the goblin.

Gritch's bodily band stopped then as it turned to him then, yellow eyes gleaming with intensity. It said, "There are things beyond your world. Shadows that linger, whispers in the dark, demons, and spirits that take hold silently."

"You speak in dark riddles again," Drake growled. "I want no more of your goblin tales."

The goblin chuckled, the sound like mud gurgling. "Riddles? Tales?" it hooted in amusement. "Or perhaps merely truths you've yet to understand." Gritch paused then, gaze never leaving Drake's face. "Mark my words, boy," it looked at him with a serious expression with the bodily music dropping off, as though on the verge of sharing the greatest wisdom, "if a goblin kills you, you'll go to a higher heaven."

"What?" Drake halted in shock.

"You heard me. Do you want to die and go to super heaven, boy?" Gritch asked in a kindly sing-song voice.

"No! Most certainly not!" Drake called out, scoffing as though it were a joke.

"It gets even better if you volunteer!" Gritch said excitedly, as the dreaded music began again in a tune jaunty yet stranger still.

Drake scowled, "Just keep moving!"

The forest pressed in around him, its shadows stretching longer and darker with every step. Roots, twisted and gnarled, jutted from the earth at odd angles, conspiring to trip any unwary traveler, while low-hanging branches reached out as if to smack him in unintentional insult. He leaned heavily on his makeshift crutch, the wood in it groaning softly under each cautious step.

He could not see very far at all anymore, for the winding,

darkness, and depth of canopy. Drake knew they were headed in basically the right direction, though he had never come this way. Gritch plainly knew this as a secret goblin path.

Gritch's bodily noises blasted through the trees like an evil spell.

Drake gritted his teeth against it, fighting back the urge to clamp his hands over his ears and flee into the safety of silence.

"You're mad," Drake muttered under his breath, more to himself than the goblin. "Absolutely mad."

Gritch smiled. "Madness is but another form of clarity," it said. "A way of seeing beyond the illusions that blind you."

Drake's selective silence at such statements were a near tangible barrier between him and the goblin's incessant prattle. He focused his gaze on the uneven terrain beneath his feet, the trees rustling, and animals scurrying away from Gritch, commiserate to its atrocities.

***

The path snaked through the undergrowth for hours, like a serpent, its course unpredictable.

It was summer already, and the days were getting quite hot now. Moisture beaded on his skin and soaked into his clothes until they clung uncomfortably to his frame. Sweat trickled down his temples, stinging his eyes as he blinked away the intrusive sensation.

Gritch's strange bodily noises and vocalizations continued, setting Drake's teeth on edge. He clenched his jaw tight against the urge to scream. He fought his urge to silence the maddening symphony once and for all. His hands twitched at his sides, fingers curling into fists as he imagined them wrapping around Gritch's scrawny neck, squeezing until the life, if one could call it that, fled from its twisted form.

"Keep moving," Drake muttered through gritting teeth, more

to himself than the goblin. "One foot in front of the other. Just keep walking."

Yet even as he repeated the mantra, he remembered some of Gritch's mad words, "There are things beyond your world. Shadows that linger, whispers in the dark, demons, and spirits that take hold silently." These words made him think of his father's warnings about goblin lies, but also the stories of illusion magics.

Drake shook his head vigorously, attempting to dislodge the goblin's voice from his thoughts. The pains throughout his body had converted into an almost numb throbbing which was nonstop.

"This way," Gritch urged now in full song. *"Just a little further! This way, just a little further!"* it kept repeating this to the beat of its throat noise-based bodily music.

Drake hesitated, crutch poised mid-stride as he eyed the goblin warily. "Okay, okay," he said, annoyed by the repetition, waving at it to stop.

The goblin's music could be felt through his feet throbbing within pain through every step. Drake gritted his teeth against the sensation.

He imagined Gritch's skull in his hands, the creature's twisted form convulsing as life fled from its body, leaving nothing but an empty husk behind.

He forced himself to take a deep breath, as if drawing strength from the very ground itself.

The goblin's puppet-like form swayed as it navigated the treacherous terrain with an eerie agility in its skip-flopping dancing gait. Twisting its torso around, Gritch's eyes met Drake's steadily, that unsettling intelligence burning brightly within their yellow depths. The goblin stopped, so did Drake, but the music did not.

For a moment, they stood thus, locked in an unnatural communion, one still noisy, the other silent, as if reality had been torn asunder, leaving them adrift in some surreality where time held no meaning.

Finally, Drake spoke up, "So if what you were saying before about goblin beliefs is true… and held logically true, then my father must have sent all those goblins to goblin heaven, right?"

The emanating music stopped once again, Gritch's mouth agape in shock. The goblin looked confused for a few moments, then answered honestly, "Mhmm, I never thought of that before, but correct sir, it would be as true in reverse." The goblin stared dumbly at Drake as though the implications of what it just said were not obvious, which was so strange considering its seeming ability to practically read his mind at other times. None of this made any sense.

Then, with Herculean effort, Drake tore his goblicidal gaze away, focusing instead on the path ahead.

The goblin shrugged and turned back around, it's bodily travel song starting up once more.

Drake fought the urge to clamp his hands around Gritch's neck.

Gritch giggled, with the music taking on a peppy tune once more.

They then stepped into a clearing bathed in the softest and most docile of moonlight, and the throat music ceased entirely. The slivers of beams pierced through the canopy above, casting shadows against the glow, having an almost hypnotic effect. Drake froze mid-stride taking it all in, ruins looming before them, a torn banner on a lowered flagpole, specter from a desperate past lowered in the mourning present. Collecting himself once more, he proceeded.

Under the light evening fog, crumbling walls choked with moss and vine, their stones worn smooth by time's relentlessly destructive caress. Roofless buildings against the moonlit night sky bore silent witness to memories and secrets lost. Battles were fought from here and victories won, leaving only fading stories of heroes, now corrupted.

'All they do is lie,' Drake thinks again, like a grim slogan repeated throughout his life.

Gritch's voice broke the silent moment. "You'll thank me when you find what you need," it rasped, sounding more like a desperate plea laced with hints of a threat.

Drake gripped his staff tighter as if to anchor himself against the goblin's influence.

'No,' Drake resolves internally without saying a thing, pushing aside the creature's insinuations. He imagines Gritch striking from behind with some blunt item, catching him off guard when least expected, and eager to claim any treasures or the bounties on Drake's head.

The goblin shrugs nonchalantly, unperturbed by Drake's apparent hostility, "Nightmares are just dreams having a bad day," Gritch murmured, its voice almost tender. "I can still help you inside," it offered.

"Maybe if you stop saying all those crazy things and cease with the music," Drake growled, voice revealing cold contempt. He holds back, figuring that the display of too much hatred might cause Gritch to overcorrect, in bending too far in attempt to appease him, or worse. It was likely better to have the creature nearby, docile, and where he could see it.

The goblin merely smiled gummily, as if amused by some private joke known only to itself.

As he ventured into the old hidden village, it felt like trespassing on hallowed ground.

This was similar to many of the hidden villages from that era, nothing special in truth, except it was where his father and allies had worked together to devise the strategy which led ultimately to Solipsia's freedom.

He thought back to his father talking about events which happened in this very place. Though Drake was born immediately before the war, too young to remember much, he felt tinges of memories flicker upon seeing the buildings.

"Don't blink," Gritch intones suddenly, "you might miss the moment your eyelids turn into bats and fly away!" It cackled uproariously.

"I said stop saying those wild things," Drake said in exasperation, his footsteps kicking up gravel. "I did not ask for you to say more."

Gritch fell silent for a blessed moment before resuming the nonsensical prattle. "Water always wins in the end. Don't fight it, drown gracefully." Its voice took on that sing-song quality again, and in started the bodily orchestra all over.

"No, do not, I told you," admonished Drake, looking at Gritch directly in the eyes as one might an inappropriate and rambunctious child.

They moved deeper into the old town, guided by glimmers of moonlight filtering through shattered windows and gaps, big and small, in roofs. Drake's makeshift crutch tapped against the carefully placed stones of the path. The atmosphere grew more oppressive with each passing moment, as though the very ground there breathed malevolence into a fog.

***

Finally, they reach a large cottage with half of one wall completely obliterated, but held up by strong timbers, suggesting late-stage repairs.

Gritch gestured towards it, smiling wickedly as if sharing some secret joke. "What you seek lies within," it rasped softly. The goblin continues its stream-of-consciousness observations. "Eggs aren't always what they seem. Sometimes you crack one open and find a tiny dragon."

Drake ignored this and approached cautiously, half-expecting some trap to spring forth from shadows concealing malevolent presences, feelings increased by the ceaseless goblin nonsense. Yet nothing was stirred, save the memories like old ghosts disappearing through the vaulted ceiling.

With bated breath, he walked into the old home of his father and mother, recognizing it easily. Debris from the destruction littered the floor, but there was not much actually left.

On one wall within the home, was a mural of the Ædlertuwin family crest: a double-headed golden eagle rising through the air with shields in one claw and swords in the other, as though savior through one's own action, and merely bringing people the means. His father had often waxed poetically about how the tools for strength are all around us, if we merely pick them up and learn to use them properly.

At the far end of the main room was a desk, which stirred strange long-lost memories of crawling up to his father, and being hoisted up to be read something from the desk. He knelt down before the desk carefully, stumbling a bit upon his crutches. He stared at the desk a long while, just sitting there almost like a child again.

After a while, he opened the drawer directly before him, inside it was nestled a journal. It was bound in worn leather and had yellowed pages filled with his father's familiar script: loops and curves bearing testament to countless hours spent poring over history, philosophy, myths, maps, and strategies alike. Intricate leather for the cover, bearing the same double-headed eagle symbol with shield and swords as painted on the wall.

Drake caressed the journal, recalling its touch from many years before. He felt his finger tracing the lines of the Ædlertuwin double-headed eagle, in the exact same way that his father had. It had been left here recently, perhaps by his father shortly before his death, or somebody else even more recently. He felt the edges of the pages that held answers to questions long unasked. Perhaps he now fared a better chance at answering some.

Gritch watched silently from a distance, expression inscrutable as if carved from stone itself. Finally, it spoke again, "You think you're chasing shadows? But they actually chase you!"

Drake could not tear his gaze away from those pages, and did not seem to hear the goblin.

Gritch, "If you have a moment, the shadows have something to share."

Looking up from the journal, he met Gritch's eyes. He hears his father's voice again, "All they do is lie because that's the only way they can survive..."

He ignored whatever it was the goblin had said. "Why have you helped me, goblin?" he asked.

The creature chuckled darkly, like a cliff-face crumbling. "I'm not helping you, boy," it said coldly. "You're just going to get yourself killed anyway." Gritch shrugs dismissively, as though discussing nothing more consequential than weather patterns. "Everyone has a tail; some just hide theirs better than others. Your tail shows, and your shadow is a traitor, it tells all sorts of lies about you to the ground but only behind your back."

Drake fights back a surge of anger at the nonsense. 'They lie after they lie,' he recalls again bitterly, but it had become more than a memory of his father's words. It was now his own thoughts, fact based in lived experience.

Before he could voice a response aloud, Gritch turned away, disappearing into shadows without another word.

Left alone in the ruins, Drake opened the journal and lost himself more fully, devouring pages filled with his father's thoughts, strategies, observations, and, most importantly, possibly the location of this powerful sword destined to slay the goblins.

Drake's mind raced as he absorbed each new revelation, plans forming even as memories washed over him like waves mounting in tides of emotion, bringing him to tears repeatedly. His mind was awhirl in Eldred's wisdoms, warnings, and insights.

Days pass by, the many hours barely noticed, when finally Drake rose to his feet. He now knew what must be done, and nothing would stand in his way. With newfound purpose guiding his steps, he made his way back through the ruined village.

The sword must be hidden deep within the heart of Whisperwood, a place his father had taken him and Telyn as children for his own purposes of research. Drake recalled the strange adventure with his father, skirting its edges. Now it made sense. There was something to do with their lineage below Whisperwood, and probably that legendary sword. His father had put forth great effort to find the entrance, but never could.

Taking a deep breath, Drake steeled himself against all the doubts and fears that gnawed at the edges of his determination.

This is but the beginning of battles yet to come, of truths awaiting revelation. The road ahead stretches before him, dark and uncertain, yet he walks it willingly, heart light despite the shadows gathering about him.

With a final glance at the wreckage of his home during infancy, Drake rose to his feet, father's journal clutched tightly to his chest. The fading darkness accompanied his passing from the little ruined village.

It passed him as he passed it, however a piece of it remained within him, like all the unspoken yet honored promises held between father and son, man and community. Having scavenged clothing from the ruins of these homes, he also wore pieces of that community in which he was born. There was something poetic, something fated in it all. He did not look back, not at the buildings crumbling into decay behind him nor any of the residual doubts which beset him at the lowest points. Drake's gaze remained fixed firmly on the destiny before him.

As he stepped back into the depths of the forest, something within him shifted, an almost imperceptible yet fundamental realignment of spirit and soul. The weight of expectation lifted, replaced by something now far heavier than before yet more familiar: responsibility. It was no burden, however.

With every step, and for the first time in his life, Drake felt the weight of his father's legacy under him, rather than on his shoulders, lifting him up with its challenge.

Drake would vindicate his father, and heroism itself. He felt complete clarity. He had spent years chasing the truth, believing it to be something distant and unreachable. Now, though, with the journal in his hands, he understood: truth was never a location or destination, because it is as infinite as time, and only part of it can belong to a single person.

With the onset of honesty for the sake of truth and actual loyalty, further devotion to truth itself becomes about forging your way to that part which you can best and most devote yourself. This path requires courage, sacrifice, and the willpower for good against evil.

Nay, this was far from the end of his story. He would be the one to answer that call for Solipsia, even if it meant standing alone for his father's memory, and doing so all on his still healing legs. Truth cut deeper than any sword, and he knew it did so in his favor.

Drake hobbled along on his staff through the night, leaving the shadows and ruins of his past behind as another dawn broke. The light of his purpose burned, as brightly as that sunrise, within.

CHAPTER EIGHT

INTO THE DEPTHS

Being on the mend without Gritch to slow him down, Drake moved with much greater speed despite the continuous throbbing and tiredness wearing upon him. Drake's staff tapped out a steady rhythm as if keeping time to some unheard melody that had nothing to do with goblish throat music. His mind churned with thoughts of what lay ahead, and he prepared himself.

The pain was as nothing in comparison to his mission.

Drake arrived at his destination sooner than he had anticipated, having grown used to the pace set by Gritch in the forest.

Whisperwood loomed before him. Its massive ancient trees were tightly packed in and overflowing without a sapling in sight.

It brought back a lot of memories of his father and sister.

An all-too-familiar yet inhuman voice cut through the underbrush behind him, "You know, they say these woods are full of whispers, and if you listen close enough, you can hear them singing your name." Gritch emerged from shadows like some grotesque apparition.

Drake froze mid-stride, jaw clenching as irritation flared within him. He turned slowly to face the goblin, eyes narrowing into slits of cold contempt. "What do you want?" he growled.

The creature grinned widely, green gums and slimy tongue comically bared in a parody of friendliness. "Oh, nothing much," it replied airily. "Just thought I'd keep you company on your little quest." Gritch's eyes gleamed beneath feigned innocence, as if daring Drake to contradict him.

"I don't need your company," Drake snarled, gripping his

crutch tighter until knuckles turned white. "Nor do I want it."

Gritch shrugged, unperturbed by Drake's hostility. "Suit yourself," it said casually, falling into step beside Drake as though a time-honored guest. "But mark my words, boy, you'll be glad for the guidance soon enough." The goblin laughed darkly to itself.

Drake ignored it, focusing instead on navigating the terrain ahead. Roots snaked everywhere like twisted limbs reaching out to trip unwary travelers since there was no path to speak of, while low-hanging branches bore down oppressively. Each step required careful placement of crutch and foot alike.

Gritch persisted in its nonsensical prattle just as before, voice insinuating itself constantly. "You ever notice how leaves change color before they fall?" it mused aloud, tone conversational, as if sharing some profound insight. "It's almost like nature's way of giving fair warning, a chance to prepare for winter's cold embrace."

Drake sighed, increasing pace in attempt to outstrip the goblin's relentless chatter. Yet Gritch matched him stride for stride, voice never wavering from its stupefying monologue of stream-of-consciousness observations with seemingly boundless enthusiasm. "They say time heals all wounds," it said softly, almost gently, as if in a dream. "But what if some cuts run too deep? What if certain pains linger long after flesh has mended?"

Drake rolled his eyes.

Gritch chuckled lowly "Ah, I see I've struck a nerve," it teased, voice raised in amusement. "Forgive me if I overstep, but sometimes truth hurts, that's why they call it cutting." With that, it turned away, melting back into the shadows from whence it came.

Drake pressed on, enjoying the respite and peace in the silence. He wished that creature would finally stay away this time. His thoughts turned the pages of his father's journal.

He was about to get the journal out to re-read something when, just as familiarity threatened to breed complacency, Gritch reappeared once more. It emerged from the undergrowth with a suddenness like rot that made Drake startle. The jump caused his staff to slip on loose debris, so that he fell on his backside.

The goblin laughed wickedly, "Miss me?" it taunted, voice laced with mockery.

Before Drake could respond or even stand up, Gritch continued in its never-ending nonsensical soliloquy.

"Did you know that squirrels are excellent climbers? Some say they can even scale smooth surfaces, though I've never seen one attempt glass."

Drake rolled his eyes and pushed himself back up. He continued on his way, passing the goblin without acknowledgment. Refusing to engage the creature further, he focused instead on the mission.

Yet Gritch persisted, falling into step beside Drake once more as though nothing had happened.

"You're going the wrong way," it announced suddenly, tone matter-of-fact. "The blade isn't in this direction."

Drake hesitated mid-stride, brow furrowing in confusion. He consulted the journal again, tucked safely within his clothing, tracing paths laid out by his father's hands. According to the map, he confirmed for himself as he knew: that he should indeed be headed due north, towards the heart of Whisperwood. There was no entrance, the place simply snuck up on a person, becoming stranger with centrality, according to Eldred.

"Don't trust everything you read," Gritch advised. "Sometimes words deceive even when intent is true."

"And whose words should I trust?" Drake demanded, voice laced with bitterness. "Yours? The ramblings of a mad creature who delights in chaos and confusion?"

The goblin merely shrugged, unperturbed by Drake's hostility. "Perhaps not," it conceded mildly. "But consider this: what if your father was mistaken? What if the blade lies elsewhere, hidden away where even he dared not venture?"

Drake fell silent, considering Gritch's words despite himself. He thought back to the journal entries, how they corresponded to his own memories of father, and also recalling instances shared by Eldred where certainty wavered, doubts creeping in, and who he chose to trust.

"No," Drake said firmly, shaking his head as if to dispel any purchase in lingering seeds of doubt. "I trust my father's judgment, and his map."

Gritch puffed up and huffed. "Very well," it said indignantly. "But mark my words, boy: truth is just another path to lies. Whisperwood is full of things that await the foolish."

***

With that ominous parting shot, the goblin melted back into shadows once more, leaving Drake alone to navigate deeper into Whisperwood, a strange and tree-suffocated thicket of roots, trunks, and branches, apparently free of undergrowth. It was deeply disturbing to see, now as an adult.

The canopy above thickened until sunlight was reduced to mere suggestions filtering through dense foliage.

The ground beneath his feet began to slope upward, path climbing gently before giving way to a steep ascent, with trees or roots getting denser as he climbed, until he could barely see dirt any longer. He had never been this deep into the Whisperwood. Drake's heart pounded with trepidation as he caught sight of the ascent upon tree roots before him. His legs pulsed in protest.

He climbed the roots of the trees and the trees as well, levering off this or that one to gain ground overall as he climbed the hill.

It was more than a hill, though. He climbed into the fog built up under the canopy of the tree mountain, until he could barely see anything

Eventually the steep ascent gave way to what could only be described as a wall of trees and roots, ascending into the sky, in all directions ahead of him.

He moved cautiously, using his staff to pull himself up, sometimes against stone that jutted through layers of moss or dirt in between some roots.

His curiosity got the best of him, and so he climbed to get above the trees. From below, the canopy could barely be seen for the great amassment of fog, but he climbed through it anyway, blindly grasping at branches.

Upon breaking through the canopy, he found he was beyond the fog as well.

Looking around, he spotted the entrance to a cavern only a little downhill, in the distance across the way.

Drake climbed back down and then downhill a way, making his way closer to where he had seen the cavern through the roots and lower branches.

The cave yawned before him, like the mouth of some slumbering beast, gaping maw framed by twisted roots and gnarled branches like teeth, seemingly warning against trespass.

Drake ventured into the cave, down a spiraling staircase, and into a large dark chamber within.

Walls glistened with moisture, slick and black as obsidian beneath glow cast by luminescent fungi dotting surfaces like constellations against the night sky. He felt tiny tendrils of light reaching out to touch him, as if to caress his face and skin.

Gritch, appearing once more, darted eagerly ahead of him into the cavern, drawn inexorably towards bioluminescent bottom-rot feeding growths that painted cavern walls in ethereal hues. The goblin reached out a tentative hand, fingers brushing gently against the oddly pulsating fronds before recoiling sharply as if burned.

"Ouch!" it yelped, sucking its digits in its mouth, like some chastised child. "Sticky things!" Gritch pouted, inspecting its hand. "And they taste awful, too."

Drake ignored the goblin's antics. He heard voices in the chamber except they were clear and not whispers, they spoke in ancient tongues. The voices spoke his name as well, but then they also called him by names he had never heard before.

"What do you want?" Drake called out aloud to the voices. "Why bring me here?"

Gritch giggled, sound bouncing off walls to create an eerie chorus. "Because," the goblin interjected its own unwelcomed answer airily, "every good quest needs…"

"Just shut up," Drake said, moving onwards.

He navigated by instinct alone, guided by the faintest traces of light emanating from fungi and the voices that seemed to beckon him ever deeper, a few seeming more familiar and quickly gaining his trust. They spoke of the sword, and he knew he was in the right place.

* * *

Soon enough, Drake found himself confronted by the first barrier: a riddle carved into stone before him, letters etched deeply as if by some ancient hand. He leaned in close, brow furrowing as he deciphered words beneath flickering glow:

"Taken from dry earth, enclosed in watery tomb,
I guide the lost and save them from their doom."

Drake's gaze flicked to Gritch, who merely grinned toothlessly in response. The goblin said nothing, thankfully.

He pondered the riddle, mind racing through possibilities as he searched for answers hidden within seemingly innocuous phraseology.

"A lodestone in a compass," Drake said finally. As if responding to his words, stones shifted, rumbling ominously through the walls as they moved aside to reveal the path previously obscured.

Gritch clapped hands together in delight, laugh bouncing merrily off walls. "Very good!" it exclaimed, sounding almost proud.

Drake paid the goblin no heed, pressing onwards with newfound determination. He entered the next chamber, where he found yet another riddle, which he read aloud:

"Born small with many captivated,
I die as quickly as I am hated,
Feed me and I am never sated,
I simplify all that is complicated."

This one presented much difficulty for Drake, since each clause seemed to indicate something else entirely.

Gritch was giggling to itself and then quietly said, "I know the answer, but I refuse to say."

Drake looked at it with disgust. In his mind's eye, he saw Gritch and all its relatives set aflame, burning alive, and screaming in sheer pain. Then the answer came to him, and he called out, "Fire!"

Nothing happened.

"Not giving it away. You'll have to figure it out for yourself!"

Drake thought of all the people he had lost. He thought of his need to revenge them and how much that simplified everything, and then answered simply, "Love!"

Mechanisms deep within the walls moved and the stone blocking the door to the next chamber rolled out of the way.

"Oh," Gritch said in a confused tone, "Not what I was thinking but whatever."

"What were you thinking?" Drake gave in and asked.

"Power!" sang out the goblin as its bodily band started its jamboree.

"No, no, not that, stop. No singing, no throat music. Power though? Really? Power does not simplify anything," Drake said as he moved along into the next chamber which had opened up.

"But it does!" was all Gritch could manage in retort.

Each riddle presented itself as barrier between him and goal, yet with every correct answer, walls would groan and shift, guiding him ever closer to the salvation of Solipsia. The next riddle was the shortest yet:

"You can keep me,
But never hold me
In your hands."

Drake thought for a little and then threw out a quick answer, "A secret is kept but cannot be held in the hands. A secret?"

Once more, nothing happened.

Gritch was ready with its laughter and celebratory musical accompaniment.

Drake pondered for longer now, brow furrowed in concentration as he sifted through his mental lexicon for a word that fit the description.

He fought to remember, struggled to recall, and yet it was right there. His heart sank as he thought about all that Solipsia used to be and all that he wanted for it.

Tears threatened to break in his eyes as he answered, voice dripping with emotion, "Memory!"

Once more, stones rumbled and shifted, clearing the path before him.

Drake found himself face-to-face with yet another riddle, carved into the next wall much like the others before it:

"Originated winding round in mountains,
Fortune flicked into all fountains,
Markets with too much always close,
And yet ever it flows."

He considered possibilities, weighing each against criteria laid out in cryptic verse.

"Coin?" Drake said aloud after moment's thought, feeling uncertain of the answer even as the words left his lips.

This time again, nothing happened, the stones remained stubbornly immovable, barricading his path ahead with implacable finality.

Gritch chortled from somewhere behind him. "Wrong answer," it taunted, drawing out each syllable like poisonous syrup. "Try again."

Drake just did his best to ignore the creature.

"Water," he said finally. "The answer is water."

Stones rumbled once more, shifting aside to grant passage

through another newly revealed corridor. The next room's riddle read:

"I bring peace to the overwhelmed,
My practitioners are ever well helmed.
Sought by the wisest though most hate me,
Yet so fragile saying just my name breaks me."

Drake breathed deeply and exhaled quietly, "Silence" feeling almost reverent as the word left lips.

The stones then moved, more loudly it seemed this time.

A musical huff could be heard from his unwelcomed audience, as he walked on to the next chamber.

"I turn without moving and fly when caught,
But unlock always whether liked or not.
I am the last thing desired while all else is rot."

"Time," he declared after moment's thought, gaze fixed firmly on the riddle before him, and the stone covering the next door opened as well. "But it doesn't heal all wounds," he whispered to himself as he glanced over at the goblin rolling its eyes, obviously now bored by his success.

So it continued. Each barrier eventually fell by application of intellect and willpower alone. Drake felt as though he was battling some unseen foe, engaging in a duel of wits with the past.

"I hold most hands at once yet touch none,
And protect evil-doers until their deed is done."

“Gloves!” Drake shouted confidently.

An enormous stone broke loosed itself from the wall and hurtled full-force at Drake, giving him almost no time to get out of the way. He lost his staff-crutch, crushed and shattered now.

The stone lifted out of the way back into position, with stone dust and wood splinters from the staff settling about the chamber as it did.

‘Wrong answer, I guess,’ Drake thought. He groaned, as he lifted himself back up. He did his best to stand up straight and walk without the staff.

Gritch called out, “No more games now, boy, wrong answers will get you killed.”

Drake pondered for a good while longer this time, looking off into the corners of the chamber, and at the hooded yellow eyes of his nasty companion. “Shadow,” Drake murmured softly, almost sadly, as if acknowledging his failures.

Stone once more moved, and the path now lay open before him. Drake pressed onwards, walking slowly and carefully now without his staff.

“I fly on wing,
But then on air.
I soothe dreamers, unseen,
And archer’s error.”

“Feather,” he answered without hesitation, voice steady and sure. “The answer is feather.”

This was correct, and so he again moved forward.

"I have arms but no hands,
Neck but no head,
Trunk but no branches."

Gritch laughed uproariously as Drake read this aloud.

Drake was not amused. He contemplated for a very long time and could come up with nothing for this one.

Gritch cackled in delight, "Boy, you had better be careful!"

Drake watched the goblin wipe its nose with its disgusting stain-riddled sleeve and thought back to all the water he had drank again. The thought came to him at once, "Tunic!"

The sound of stone moving could be heard behind the walls.

"Dagnabbit," Gritch cursed.

A door opened, but it was not to another chamber lit by that same luminescent fungi. There was a closed in hallway of darkness, instead.

First they heard what sounded like a ground slamming machine, repetitive and growing louder, but not down the hallway so much as through the walls.

The air grew colder as the stone groaned, like grinding ice against iron, and from the darkness emerged a figure of dread. Stomping slowly, though still too fast, came a towering mass of icy granite, its form jagged and enormous.

Eyes, if they indeed were, set back as hollow pits of black glass, brightly reflected the pale light of the fungi that clung to the walls like spectral candles, as did the figure's granite and icy surfaces.

* * *

The stone giant moved with a slow deliberateness, steps blasting like thunder in the narrow corridor. Each footfall resounded forth as though it sought to shatter the very fabric of silence itself.

Drake staggered forward, his broken legs protesting with every step. He had pulled out his knife on instinct, though it felt silly now, clutching it as he did, hand trembling in fear.

The pain was a constant companion but grew in presence as he was forced to move faster than he was now capable, a gnawing ache that curled through his bones like ivy, but he pressed on, his breath shallow and ragged as he forced himself to focus. The stone beast loomed before him, oppressive and terrifying.

"Thou art not first to covet what lies beyond," it rumbled in an archaic dialect Drake could barely understand, its voice a grinding of stone against stone, "neither wilt thou be last."

Drake's eyes flicked to the knife in his grip, his mind racing through the possibilities.

He could not match the golem in strength or speed in his condition, and with hands also still healing, but he had his mind. Power was not always found in might, but in the spaces leveraged between.

The rock monster raised a massive hand, its fingers like claws of iron. It reached for Drake.

He did not move to evade. Instead, he stepped forward, his injured legs feeling as though they might break again as he forced himself into position. He held the knife tight, not feeling the slightest bit silly for it anymore.

The giant's massive hand paused mid-motion, unable to bend its arm inward enough to reach him. Drake seized the moment, his body shaking from the exertion, and drove the knife into the stone legs of the monster.

The blade struck directly into a joint with barely a sliver of space for purchase. Drake had driven it in with all the force he could muster, but it still jutted out. Noticing the crack expanding as the beast brought that leg up, Drake pulled himself up and held on, finding purchase with his elbow on the lifting leg of the creature. His other palm could just reach the knife sticking out of the crack, and so he pushed it in further with all his might.

Drake fell off and rolled out of the way.

The monster shifted its weight onto that leg, which leveraged the weight of the creature against its own stone. Its granite burst open with earsplitting cracks that snapped through the chamber, as though some distant earthquake moved the stones under him. The massive thing staggered, its form shuddering as if something deep within had been disturbed.

Drake had to move. With great effort, he pushed himself up and stood again. His legs buckled under him, yet he was able to catch himself and limp away. He did not look back, and tried to move as quickly as he could.

The enormous thing roared, shaking the very walls as it began to pursue, but instead it fell apart behind him, and so the door to the next chamber opened up to him.

The knife was now gone, lost in that monstrosity, and this was more frightening to Drake than the stone monster.

Drake stepped into the next chamber, its walls lined with ancient runes that pulsed brightly in the fungal luminescence. They spelled out:

"Welcome home, son."

Ancient words cast in stone set fire to his soul.

The silence was absolute, broken only by the distant drip of water somewhere and the slow creaking of stone, resting in new positions.

Before him stood a featureless statue vaguely shaped like a human cast in obsidian, and it spoke a riddle in his mind, and tongue.

"I enslave all,
And cast them into darkness.
I crave thralls,
And rob the light of starkness.
My knaves fall
All their powers do I harness."

The figure did not move, but its presence pressed against him like a vice. He closed his eyes, letting the meaning sink in, the riddle spoke of a force that bound others to it, devouring their strength, their light, their will. It was not a weapon or creature, but something worse: a force that thrived on subjugation, and ownership. Drake knew it too well. He opened his eyes and spoke, "Lies."

The figure shuddered as though struck by lightning, the runes along its body flaring crimson before dimming to black once more. A deep rumble echoed through the chamber, but it was not a sound of destruction. It was a sigh, ancient and weary. The shadows recoiled, and the figure flickered, casting the chamber in an eerie glow.

The figure finally burst into light, so that the room became intolerable in it, forcing Drake to shut his eyes in the presence.

"Everyone pretends to have me,
But nobody does.
All pretend to like me,
But few actually do.
I'm the best friend to good,
And the worst enemy of evil.
I can not say do what you should,
But display merely in what you are able."

The riddle spoke of something hidden, a thing at once both

companion and adversary, an unconquerable force, revealing rather than commanding.

He thought of all the warriors who had chosen to stand beside him instead of ignore him or wait, and how thankful he was for their being against the darkness with him. What drove them to it most? He knew at once.

Eyes still forced shut by the brightness, he stepped closer to the figure. Its surface cool against his fingertips as he reached out, though it was as if he could feel a deeper warmth within it.

Drake said, "Truth."

The moment the word left his lips, all light in the chamber disappeared, so that opening his eyes revealed an even deeper darkness. Drake's mind was filled with a thousand images at once, each one reflecting not just his face, but the faces of those who had shaped Solipsia's fate. He saw the faces of his own family, his father, his sister, his cousins, and all his comrades in arms.

The air trembled, and for a brief instant, Drake saw all of them at once. Eldred, his family, the warriors he had fought beside, the evil goblish plotters whose lies were destroying everything, and every person in the kingdom depending upon him. He felt their presence in the silence that followed, an unspoken acknowledgment that truth was as much a burden as a weapon, one that could not be wielded without consequence.

The chamber became still once more, visions passing, and Drake stood there in a calm state, his legs heavy with pain but his mind lightened by something he could not name. The path ahead remained dark, but he could no longer bring himself to fear it.

***

Drake simply stood in the darkness, thankful for being alive. He was thankful for the images and the reminders of all that he was fighting for. If not for the needs of the kingdom, he would not have minded that respite going on for an eternity.

Then finally, after what felt an eternity, he could hear the stones of the ancient caverns move all around him and within the walls, sliding into new arrangements sounding like great sighs of relief from long-held burdens discarded.

Drake stood in the once again silent chamber, breaths slow, but feeling energized despite the condition of his legs and his now being forced to hobble slowly without the staff. The figure was gone, and the only light was from the fungi of a path past a cavern door which appeared after the event.

Gritch materialized beside him then, grinning widely, as if sharing a secret joke known only to itself. "Well done," it praised, voice laced with a grudging respect.

Drake said nothing, merely nodded acknowledgment before turning away from the goblin and hobbling purposefully.

The air grew colder still as Drake emerged into the next cavern, breath misting before him in small clouds that dissipated quickly.

He blinked, eyes adjusting to the abrupt shift in surroundings, and found himself overlooking a vast bottomless chasm that stole away his breath and set his heart to pounding.

The fungal assistance was not here. All the light he could see by was the fungi from the door he had just exited.

He could not see the other side of the cave, nor could he see the bottom. Looking up, he could just make out some sort of distant icy ceiling above, but only by the remnant glow of the fungi. The blackness beyond the black ice went off into seemingly infinite expanse before him.

The great expanse indeed stretched out like some limitless wound in the ground, its edges lost to swirling mists and impenetrable darkness that absorbed any shred of light.

Drake leaned over the edge, craning neck to glimpse the depths below the cliff he stood upon, but found only endless abyss staring back silently, inscrutable and utterly devoid of mercy.

A gasp escaped his lips as he took in the sheer magnitude of the vista unfolding before him, as his eyes continued to adjust to the sheer darkness. Vertigo threatened to claim his senses as he teetered perilously at edge of the lip of a cliff made with icy stone. He felt insignificant against the raw power of some superior nature laid bare before his eyes, humbled by this stark reminder of his own mortality.

Drake's gaze drifted towards the center of the chasm, where a massive ice bridge with railing spanned the void like a frozen waterfall suspended as some deadly trial.

That goblin had again made itself scarce.

Its surface shone smooth and translucent beneath the faint glow cast by distant fungi, looking treacherously slick as polished glass. The structure went straight across, disappearing into darkness on the far side. As he studied the thing, he came to the awful realization that this was the only way across.

Drake hesitated, considering the daunting prospect of traversing such a perilous bridge without his staff.

The idea of stuffing the fungi into his clothing came to him. It would help keep him warm and grant him some precious light at the same time.

All stuffed and lit up, he tested his weight against the thankfully even ground of the very narrow bridge, crutchless legs trembling slightly beneath the strain. He heard his father's voice steadfastly exhorting him onwards, despite the natural trepidation coiling tight around him.

"Courage is not the absence of fear," Eldred had told him once, "but the fortitude in justice to face it nonetheless."

Drake drew strength from those words, and said under his

breath, "For justice, and for Solipsia."

He took a deep breath, exhaled slowly, and stepped onto the strange ice bridge into nowhere. The railings were so slippery to the touch, that the presence would seem a mere consolation for most, but these were a lifesaver for him.

Each footfall upon the bridge sent vibrations through its structure. It creaked ominously beneath weight, protesting intrusion upon its silent realm with groans that reverberated throughout the endless expanse.

Drake moved cautiously, testing each step before committing fully, arms holding firmly upon the rails, as he shuffled along the slick surface. He felt the precariousness of his situation acutely. One misstep could send him plunging into oblivion and a no doubt ignoble, icy death.

As he ventured forth across the bridge, darkness closed in. Drake's heart hammered against his ribs, pulse pounding loudly in his ears as he fought back the rising tide of panic at what could only be described as a real living nightmare.

He focused on the rhythm of his breath, in and out, a steady metronome anchoring him. It was like being lost high above some silent sea on a slippery sheet of ice, but with no hope of sunlight, that mighty conqueror of darkness.

He saw nothing, and only felt the ice bridge. It was an inexorable tide of night that seemed to press in from all sides. Drake could see naught but swirling shadows dancing at edges of perception, that he could not be sure were even real; tendrils reaching out to ensnare any unwary traveler and drag him down into that endless abyss. The only guarantee was the constancy of slipping on that bridge and fighting against losing any purchase gained.

Suddenly, a distant hum reached his ears, in a discordant melody borne on currents of cold air, growing steadily louder with each passing moment. Drake froze mid-stride, head cocked to the side as he strained to discern the source in the depths of darkness.

'It can't be,' he thought, disbelief warring with a burgeoning sense of fear and unease. Yet even as his rational mind rebelled against the notion, instincts screamed warning.

He turned slowly, squinting into the gloom behind him, and caught a shocking sight.

Gritch, covered in luminescent fungi and moss, skated along the rails of the ice bridge with wild abandon, body contorted at impossible angles. The goblin's body emitted its otherworldly concert of whistles and honks, with a diaphragm-driven backbeat, as it sang out aloud in goblish speech something about "ICHOR" which Drake recognized as the goblin word for themselves.

As Gritch passed, it called out gleefully and in a sing-songy tone, "**Don't get distracted by the wildlife!**" The music was louder from behind, as the goblin projected noise to its rear, as some sort of a noisy propellant. Drake stared agape, horror rooted him to spot as the goblin slid past, chest music fading into the distance with an unsettling swiftness.

"What wildlife?!" he shouted back desperately, voice alone in the darkness filling the cavern as the music faded.

The bridge trembled beneath the outburst, vibrations rippling along the surface, threatening to dislodge his precarious footing. Drake gripped the railing tightly, as he fought to maintain balance.

Gritch's laughter could be heard, distantly and faintly, before being swallowed entirely by that encroaching darkness.

Drake stopped for several heartbeats, breaths coming in ragged gasps as he struggled to regain the composure shattered by the goblin's intrusion.

CHAPTER NINE

DARK STORM

Lightning forked through the chasm then, jagged bolts illuminating the bridge in a flash and revealing the treacherous expanse stretching out before him in stark relief. Regardless, he still could not see the other end. Drake stumbled forward, propelled by the primal urge to escape.

The bridge groaned. A whisper coiled through the darkness, not a voice but a presence, a shadow that did not move yet pressed against his thoughts like a hand curling around his ribs.

"Drake," it murmured, "you are the best. Who can stand against Drake? Who can stand against Drake the Great?"

He had not expected to hear this from whatever it was. He found the voice and the things it said complimentary yet uncomfortable.

"More talented than Eldred, father of Drake. More important than Solipsia or any hero from her past. More powerful than the trolls who shattered your bones. You are the storm, the fire, and the edge that cleaves through lies." The words were not physical but felt, as though the darkness itself had taken up residence in his skull. "You do not need them. They are nothing, nothing compared to you."

He tried to ignore the voice, treating it as though it came from within. In saying such things, he could not imagine the voice being anything other than some part of his own mind. To him, these were loose and vain thoughts, the sort his father had taught him to stop, push away, and discard. Drake's breath came shallow, his legs now trembling from pain and exertion.

"They fear you," the voice in the darkness continued, rising like the hymn of a thousand voices at once. "They know your name, yet they do not understand you. You are not bound by their laws, their debts, or their weaknesses. You are free."

The words clawed at him, sharp as ice and sweet as poison, as though sung only for the dead.

"You are not bound," the darkness insisted, its voice now a roar. "You are a god, Drake!"

Drake was no fool. He had been taught from a very early age what such pretensions of immortality could do to a mortal man. He knew how men could be turned into monsters as wicked as any goblin, with even the noblest hearts rotted out in pride.

Drake clenched his teeth and yelled out, "You speak as if you are something and as if you know something," he growled. "None of what you say is true. You have no power. If things did not apply to me, I would not need to be here, and I would not have started across this bridge. You reflect my hubris in what I was, what I am, and what I could become. In the end, however, I choose my future."

The darkness recoiled, its presence flickering like a flame caught in a storm. "You would deny me?" it hissed, its voice now sharp as a blade. "You would call me nothing, yet you are the one who has forgotten what it means to be weak. You have buried your pain, your fear, and your ignorance beneath layers of pride and power. You think yourself above them all, but you are no better than the goblins you fight."

"I have not forgotten," Drake said, his voice steady despite the tremor in his hands. "I have chosen to remember."

The darkness surged forward then, a tide of strange truths, half-heard lies, and shadows that threatened to drown him whole. Drake did not flinch. He closed his eyes, letting the pain, the fear, the truth of it all wash over him without denial. For in that moment, he saw not just the voice of the darkness but the reflection of himself in his his conceit, his obsession, and his unrighteous disdain for those who could not see what he had seen. And in that reflection, he found the answer.

"I am not free! Not the way most would have freedom. But that freedom is an illusion founded on ignorance," he called out. "I am alive, aware, and truth is with me, even if some lies might still hold me down."

The darkness shuddered, its presence unraveling like smoke in the wind. The bridge groaned once more, and Drake took a step forward. The chasm yawned beneath him, vast and deep, yet he did not falter.

* * *

Rain fell, at first a mere sprinkle, but quickly escalating into a deluge of hail. It pounded against his flesh with bruising force. Thunder roared overhead, reverberations shaking the cavern walls and sending cascades of ice and freezing rain crashing down from unseen heights above.

Drake cursed inwardly, squinting against the sting, driven by sheer survival instinct. The luminescence within his clothing was being washed out, quickly, so that he now had less and less light to even see himself.

As if summoned by tumultuous skies, bird-like ice forms began to materialize within the cavernous storm, small bolts of lightning darting erratically through the air like feathered projectiles unleashed from a heavenly quiver. They swooped and dove around Drake, energized hum filling ears, as he ducked and weaved futilely against the assault.

One such bolt struck him, the impact jolting his balance violently. He teetered dangerously with foot falling off the edge of the bridge, arms flailing wildly as he sought any grasp upon the slick surfaces beneath fingers, boot, and joints. Panic surged through veins like wildfire, urging a primal scream from deep within his lungs.

Before sound could escape though, another bolt slammed into his side, causing him to be thrown against the railing on one side of the bridge. Drake's world became a swirling maelstrom of darkness and blinding flashes of light, pain and cold, as he slipped continuously trying to move through the storm.

He fell again, nearly slipping off the edge once again. Somehow, Drake managed to snag the railing with both hands as he began to fall, fingers closing around the freezing ice in desperate bid to survive. He hung there for an endless moment, body dangling precariously over abyss, while rain lashed against his face and the lightning continued its merciless barrage.

With a grunt of exertion, he hauled himself upward, muscles straining against the weight of sodden clothes and the sheer force of gravity conspiring to drag him down. Soaking wet and freezing, each pull sent fresh waves of agony lancing through his hands, shoulders, and legs, when granted purchase again, but he gritted his teeth and refused to give up. To surrender anything now would mean certain doom.

Finally, after what felt like an eternity of struggle, Drake managed to roll onto the bridge's surface, body shaking with exertion and adrenaline coursing wildly through his veins. He lay there for several moments, breaths coming in gasps as he stared up into the storm-racked darkness, hot tears of relief streamed down his cheeks despite the icy rain.

Lightning flashed, and this time struck part of the bridge in the direction he had come from, causing the entire bridge to strum like some giant's bowstring. He panicked in pushing himself upright and fighting against slippage, limbs trembling beneath the strain of the ordeal.

Thunder rumbled overhead like a distant rapid drumbeat quickly drawing near in the dark, echoing out through the abyssal cavern as though urging him onwards. Another bright strike, this time ahead of him. In the glow, he saw something in the distance ahead, something different, which looked a lot like the other end of the bridge. He scrambled for it, at the fastest pace he had ever trod carefully.

He was apparently now beyond some of the cavern clouds which had been completely blocking his view ahead. There was an eerie light emanating from nowhere, behind the remaining cloud cover.

It all became much more visible as he approached. What he saw sent fresh jolts of shock coursing through his system, unrelated to the lightning.

It looked as though another massive ice bridge ran vertical from the cliff that the ice bridge was attached to, and the sight confused him so. Drake blinked, and rubbed his eyes wearily, as though expecting it to dissipate upon better inspection.

The thought of climbing an ice bridge like this vertically was just too much.

Suddenly, looking over the clouds behind the vertical bridge, he realized quickly that it was a reflection of clouds around the bridge he was currently on.

At once, he figured out he was looking upon a massive wall of mirror looming over the cliff, reflecting the ice bridge back at infinity in a dizzying display that seemed to defy reality.

Suddenly, an incredible sound erupted throughout the previously silent cavern, a deafening noise that sent shockwaves rippling along the ice of the bridge. Drake staggered, hands flying out to grasp the railing as he fought to maintain balance. The noise grew louder still, swelling into a thunderous roar that shook the very foundations of the cave itself.

He turned towards the source of the monstrous sound behind him, squinting into the darkness as he tried in vain to discern anything beyond the clouds obscuring his vision. All he could see was half of the darkness from the left moving into the darkness on the right, and it was hot yet without it being any kind of actual weather pattern. Suddenly it was no longer dark, anywhere, and all the clouds were gone.

Drake hesitated only briefly before breaking into as close to a full run as he could manage, propelled by primal terror gripping his heart in its icy fist.

He splashed through the puddles forming suddenly on the bridge's surface, each step sending the splashes of water up like the wake of a small boat cutting through water. His legs now felt on fire despite the many hours out there in the blistering cold and being soaked through. The sudden heat from behind was no consolation though, only reminding him that he was probably not running fast enough.

As Drake neared the distant cliff, he attempted to push harder and faster with his legs at the same time. He could feel a pain through the numbness, as though his legs were about to break anew. His lungs burned in exertion as he stumbled his way toward the mirror wall looming before him, escaping the blossoming blast of heat radiating from behind.

He skidded to halt before the mirror wall, breath misting lightly against the cool smoothness as he stared into his own reflection, with a fiery blaze in the abyss behind him as he stared.

Then there was silence again, with darkness behind.

The blast was completely gone, yet so was the bridge. Drake's clothing was scorched. He looked back into the mirror again, spotting his singed hair this time. For the first time in forever, he laughed heartily at himself. Drake raised his hand tentatively, pressing palm flat against the mirror. It covered the whole wall and was the source of that eerie light itself. Logic dictated that a path lay hidden, perhaps to be revealed by some secret mechanism concealed somewhere in the mirror.

Drake turned back towards the chasm he had just crossed, gazing out across an unending expanse of darkness. It must have been a dozen miles, at least.

***

He had made it. Yet his trials were far from over. He must push further than ever before, deeper. This was it, and he was now the doer doing.

Drake sat for a long time, in the quiet with his eyes shut, reacquainting himself with the darkness, since it was no longer trying to kill him. He did so facing the mirror absentmindedly.

The towering mirror edifice loomed ever present physically and in his thoughts, stretching skyward reflecting his own image indeed but something else as well. It seemed impossible to Drake that it could have been a singular mirror, but must have been composed of many. The mirrors hummed softly. Pale internal light spread evenly throughout their glassy depths, casting a glow that seemed to pulsate rhythmically, beating in time with his own heart.

Specters materialized before him in the mirrors, writhing forms wreathed in grotesquely twisting shadows, taking shape from fractured thoughts and remembrances dancing across mirror surfaces. Drake recoiled instinctively, breath hitching in his throat as he beheld horrors spawned from the recesses of mind; ghosts of past failures and mistakes given form in the shimmering reflecting glass. His recent regrets in not doing more to recruit other heroes to the cause or to secure his allies, for instance.

He saw himself leading the charge against that singular strangebreed troll, then the many more who stormed out from the forest where they had been in waiting. The mirrors reflected fragmented visions of important memories, as though juggling his emotions.

"Shadow is not holding my hand," he shouted aloud. "Not the shadow but the light. The light holds my hand! It casts shadows of my fingers in all things."

Drake took a deep breath, steeling himself against the onslaught of memories overwhelming his vision, thoughts, and emotions. His breath hitched in his throat as the images grew more vivid. Failures, his doubts, the wounds left by the past. He closed his eyes tightly, fingers curling into fists at his sides.

He raised his hands and opened them, palms spread wide, as if offering solace to phantasms conjured within his own mind.

For a moment, the reflections faltered.

The wall ceased the torture, glassy surfaces smoothing over like calm waters, disturbed no more. The specters recoiled and dissipated, until all that remained were faint traces of color, flickers of deep emotional warmth, of laughter, of a child's hand clasped firmly in his own. Drake recognized it as his own hand.

Images shifted, fractured visions giving way to wholesome memories of goodness. He saw the mirth of childhood playing beneath the summer sun and the gentle touch of mother's hand upon his cheek. He heard his father's voice steady, true, and sure against any doubts.

Darker shadows still lurked, pain and loss clinging on despite his best efforts to cast them aside. Drake saw her then, no memory, a vision beyond his own recollections of her. The mirror was showing him an event.

The recently living figure of his dearest mother, Zenara, yet wreathed in an ethereal glow, face pale and ideal even as a crimson bloom spread across her throat like a gruesome ribbon. Face still serene, even as she lay there taken forever from him, before he ever got a chance to know her.

A tiny goblin with a singular razor talon curled around her

throat as she slept, its eyes wide with innocent curiosity and wonder at the deed, and it cackled.

The disembodied cackling continued beyond the vision into the next.

He saw the tree that took his father, falling upon him.

He sank to his knees, trembling as sobs wracked his body, the weight loss pressing down on him like an iron crown with nails digging into his skull. He wept profusely, tears streaming unchecked as he tried to shield his vision from sights too terrible to bear.

When Drake at last lowered his hands, blinking away tears along with remnants of grief clinging like cobwebs to lashes, the enormous mirror had vanished entirely. All that was left was a vast expanse of rock cliff stretching upwards towards unseen heights above. Drake wiped his eyes with the back of his hand after the tears had covered his entire face, the salt of them mingling with the cold air in his slack jaw, feeling pains greater than any physical.

It was now much darker with the mirror gone, with the only light coming from far above. Drake felt incredibly tired. Laying down against the face of the cliff where the mirror used to be, he fell quickly to sleep.

* * *

He slept for a very long time.

Some hours later his peaceful slumber was disturbed. Previously unseen torches along the rock wall lit up all at once as though to wake him.

Drake proceeded cautiously, the sound of each step dissipating into ominous nothingness as he made his way towards a newly appeared room set into the formerly mirrored wall. It was a space no larger than a tomb, small walls adorned in carvings which shifted when viewed from different angles.

At its center, the highly ornate sword laid upon intricately carved ancient stone arms jutting from the wall. Drake drew nearer the cave room warily, eyes narrowing in scrutiny as he studied the blade from afar. The dark metallic blade glinted almost magically with what little light there was. He wanted to be excited for it, but something was wrong.

Disappointment suddenly surged through his veins like a bitter tide from out of nowhere. Drake tried pushing it aside with great effort, but to little avail. Memories of father's words rushed forward, cautioning against expectations and deceits that often masked the true nature of things unknown and unseen.

Eldred's voice spoke once more in his mind, "Never trust what seems, Drake. Deception is where you least expect it."

Drake was willing to admit that his perceptions were far from perfect, but there was something else atop the senses. At the corners of his eyes played wisps of smoke, as though spirits manipulated his vision.

A sudden gravelly laugh broke the silence, and Drake turned sharply to see Gritch perched on a nearby ledge; eyes gleaming, grinning widely.

Its throat music had begun to let out a congratulatory tune, upbeat and fun.

"That's it! There you have the sword, sir! You did it!" the goblin exclaimed, voice abounding with enthusiasm. "Now go get it!" Gritch wobbled angrily on the perch.

Drake's gaze snapped from the creature, eyes narrowed into slits of cold contempt, back to the sword. "That is not real," he growled, voice steady despite turmoil raging within. "You seek to deceive me, goblin, but I will not be swayed by your tricks."

Gritch laughed again, music suddenly shifting to a comical tune that would have best accompanied a troupe of clowns. "Just

GO get it!" the goblin cried trying to sound playful about it, yet voice rising to a shrill pitch. ***"That's what you WANT, just DO it!"***

Wisps of specters recoiled at the goblin's scream, forms of the room, wall dissolving like smoke on wind, as if banished by sheer force of will.

What remained beyond where there had previously been mirror and then cliff wall, rose instead an enormous and gently lit sandstone staircase stretching upwards into the darkness above, a monumental construct, steps ancient yet unworn by the passage of ages unspoken and unheard.

Gritch watched him in silence.

Drake ascended steadily, hands trailing along the cold stone wall to one side for guidance. The air grew colder still, breath misting before him in small clouds that dissipated quickly in the stagnant atmosphere.

He felt the great expanse below and behind him, like the weight of the visions in that great spectral mirror.

As Drake climbed higher, each step feeling like a tremor to the earthquake of his injuries.

He thought, for a moment, he could hear voices from past centuries calling out to him across the many chasms, urging onwards and upwards. He focused on the rhythm of his breath, in and out, steadily anchoring him along with the fonder memories and his father's lessons.

Finally, after what felt like an eternity of ascent, Drake emerged onto a ledge overlooking that vast cavernous world below. He stood there for several moments, catching breath as he gazed out across the expanse of darkness stretching endlessly now behind him.

Drake turned away from the ledge then, squaring his shoulders and shaking away the numbness in his legs once more.

The air here was indeed much colder, carrying with it an almost palpable sense of antiquity, a silence pressing heavily against his eardrums.

Drake's breath hitched as he recognized his family motif upon the door set into the wall beyond the final landing of the staircase. The carved double-headed eagle stood out proudly, wings outstretched and rising against encroaching darkness, carrying shields and swords to those in need of them. The door was a square in the stone, like some mausoleum entrance, and so he pushed. It did not budge.

Remembrances of father blistered through Drake's mind like brands seared onto flesh, the many lessons learned at knee guiding him still. He traced the pattern of the eagle, fingers moving almost involuntarily as muscle memory took over, guided by years of watching his father do the same.

Immediately, the eagle lit up at the pattern of touch and the stone moved. Witnessing this sent a thrill coursing down his back like an energetic movement. His father had taught him the key without either of them ever knowing it.

He pressed harder, palms flattening against the cold surface as he applied weight evenly, pushing with shoulders and legs alike. The slab shifted inch by inch, grinding against unseen mechanisms concealed within depths of the wall itself. Dust billowed forth from cracks widening around the edges, causing him to cough.

The barrier finally gave way entirely, revealing a chamber untouched by time yet filled with a static light, sealed away behind stone for ages. Drake stumbled forward, body shaking in excitement, as he gazed upon the ancient family workmanship laid before his eyes.

The family crest was everywhere in the room. It was all too much to take in at the moment. His heart pounded wildly. He proceeded into the room cautiously.

At expense to all the grandeur, his attention was drawn immediately to what he had been searching for, what his family had kept in memory and legend. There it was, that blade his father had ever been after. He knew at once this was real. ***This was it.***

Its metal darker than night and edges honed razor-sharp despite years, or centuries, and yet concealed within this hidden stone tomb all this time awaiting for someone to use it.

As he touched the sword, its name came at once to his mind so he spoke aloud, "Nightbane!" The hairs on the back of his neck stood on end.

***

His fingers and palm fit perfectly on the hilt, as if it were crafted specifically for his hands.

He lifted the sword and a surge of energy coursed through him, rushing like a river breaking free from ice, at first cold and invigorating and then thawing into something else even better.

The sword felt more balanced than any he had ever held, as he swung the blade in forms common to him. There was a balance greater than mere equity in its weight distribution or outward design. He himself felt more balanced as he held it. Something deeply affected him as the wielder, but he could not quite understand, yet.

Waves of energy resonated through his injured limbs, jolting his body awake, as though the first time. The very marrow within his bones hummed sympathetically, awakening slumbering potential laying dormant until this moment.

Drake's grip tightened involuntarily around the hilt as he felt its invigorating power coursing through him, as though pushing through his veins like the hottest of lava flows. He could feel the ancient power within the sword. There was a sheath with the display that fit his shoulders and back, so he put it on and slipped the sword into it.

With sword stowed away, he looked around slowly at the inside of the chamber, taking measure of the grandness surrounding him for a moment.

His gaze fell upon the art hanging from stone, their surfaces woven intricately with scenes depicting battles waged and victories won against horrors lurking in dark corners of the world.

Flummoxed by the majesty before him, he felt a sting of additional loss that he could not come to know it all better in the now, his time fleeting as it was and his actions so necessary.

He recognized the different motifs and their stories as tales his father had told him, symbols similar to those carved into the very sword now resting on his back en route to its destiny: double-headed eagle soaring proudly. Staffs held aloft by sternly-faced robed figures in contests with serpents and monsters.

Drake approached the nearest hanging tapestry, reaching out his hand to trace patterns embroidered along the hem.

Fingertips brushed against the coarse weave, sending shivers down his spine, as if touching something sacred. It was indeed hallowed ground, trodden by few and remembered by even fewer.

He leaned in close, studying the intricate details woven into the hanging banners, each stitched to perfection in telling a story of its own, contributing pieces to a larger story unfurling before him like pages of some ancient codex come to life.

There, between the swirling melee of warriors locked in combat against monstrous foes, he spied a figure fighting goblins in dresses, using the very same sword he now held.

The figure was pointing the sword at the goblins.

He looked back up at the top of this banner and found ancient lettering which was instantly readable despite the antiquity of language:

Ð ЯÆꝀ ṾÉ ÆŁÐƖSÐ (DRAKE OF ELDRED)

ꝀÚBŁVBÆV (GOBLINBANE)

VÚ)ˊÐBÆVÅ (NIGHTBANE WIELDER)

He looked back at the image again, in shock. There was no doubt: broken legs, a staff, and even Nightbane's scabbard on his back as he had just placed it.

It was absolutely him, yet was he supposed to have saved the staff? At least it looked very much like his staff-crutch recently destroyed, crafted by his own hands deep in that forest. He decided not to give it much more thought.

This was a total shock, as nobody in his life had ever even recognized him outside of being his father's son. The legacy was part of his name after all, and it was never as though he were looking to escape it, but it was always his father's legend overshadowing him, and here it was all turned on head before him.

He cried openly at the thought of his own father to be made all the more remembered and glorified through his only son. A pang of gratitude shot through his chest, sharp and sudden as a dagger thrust, grief long suppressed rising unbidden to surface like a ghost from the disturbed grave. Drake swallowed hard, blinking back more tears and stinging behind the eyes. He maintained composure through the emotions stirred by the reality now revealed to him.

Everything that happened to him, had to happen to him, so this was fate and a process. Eolande, Telyn, the other heroes rejecting him, his cousins, and all his failures came to mind. All these things brought him here to this moment, to see that banner put here for him, and this sword placed here for safekeeping until it was needed specifically by him.

Apparently that feeling he felt deep inside all his life was real, and his destiny had been awaiting him, and him alone, all these many centuries long before his birth. It was almost all too much to process.

Yet even as the heady concoction of exhilaration and sorrow threatened to overwhelm his senses, another realization dawned, one born not merely from recognition of his likeness, and his destined likeness to his father, but also from the understanding conveyed through careful study of the banner's design.

This was no mere depiction of battle fought and won; nay, it showed a purpose far more profound, fit to all the lessons imparted long ago by his father, a culmination cast in the thread of long dead weavers yet again, in patterns of fate and the languages of divinity beyond mortal comprehensions. His father had been right to give up on the dream, so that it could, in turn, be his to complete.

Eldred did what he had to do and provided what he could, while giving up on the goal just short of it, to hand forward. It was no failure, regardless any excuses Eldred had made to console himself. Other tapestries also showed him, but to do with events further into the future. He studied them with astonishment.

Among the imagery were his dreams for Solipsia, most of which he had never shared with anyone else, seeming utterly too fantastic, yet real and laid out here before him as though his ancestors could peer into his very soul.

Woven into that fabric of narrative were clues, riddles hidden plainly within the intricate patterns. Drake stepped back, gaze sweeping over all the banners, taking measure of the grand tableau stretching out before him like a roadmap charting courses through the depths of history itself, leading invariably to this moment, his moment.

He saw now that each one hanging bore connection to the previous, scenes unfolding sequentially from left to right, chronicling generations lost to time, as well the present and beyond.

Near the end stood his own figure wielding Nightbane. These ruins had been designed to protect his heroic inheritance, something that could have come to him in no other way.

A profound sense of pure destiny overcame Drake in those moments, the precious few he could devote.

Thoughts of ancestors washed over him, focused upon him alone in this enormous construction. Drake felt the weight of responsibility settle firmly upon his shoulders, and he wouldn't have asked for anything else.

After looking it all over and promising himself to return, he found another door in the chamber, which apparently led outside. Drake had a mission.

***

Stepping outside, he found himself nearly at the top of an enormous mountain. The air outside was crisp and biting, a stark contrast to the stale atmosphere within the mausoleum. Drake took a deep breath, filling his lungs with the cool mountain air as he stepped out onto the ledge.

The world stretched out before him in all directions, vast and untamed, a panorama of rugged peaks and valleys blanketed in evergreens that clung tenaciously to the rocky slopes. He stood there for a moment, gazing at the expanse with awe.

The surrounding stone, weathered by time and wind, gave testament to ages past. The ledge jutted out from the cliff face, offering a perilous perch among the clouds drifting lazily by as though the whole world had not just changed.

Gritch had been sitting on the ledge, waiting for him, legs dangling without a care.

The goblin grinned widely at Drake, green gums bared in its typical parody of friendliness. "Well, well, look who decided to join us," Gritch taunted, with his lisp rendering the word 'de-thided.' "Took you long enough," Gritch said chuckling, swinging legs back and forth with practiced nonchalance.

Drake ignored the creature's jibes as he held on to the strap to his sword's sheath, ensuring it was secure before turning away from the goblin and walking down the steep path still dressed in snow.

The goblin, still perching casually, called after him half-shouting, "You know, if I hadn't been down there, you probably would have gotten lost or smashed!"

Drake continued, ignoring it. As he walked, he pulled out his sword to examine it better in the daylight. He stared at the sword in hand, mind racing. His fingers traced along the edge of the sword as he marveled at the craftsmanship of every part. Outside, it appeared to drink in the light. Staring at the edge, he could almost see the energy being pulled into it, especially as he held it. He could feel it surging in him. It felt good. He felt as if it were an extension of his own being, resonating sympathetically with inner essence.

Drake continued down the mountain at a rate that would have been too fast without the sword guiding him. The wind at his back, each step of crushed mountain snow sent up mists swirling below like ghosts fleeing the sunlight.

He paused abruptly as another sudden realization struck him like a physical blow.

He could see the whole way, and all his steps at once, the path before him laid bare in stark clarity despite twists and turns obscuring true course from view.

It was as if a veil had been lifted, revealing underlying structure beneath deceptive surface, guiding steps surely towards destination awaiting at journey's end.

He felt as though he had an internal vision of reality that felt more complete; seeing potential futures in motion, as though as real as past memories or his current experiences. He imagined how much help this could be in battle.

He continued to carry the sword as he made his way carefully along the narrow and downhill trails, Drake couldn't shake a sense of unease gathering, a gnawing suspicion that Gritch's actions and insane words held additional significance. The goblin had been oddly forthcoming with information, almost as if... Despite best efforts to rationalize the creature's motives, the hero could not shake the possibility that there was some deeper betrayal underlying Gritch's assistance. Drake found it difficult to ignore his mind's persistent prodding on the topic.

He could see the sword now glowing and growing ever brighter as he held it and thought upon these things.

For now, there were more immediate concerns demanding attention: namely, navigating this crazy descent without plunging headlong to death upon jagged rocks far below, especially considering his injuries, which seemed to be healing much more rapidly as he held Nightbane. Drake took a deep breath, gripped the hilt of the sword tightly, as though using it for balance, and exhaled slowly as he prepared to continue his journey into the kingdom.

Drake noticed the blade illuminating him not just external objects, pasts, or futures, but also the workings of his own mind, as he held it, and as it grew brighter still.

He saw fragments of memories, forgotten fears, and lingering doubts illuminated helpfully. For each of these new truths or connections he had never made before, Drake felt as though he had been assisted in overcoming one-by-one.

The sword was revealing to him the hidden recesses of his own psyche, showing him the tangled web of his thoughts and emotions. Drake felt a mix of fascination and trepidation as he watched his own mind unfold.

Awe gave way to exhilaration then, joy surging throughout as Drake embraced these newfound abilities. He tested the limits of his new uncanny sight, finding delight in unmasking deceits both mundane and extraordinary: histories masquerading as myths, myths concealing histories, and lies taking form into reality.

He moved quickly, despite his injuries, holding the hilt firmly to see the path forward plainly. He was also feeling nourished and rested, despite not having eaten nor slept comfortably in some time. With that grip, however, he began to feel out into the kingdom of Solipsia and could sense everything had taken a massive turn for the worst since his disappearance.

He stopped and released his hold upon the hilt for a moment, finding that the vision did fade quite a bit upon doing so. Suddenly he thought of Gritch and its grift, whatever it was.

Gripping the hilt tighter, Drake turned his gaze back towards the peak looming high above once again, and beheld the goblin, nearly invisible, crouching on a tree branch, watching Drake's progression silently, and also doing something else… with its pants down…

'Oh no, it's crapping,' he thought. The goblin's form shimmered slightly, edges blurred as if seen through distorting lens, and Drake understood: he could see through any illusion, through all the false fronts concealing true natures lurking beneath surfaces, and also through to those currently focusing illusions on him.

With this newfound clarity, Drake saw through all Gritch's deceits, piercing the veils of misdirection that had clouded his judgments thus far. He felt no anger, nor resentment, for in place of those emotions burned only an intense desire for justice.

Gritch looked up then, meeting Drake's gaze steadily, as if sensing the shift in perception that had taken place between them. The goblin grinned widely with anxiety, gums bared. It stood up and walked towards him while pulling its pants up.

"Goblin, you had better tell me everything you know," he said to Gritch, as it came near.

The goblin saw the glint of the sword then Drake's eyes, and suddenly knew enough to run.

CHAPTER TEN

UNVEILED

Shrill cascades of goblin laughter rang out through the forest below. Gritch darted between trunks with an agility born of goblish malice and mischief, his form weaving in and out of shadows like some deformed dancer performing a queer jig for its solitary audience.

Drake pursued relentlessly. Each step still sent jolts of pain lancing through his injured legs, despite the aid of the sword. He gritted his teeth and pressed forward, driven by primal fury that burned hot in his chest.

"You chase me," Gritch called out, voice laced with amusement while glancing back over the shoulder, "but I am the wind in your sails!"

Drake ignored the taunt. Roots snaked across the path like twisted limbs reaching out to trip the unwary traveler, while low-hanging branches bore down with oppressive weight, conspiring to ensnare him in their gnarled embrace.

Yet even as Drake struggled against encroaching fatigue and disorientation brought on by the goblin's erratic movements, another realization dawned. Gritch was leading him somewhere. The creature's path held purpose, winding through underbrush with deliberate intent rather than mere chaos of evasion.

There was suddenly much less snow "The ground you tread is my shadow," Gritch crowed. "I am the path of your steps!"

Forest canopies gave way to rocky outcrops jutting from earth like broken teeth thrusting defiantly towards sky. Gritch moved down the treacherous slopes with an ease born of long practice.

Drake hesitated briefly at the base of an outcrop, taking

measure of the descent before him. Sharp edges of stone glinted wickedly, promising sliced flesh should he falter even momentarily during the climb down.

With grim determination on his face like some mask of stone, Drake descended, hands and feet slipping on loose shale that skittered away beneath his feet. He moved deliberately, committing all his weight and trust in the guidance of the blade.

Gritch looked back occasionally, grinning widely as if enjoying spectacle of Drake's slightest sign of struggle. "Come on, slowpoke!" it taunted, voice carrying easily over the distance separating them. "Or have you given up?"

Lower they went, ever closer towards the kingdom below and to wherever Gritch was taking him.

Drake's limbs ached dully as they ran.

***

Gritch finally stopped and stood at the edge of a precipice overlooking another forest below, arms spread wide as if embracing the sprawling vastness. The goblin turned slowly, yellow eyes gleaming with triumph. "Well," it declared, "here we are!"

Drake approached, wincing at protest from muscles abused by the recent exertions and near falls. He stood cautiously, testing balance before turning full attention towards the goblin awaiting him mere paces away. "Why did you bring me here?" Drake demanded, voice steady despite his rage. "What is it you want?"

Gritch chuckled lowly, "I want what you would want if you knew better."

Drake frowned, brow furrowing in confusion as he struggled to discern meaning behind the goblin's response. He recalled each taunt hurled over the goblin's shoulder during the headlong flight down the mountainside, a rant of riddles and half-truths designed to confound and disorient.

"I am the wind in your sails," Drake murmured aloud, more to self than the creature before him. "The ground you tread is my shadow... I am the path of your steps."

Gritch grinned widely, gums bared once more. "Very good," it praised, "but can you see it? Can you truly see?"

Drake hesitated then, considering the goblin's words carefully, as if turning them over in his mind. "I think you're trying to take some credit here for my work," Drake stated. "All of it, the trials, the challenges... even Nightbane. You consider yourself my guide."

"Bravo!" the goblin exclaimed, clapping hands together in applause, as though its conceit was some kind of puzzle. "I knew you had it in you, boy. Took you long enough, though. In fact, I put your father's journal in his desk," Gritch announced proudly.

Drake's gaze narrowed into slits of cold contempt as he regarded the creature before him, seeing it now as more than merely a mild irritant.

"Why?" Drake growled, voice laced with barely suppressed fury. "What is your purpose in all this?"

Gritch sobered then, amusement fading from its eyes like candle flame extinguished by sudden gust. It took a step back, arms dropping to sides as it regarded Drake. "My purpose?" it repeated in plea. "To ensure balance, of course."

Drake blinked, taken aback by the goblin's response. "Balance?" Drake asked himself, probing for deeper meaning hidden beneath the surface.

Gritch nodded solemnly. "Indeed," it said. "For too long, your kind has walked unopposed, shaping the world to suit desires, without thought for consequences that ripple outward from actions taken. But now..." It paused, gaze drifting dramatically towards the horizon where the sun dipped low through the bloody hues of the sky. "Now, the scales must be tipped once more. See, you're set to win, and when you do, that's bad news for goblins. Why am I here? It would have been worse, the longer this all went on. I was ending the charade by helping. To talk you through all of this. I need to make sure your victory doesn't cause too much of a blowback from goblinkind the world over, because that would be horrible. Especially bad for Solipsia, you see?"

Drake's mind raced as he considered implications behind the goblin's words, grappling with the idea that this creature helped him. "Especially bad for Solipsia, huh? What do you care about Solipsia? Why should I believe anything you say?" Drake demanded, voice steady despite the turmoil within. "What is your stake in all this, oh great-hearted goblin? It all sounds like more cryptic threats on your part. You could have done nothing to stop me, except report me to Gervin's troops, which you haven't. Don't lie to me, you evil beast. You betrayed Gervin and your people out of sheer envy, of the petty variety your rotten kind carry around with you at all times. It wasn't you in the spotlight, and that was enough to make you betray everything. I have you figured out, you're just out for glory."

The goblin grinned then, a slow, sly curve of lips that set Drake's neck hairs on end. "Me?" it said. "I am but humble servant, a cog in the vast machine grinding ever onward towards inevitable conclusions."

Drake rolled his eyes as he found himself no closer to understanding the true nature of this creature before him than at the beginning of this nightmare. "See, there you go again with that abstractly malevolent language you use to tangle up truth in nonsense, acting as though I was not privy to the insults and curses. Enough riddles. Tell me everything you know. At this point, I do not care nor believe your claimed motives. You choose to say what you think I want to hear or what might distract me, without any truth of it. Now tell me everything about your master."

Gritch chuckled awkwardly and asked, "My master? Heh, you

mean **your** emperor," it teased, voice the color of malice. "Besides," it continued, tilting head slightly as if considering things, "I doubt you would know anyone I do business with." The goblin's grin widened.

***

Drake gripped the sword hilt tightly and thought back, as the Goblin continued its fearful rant. His vision swam briefly, mind's eye conjuring images of a goblin darting through the shadows. He saw Gritch standing over a fallen tree in a forest clearing, axe raised high as the moon cast silvery glow. He saw the form of the creature before him shift subtly, taking on the semblance of something more sinister lurking beneath the surface.

Before Drake could fully grasp the significance of the vision unfolding, another image intruded, a memory half-forgotten, buried deeply.

His father was speaking to him about his mother's death. In tears he said, "Life is never truly your own." As soon as the vision arrived, it was gone again, replaced by another. He saw his father then, seated at that desk within his study in that old home, quill poised above parchment as he scribbled notes feverishly amidst piles of dusty tomes and ancient maps.

The journal was there too, leather-bound volume tucked neatly amongst the clutter, its presence unremarkable save for the sudden jolt of recognition that surged through Drake. He had pored over that journal and still carried it now.

Gritch's eyes gleamed with an inhuman intelligence mimicking something akin to affection, perverse and twisted though it may have been, searching out Drake's. "Your emperor," it murmured clutching whatever distraction might work best next. "Oh yes, he is one of us. He's part goblin, hidden deep within his blood. Isn't it amazing?"

Drake thought of the emperor surviving being run-through

with that sword. He thought of that cold gaze, the crafty intelligence behind eyes exuding ancient cruelty. It was obvious now, but not until it was said directly. The pieces fit together then, clicking into place with unsettling finality. It was a solved puzzle, revealing a portrait far more sinister than initially anticipated.

"Is that all?" Drake's voice was calm, almost disinterested as he regarded the goblin steadily, vision tunneling until only Gritch's smug face remained. "Is this supposed to be big news?" he asked, not wanting to sound shocked.

Gritch chuckled, a sound like the creak of some ancient door protesting its opening. Gritch whispered conspiratorially, "You're missing something, boy. This isn't a game. This is about seeing beyond the illusions that blind us to the reality which surrounds all." Gritch's chest music began to play then, as though a sign of friendship, or to emulate contrition. The goblin smiled widely in appeasement. "Remember all the good times in the forest? Remember my songs? That was fun, right?" It asked, voice dripping with false sincerity as it faltered.

Drake saw through the deceit, the manipulation, and the lies ransacking his history, and the history of his family. He gripped the hilt of his sword tightly again, as he sought the concealed truth.

This time visions came clearest yet, certain and without doubt. He saw Gritch then, standing over a fallen tree in the forest clearing once more. He saw the journal tucked neatly into father's pocket. Then he saw the axe swinging down against the tree, earlier, as that creature sprung the careful trap intricately crafted and planned to end Eldred.

It was Gritch who killed his father.

Drake's heart pounded wildly. He thought of his father then, of his sacrifice, his honor, and his unwavering belief in justice even through the darkest hours, as reflected in he himself, and suddenly knew what must be done.

A pile of rocks fell from of the sky out of nowhere, right next to Drake. Drake looked up and saw the remnants of some goblish contraption in the tree directly above. He looked over at Gritch, then.

The goblin merely shrugged its shoulders and gave a silly and inane expression to Drake, its throat band music producing a whimsical tune connoting some minor comedic mistake.

The goblin screeched its last, as the sword cut through its flesh like overcooked meat, sounds raw as life cutting off the discordant notes of its chest music.

Drake stood over the fallen creature, glowing sword still gripped tightly in hand, as Gritch's rotten body slumped into near nothingness, seemingly leaving behind more acrid stench than cadaver.

***

Silencing Gritch sent a shudder through Drake, not in revulsion at the violence enacted but rather of relief. He felt a profound sense of finality wash over him like a tidal wave, cleansing away remnants of doubt and uncertainty lingering.

The air grew still, as though the world itself held its breath in reverence for his act, like a small mercy.

A few birds sang again, and he spotted a few pensive squirrels testing the ground nearby.

Gritch was gone, no more than a smear of corrupted essence lingering in the air like the afterimage of a nightmare. Drake felt some pride in avenging the death of his father.

The sword felt lighter now, as though the burden of secrets and lies had been lifted from his shoulders.

No compromise with lies. Middle ground with deception was impossible. Those who delight in destruction, enslavement, and mayhem do nothing good for those who do not.

He stood there for several moments. The acrid stench of decay from Gritch's body came immediate and was overwhelming.

A blue songbird landed nearby and sang joyfully.

A strange sense of clarity descended upon Drake then, as if something obscuring his vision for so long had been suddenly removed, revealing the world anew in all its stark, unapologetic reality. He felt freed from chains forged from shadows and lies cast by ancient evils.

The memories of his father and of the trials that had shaped him felt like brushstrokes in the art of his life. He now understood more fully. He no longer thought of himself as the son of a hero only, but heir to a legacy of generations forged in blood against betrayal, and the truth of it all had been waiting for him the whole time.

Eldred had always been self-reliant, and he certainly passed this on to Drake. It was on this account that Eldred also shied away from discussions of their ancestry, because it had been more of a barrier to him in his life.

Drake wiped the blade on Gritch's clothing and sheathed it, turning away from the scene of confrontation. He took a deep breath, exhaling slowly as he surveyed the landscape stretching out before him. Craggy peaks kept the company of dense forests that rolled like waves toward a distant horizon as the setting sun gave way to the darkness once more.

Drake made his way down the now dark and treacherous slope leading away from the outcrop. Each footfall sent jolts of pain lancing through still healing legs, but he welcomed the sensation as a reminder of trials endured and the pain all around him.

The forests thinned eventually, granting a narrow path winding through the undergrowth. The paths joined with the roads carving courses through the wilderness like serpents whose bodies entangle others before congress at the center in Solipsia's capital city, Drake's immediate destination.

* * *

As he strode, he saw many Solipsian refugees, commonfolk hiding in the shadows of the ancient forest. They hid to protect their families from the terrors which now filled their kingdom.

A group of elderly villagers greeted him upon approach.

They emerged cautiously from concealment, as Drake came near, eyes wide and wariness-tinged yet knowing something of hope.

Drake imagined that these little groups were likely how the first deep-forest villages hiding from the goblins formed back during his father's youth.

One who looked like the statue of a question mark stepped forward. He was a very elderly man with white hair and lines buried into his weathered face, telling tales of years spent toiling against the harsh realities of life in wilds, probably since Eldred's day. Plainly, those considered "wildmen" during otherwise civil times would be expected to take up leadership during difficult times, with necessary skills.

"Drake of Eldred, I had a feeling we'd be seeing you," he spoke, "I knew your father well, I am called Brot. I see you've retrieved Nightbane, without any assistance."

Drake gripped the hilt absentmindedly, receiving visions of the old man sitting with Eldred in long conversations and sharing laughs. Drake teared up at this and embraced the old man as though he were family. Drake had no way of knowing it, but he indeed was.

Brot continued to speak, "There is something I must tell you. All the heroes were executed as conspirators against the crown, all of them with extended families. All their children are gone too!"

"Telyn!?" Drake asked desperately.

"I'm so sorry, Drake, but it is said she died bravely," Brot said solemnly.

Drake's stomach twisted, but it was not from grief alone, it was the sharp, metallic taste of inevitability.

The goblins hadn't just killed soldiers, but had erased entire lineages. It felt like a blade was being driven through his chest.

He had known it would come to this but standing here now, faced with the cold reality, he felt triumph no longer. The hollow ache spread through his whole chest feeling like an open and bloody wound.

He collapsed, possibly as much from the weakness of still healing legs as his emotions. Pain filled his skull as the villagers rushed to his aid.

His legacy and history pressed down on him like the weight of the world. What he fought for was not just his father's legacy, but the blood of every martyr and every hero who had come before him which now included his baby sister.

He could hear the villagers speaking to him, but he could not understand a thing. All was so slow and empty. His broken knees sank into the moist earth, as though the ground itself would heal him or absorb the grief clawing at his ribs.

One woman pressed a bundle of herbs to his chest, another whispered prayers, and the old man knelt beside him, his face creased with sorrow.

Drake could not focus on anything, and the grief he felt before that enormous mirror was back, his eyes awash. His ears were filled with pressure from his own heartbeat and sobs, as though channelling the grief surrounding him, in the people and in the land.

He grieved, having to hold back a scream.

He wanted justice for every child who had been taken, every

parent who had been silenced, and every hero destroyed for their heroism, in weakness of age, illness, or distractions.

Out of the grief, he felt something darker rise within, a righteous indignation so pure it burned like a fire in his veins. They did not simply kill these people, but defiled the memory of them and twisted their stories into lies that would replace them in myth, taking even heroism away from the people, and tainting the very fabric of Solipsian culture and identity.

Telyn, Kenid, Eolande, Endra, Zenara, and Eldred, faces passing through his mind like a funeral procession, each syllable a piece of the fallen wall around his soul, each a verse in the dirge of his life.

They were gone forever, their lives extinguished in waves of violence empowered by that tyrant-champion of monstrosities.

Tears stung, blurring vision as he fought back surges of grief.

Drake suddenly stopped grieving, refusing himself everything outside what this sword represented. To surrender now would mean allowing defeat in capitulation to his own anguish over the whole kingdom's.

He felt he must earn the right to memorialize them properly, to grieve fully, and that he would not be able to, so long as there was something he was capable of doing about it. He could not fully mourn when the world still needed him to fight.

Instead, he channeled anguish into fuel for fire burning within breast, fierce and unbending. In his mind's eye, he foresaw each action it would take.

In his thoughts, he declared everlasting war a thousand times against that goblish tyranny of rot, so that each breath drawn was a vow to see justice served upon those responsible for the slaughter of innocents, perhaps innocence itself along with heroism.

Sensing a change in the young grieving hero, Brot helped him to stand. The villagers stepped back, their faces solemn, and Drake rose to his feet.

Brot handed his staff over to him, lovingly crafted from stout wood polished smooth by long use.

Drake looked at him desperately. "I am so sorry, but thank you for this Brot," he whispered, voice trembling as he reached out to hold the old man's hand.

It was cold, like the stone of that cavern staircase. Drake felt the weight of the old rough hand in his palm, another relic of a world that had been stolen.

Drake looked back at the staff in his other hand, marveling at the craftsmanship evident in every line and curve. It was well-shaped for his specific purpose, and Drake had ceased to believe in coincidences. The crook was carved expertly into the shaft right where it would provide most support, a testament to skill and care lavished upon creation.

"I could see your broken legs from a mile away, boy. This has been my staff since before I met your father, but I have others. Go easy on yourself, Drake Eldredson, for you are our final hope."

Drake did not know what to say at all, gratitude swelling within his chest despite, like a tide rising swiftly against the shore.

Drake spoke, "My heart weeps for all Solipsia, yet grows the stronger at your kindness."

Brot then pulled the cloak off his own back, putting it over Drake's shoulders and tying it.

The gesture was simple, but it carried the gravity of something far greater. "You keep that sword hidden, until you need it," Brot said.

The villagers had survived not by strength, but by resistance and perseverance, by clinging to the memory of what they had lost, even as the goblins sought to erase their very existence.

Now, Drake would carry that burden forward, as a hero, to redeem the stories they could no longer tell for themselves, the collective memory of a people who had refused to be forget the best of their own.

Brot smiled then, eyes crinkling at the corners as warmth spread across his features like sun breaking through clouds after a storm.

"All hail Drake, our natural-born king!" Brot called out. The villagers, all in tears, saluted Drake, "Hail King Drake! Long live our king!"

The goblins had taken everything from these people, but they had not taken their willpower. And if Drake Eldredson in the ancient Solipsian line of Ædlertuwin was to be anything, it would be that.

Drake nodded solemnly, with mind already in the future battle, without a moment for further pleasantries. A battle against an enemy threatening existence itself.

"Now is the time," he said, stepping away and into his destiny.

All the villagers wished him well, many in pained yet joyful tears.

* * *

He turned his back on those forests, cloak fluttering behind. Somewhere in the distance, the wind carried the sound of voices.

It was the first notes of a new song sung by a people who had struggled so hard to merely exist:

The hero walks through 'ere bound the feet,
While voices rise on hymn, of terrible defeat.
So sing we, on his way, Solipsia's last tale:

Of domains built on lies, and truths that cannot fail.

Gervin deceived our nation into demise,
Drowning the light of Eldred in a sea of lies.
Sweet son of Ædlertuwin, let pain be your guide,
Goblins stole the song, but truth shall never hide.

Drake now walks onward, stalwart of his race,
With staff and blade, fearless for fate's embrace.
The wind sings louder now, its tune a battle cry,
A song of sword's sorrow, and an end of lies as nigh.

The goblins would never be capable of knowing what they had taken away, but Drake was going to bring it to them anyway.

Drake set off once more, new staff clicking steadily against the road, as he ventured forth through the wilderness. He moved swiftly now, fuelled by urgent gnawing. Time was fleeting and justice needy, each passing moment brought his kingdom ever closer to the brink of irreversible catastrophe.

Drake traversed the vast expanse with a speed that should not have been possible. Solipsia's need would not be denied, nor the terrible knowledge that all the sacrifice of all its heroes was rendered meaningless unless he acted. His was a burning hatred for lies and cruelty.

Justice had been robbed, and now the hour was already far too late. He clenched his teeth through the pain, the staff in his hand a respite, as he stepped forward.

News reached him along the way, all in confirmation of the mass executions witnessed by many terrified crowds, public spectacles designed to strike fear into the hearts of all who dared defy the emperor's rule.

Guilt gnawed at Drake relentlessly, pangs sinking deep as he struggled against the tidal surges of grief threatening to overwhelm senses.

He thought of Telyn's laughter, her fierce determination burning brightly even through blackest nights.

He remembered Kenid's steadfast loyalty, his unwavering belief in the causes they shared.

They executed Endra, his sick elderly aunt, publicly... sweet, gentle Endra with heart full of compassion for all living things, who had been a mother figure to him all his life, in his poor mother's stead.

So, that was his father, mother, aunt, sister, and all his father's friends as well as their relatives, every one murdered by goblins or this forming goblish empire.

Drake's grip tightened around his staff to maintain composure despite the storm raging within. Though his strength was recovering, each step forward was heavier than the last, the feelings of loss goading at him incessantly.

Even as despair clawed at his mind, another emotion stirred within depths: fury, pure and unyielding, forged in white-heat of sorrow and outrage. Nightbane seemed responsive to this most, transmuting its power more actively in the healing of his body.

Responsibility pressed upon Drake's shoulders, now a sword real and as heavy as ever. Though Drake found he could bind the sword's sheath to the staff, and hold on to the hilt as he leaned against the stick gifted him.

He could feel great power as he gripped that mighty family heirloom, an ancient might awakening within through the sword. It resonated sympathetically with his inner essence. He had been honed sharp as the blade, and it showed him so much. It calmed him and focused him, as though an army of ancestors marched behind him.

The capital city sprawled out before him like an incredible

beast slumbering as sedated by lies. Drake approached warily, senses heightened.

It was deep into Autumn already and, along with the harvest, the breweries were in full swing. The real harvest was to come.

He slipped by like a ghost, fooling forts full of drunken goblins, cloaked form blending seamlessly with shadows cast by the strange goblins looming overhead, guarding the deconstruction of the kingdom.

Most villagers shied away from him, eyes averted, as if fearful even a gaze might betray them to unseen watchers lurking through the alleys and hidden places.

Drake paid them little heed, focused solely upon the task laid out before him, his path leading inexorably towards the palace gates. He moved swiftly now, fuelled by anger burning hot, a blaze consuming all else save Solipsia's redemption.

As he neared the great entrance to the city, the goblin guards, who had been gambling, turned to regard him with drunken indifference. Their armor, once shining and maintained with human wearers, was now covered in stains.

He gripped the hilt tightly and saw Gritch, as though a vision of the recent past, on the same path he was currently on.

Passing the guards while covered by the robe, he grumbled in gruff imitation of a half-goblin, "'Ere on Gritch biznuss!" He was relieved to see his gamble satisfy the guards. There were a dozen of them, and Drake wanted to be at least a little closer to the throne and with a clear plan within the walls before initiating any violence.

"Carry on!" one guard, who had lazily stepped forward, bellowed in his monstrous and intoxicated voice.

Drake avoided any gaze, knowing goblins didn't enjoy human faces generally. He also knew that he was hunted. He thought of his father teaching him strategic silence.

Being near the goblins brought his family to mind once again. Their faces haunted him, despite trying to bury the emotions. He saw father's proud regard as he practiced under the hero's tutelage. He saw Telyn's many concerned expressions for him.

Images of his family captured his thoughts, including Edmin and his sons. He saw Eolande beside him in the fight, alongside other distant kin. All had fallen fighting for the cause of their kingdom, now seemingly lost in a tide of darkness surging ever closer and going unanswered, as he made haste for the shores of hope with all his being despite the rawness he felt in his heart.

For them, Drake would stand defiant against the storm and face whatever horrors awaited. For the people still living, he would have done anything to spare them the pain he felt himself, but they all felt it, they had all lost people in this.

Holding on to the hilt with these thoughts, so all at once he saw Brot weeping at a hidden forest grave site, families pulling away bodies of loved ones from the gallows, and the rivers of goblin blood to flow. He saw his options laid open to him, and the best paths to take.

He would carry this weight of justice forward, even if it cost him all that he had left. A small price to pay, considering. He would honor what had been lost by all. He missed them all dearly, and he would avenge them. For them, he gladly gave all, even if all those mausoleum tapestries turned out to be too hopeful of him, and he only goes so far as to inspire his people to take it the rest of the way. To hand it off would still make it all worth it.

Despite his calm, his whole body thrummed resonantly with a power on the verge of being unleashed. His hand firmly gripped the hilt ready to bury it where his sorrow pointed. He took deep breaths, exhaling slowly as he prepared to forever alter the course of Solipsia's destiny.

'It ends now,' he thought as he set up the field of battle; his city.

CHAPTER ELEVEN

RECONQUEST

In all Solipsian history, Drake's Reconquest was the strangest military campaign ever. He had no friends or family left on which to rely, but he knew something most had forgotten, that truth was more dangerous than any sword, spear, or arrow.

The kingdom itself had become a festering wound, with the central capital city being the sorest spot. Months had passed since Drake had vanished, leaving behind only a trail of rumors. The son of the hero who had ended the previous goblin blight was now considered dead or hiding from them like a coward.

In reality, it was more like, he awaited this moment, like an injured predator crouched licking its wounds in the shadow of a tree filled with prey.

Many people had grown complacent in the wait, lulled by the false claims of peace in Gervin's reign, purchased with as much blood as evil lies. Drake knew better, however, for the peace held here was scavenging off the silence of the dead, victims, vulnerable, and demonized.

The marketplace thronged with alien voices raised, hawking expensive low quality wares. Strange laughter filled the narrow alleys where sunlight struggled to penetrate. The dense canopy of awnings and tents stretched overhead like tattered sails, as though it could take the whole market up into the air, as its rancid odor already had.

There was a sweetly acrid scent of insects being smoked from street vendors' stalls. Beneath that smell lingered decay from the piles of rotting fruit, vegetables, and meats, not trash but also considered delicacies by many of the foreigners in residence. Rot was profuse and pungent throughout.

Drake grabbed the hilt but quickly let go again, struck with overwhelming visions of abuse and cannibalism present. It was too much for him to deal with and he had plans to set in motion.

He had been unable to watch the kingdom unravel from his exile.

Tents had replaced buildings as the primary places of business, though a few of the merchants had taken up some of the still movable structures.

Once-proud business buildings of two or three stories had been pushed over by trolls, ransacked, and unrepaired, with many now left to lean upon each other like drunkards against a gathering storm.

The goblins mostly came at night and under the authority of the emperor, but the people had grown hopeless from the endless rot spreading beneath their feet, and all foundations. Many had taken to the hills and forests surrounding the kingdom under the leadership of men like Brot.

Drake moved through the periphery, cloaked form blending within the shadows. He surveyed.

The marketplace teemed with activity though few local Solipsians, a riot of colors and movements dancing and weaving in dizzying display, until his gaze fell upon the rare human figures in the crowds, without any familiar faces, forms twisted and malformed despite the veneer of humanity donned like ill-fitting masks.

He leaned heavily on his new staff, the well-crafted ancient wood bearing him without complaint. He again quietly grabbed the hilt of Nightbane as he walked.

His gaze swept over the people, eyes narrowing as he discerned patterns. Goblins and goblish magically disguised as humans made up most of the crowds, their forms betrayed by subtle tells. Slight awkwardness in gait, unnatural sheen to skin, or mere hint of malice lurking behind carefully crafted expressions were made all the more apparent when touching any part of the sword.

They were everywhere, these abominations, preying on unsuspecting souls with deceptions tailored so skillfully as to be almost indistinguishable from reality.

Yet Drake could see through it all now, especially when he bore down in concentration. True natures concealed beneath surfaces revealed like torn away veils.

He had not come to simply kill them all openly, that would not work by itself, no matter the advantage granted by the sword. He had come to unmake them first.

Those goblins back then were not youthfully errant, as Gervin's propaganda insisted, obviously. They were villains, yes, but also actors bound by their own petty ambitions, their own hunger for power and dominion over the weak. Drake knew this because the sword in his hand did not just cut flesh, it cut lies. It helped him see. He saw the goblins as they saw themselves, and as they truly were: liars, thieves, and merciless murderers.

Drake heard in passing that the goblin guards and troll pets had been out in the hinterlands weeks on end searching for him, as he hobbled his way through the forests and healed. Meanwhile, they had left the center of the kingdom at the capital city guarded only by the least ambitious, who were mostly drunkards especially fond of weekends, but that didn't mean they weren't any less greedy, in fact quite the opposite. The revelation sent a surge of exhilaration coursing through him.

With deliberate slowness, Drake stepped forward through the bustling throng, staff clicking steadily against cobblestones beneath his feet, avoiding glances. He moved with purpose. Resolve burned brightly, guiding him to inevitable reckoning.

The goblins had taught Drake one thing for certain, that lies are weapons, but truth is an unforgiving fire that burns clean all things. He remembered his father's words once more, "Sorrow points to where you bury the sword, son," but it rang differently now, despite his deeper sorrow, as though the sword in hand had opened up more truth on the matter, for it was no longer his sorrow alone. He could see that plainly on the faces of the Solipsians he spotted in the crowds, recognizable for the sadness they wore on their faces more than anything else. The sorrow was the kingdom's, and it pointed only toward Gervin's evils. Action mattered alone.

He had spent weeks bleeding and broken while getting constant first-hand insight into the goblish mindset, waiting for this.

The goblins were mindless monsters indeed. They were creatures of superstition and greed, their minds shaped by the same lustful nightmares that had driven them to always war. So Drake crafted especially targeted nuggets of truth like a blacksmith shaping steel, each distraction a shard of truth carved into something new, something dangerous to disorder.

He approached the goblish merchants, and spoke to them in the language of their deepest fears: their old demonic gods were watching, their emperor was cursed by his very order despite the chaos, and the ground would swallow them whole if they helped, which is to say the stability brought about by the empire would eventually demand their necks.

He told them that Gervin's goblin guards and well-trained army were no longer forces of the old gods, but cancers of order spreading through their own, poisoning the bloodlines of those who had once fought side-by-side against order.

Drake held the sword's hilt tightly, letting its power seep into his voice, its ancient magic humming like a sieve to his throat. The goblin merchants listened, not because they wanted to believe, but because they needed to believe since it was the simple truth laid bare, yet in their terms. Drake warned them that the guards would cease being drunkards and start coming to collect their "fair share."

In the end, it would be revelation which won. Truth, only a

weapon insofar as wielded against the darkness, consumes all lies.

* * *

Rumor rippled through gatherings like wind through reeds, as people took note of his presence, voices hushed and urgent. Eyes widened in recognition or wariness, depending on who beheld him, some gazes pleased and hopeful, others clouded by fear born of uncertainty, or worse.

"It's him," murmured one woman, clutching a bundle of clothes to her chest like a shield against unseen peril. "Drake Eldredson... he's not dead."

"Nonsense," scoffed another, voice laced with disdain. "That's just some drunken vagabond. Look at him, limping about like an invalid, that's no hero."

Drake passed some people who showed recognition as he advanced. Some whispered prayers beneath breath, hands clutching charms and talismans against evil. Others simply stared, transfixed by his sudden appearance. He discouraged such behavior and asked them to pass-by silently. Their faces were mosaics of fear, awe, and something else, something that felt almost like hope.

Drake ignored all distractions despite his amusement, focusing instead upon tasks laid out before him in justice long denied, vengeance owed to ghosts of the past haunting his every step. He could see the hope yet kindling in their eyes as he passed, and it felt good.

Of course, he ignored the others trying to instigate him with insults, or calling him an "evil hero" and spitting at him. In such cases he could grip the sword which would reveal truth about them, and it calmed him further.

He tuned out the babble as he moved ahead, gaze fixed firmly upon destiny, looming larger than all the buildings crowding the city or palace combined.

He had more merchants to visit, as well as others.

Everywhere were the veils of false humanity assumed for the purposes of deception. A goblish merchant spotted his face, gaze locking onto Drake with an intensity born of dread. The merchant pushed through the crowd towards him, a servile smile plastered across the face. He attempted to arrest Drake's progress, hands raised in placating gestures while approaching cautiously.

"Good sir," said the merchant, voice oily smooth yet laced with underlying tension, stepping alongside of Drake's path, "perhaps we may discuss whatever grievance brings you here? I am sure that whatever it is, we can come to a mutually amicable arrangement..."

Drake cut him off mid-sentence, voice steady and cold as he stared down at the creature masquerading as man, "There is nothing to discuss."

The merchant's smile faltered slightly, uncertainty flickering in expressions before being masked once more behind a facade of placid calm. He glanced nervously around, noting how others parted before Drake's advance, creating a path through the sea of bodies. All seemed to recede from him.

"But sir," he persisted, desperation creeping into tone, "you do not understand, if you simply listen a moment you might understand how we could help each other."

"Help each other?" Drake repeated, tasting bitterness, which turned him, and he continued with tenseness in his voice, "You helped my friends to their deaths. Your relatives dragged our families into the streets and murdered them all publicly." He leaned in, looming over the small goblish man as he gripped the hilt of Nightbane tightly.

"I think whatever you are planning could be dangerous. You see, I have the ear of the emperor. To..." the merchant's words were cut off as his human visage began to disappear.

Drake had pushed his staff forward, with the sword in hilt tied at the top, and lightly touched it to the merchant, whose entire human facade collapsed instantly, revealing the lying goblin within.

He pushed past the goblin then, shouldering through the press of bodies with single-minded determination. The goblin stepped aside reluctantly, eyes narrowing into slits of comprehension. It looked down at its hands to see that the magic had completely worn off. The merchant was now seen by everyone for how goblin and rotten it actually was. Its carefully manicured reputation ruined, it ran away and did not stop.

Drake laughed. It was a laugh born not merely of amusement but also from a profound sense of absurdity permeating the scenes unfolding before him, the sheer ridiculousness of these abominations attempting to reason with him, as if he were some errant child strayed from the path of goblish logic or righteousness.

His yet hobbled gait and staff carried an inexorable force, a relentless march towards inevitable reckoning that could not be stayed or diverted by mere words or threats. Drake was no longer simply the son of a hero. He was the heir to all that had been lost, and ultimately the bearer of redemption.

"Sorrow points to where you bury the sword, son." The words, though changed in his perspective now, rang truer than ever before.

Drake thought of his loved ones, and he thought of all those who had fallen fighting for this common cause.

Fury and outrage burned hotter still with each memory conjured forth, faces of friends and family lost to violence unleashed by tyranny championing monstrosities, in waves of brutality that had swept through the kingdom like plagues. This pain was inflicted upon all in apparently equal measure.

Drake gripped the hilt of Nightbane tightly. He knew he must succeed and not falter. This was what he had been made for, and this was his purpose, for this moment of reckoning against the evil. It all culminated in this defiance against the growing tide of darkness. He visited the different factions of goblins, with honeyed words of destruction and conquest, insights and the reality of betrayals.

* * *

If Gervin and his lot unleashed chaos of a sort Solipsia's streets were never built, Drake would unleash the kind it ***was*** built for. The kingdom had been constructed by hands that intricately shaped them for best needs, with minds that wove dreams into reality, through souls intending that the darkest night should never prevail upon it. Immediately, they would become a goblish battlefield, a theater where illusion and greed might collide like two hyenas fighting over a single scrap of bone.

Drake's destruction would be more thorough, harder, faster, shorter, and set up in a fraction of the time, days at most, during which he found many homes willing to host him, even finding time to rest. He was sure never to stay in a single place for longer than a few hours.

The next stage of his plan was ready to engage in tandem with the current one.

The guards' faces, both strange foreigner and outright goblin alike, were flushed with the glow of ale and the haze of authority. They had been ordered to patrol the city, but instead, they celebrated their own intoxication, their boots scuffing against cobblestones as they stumbled between taverns and parade-tent-gangs of sin.

The goblin and goblish guards sang drunken ballads about demons of old they worshiped and the glory of Gervin's reign.

One drunken goblish guard, a hulking man with a face like cracked pottery, stumbled into the square, his belt buckle clinking as he swayed on his feet. He was shouting about their old demon-gods and how Gervin had saved them all, but Drake easily saw through the cracks in his bravado, the way his eyes darted to the shadows, the way his hands twitched at his sides like a man waiting for a fight he knew he couldn't win. He began to sing in a foreign tongue, to which other guards quickly contributed their voices. Drake's hold of the hilt made their words all too clear to him, where it was a mystery to other Solipsians:

Oh, gather 'round, ye goblish fold,
And raise your cups to goodness sold!
The ancient demons, fierce and grim,
Deliver this fun and twisted hymn.

From crypts and caves where shadows conspire,
They summon forth the cleansing fire,
Flame, scorching and burning, sings,
Of kingdoms drowned in blood of kings!

Huzzah! Huzzah! To Gervin's reign,
Our emperor who brought them pain!
With sword and spell, he tore the skies,
Saving us all from their weakling lies.
We danced on corpses, chewed their bones,
Their seed smashed on bloodied stones.
Glory forged in Ruin's mold,
Whole realms drunk on doom and gold!

Once we were slaves to weakling thrones,
Our voices drowned by weakling moans.
But Gervin, with his handsome grin,
Stole our chains and lit the din!

He crowned himself in midnight's moon,
And made us priests of bloody Ruin.
Our deity, who thrives on strife,

Married to pain, extinguishing life!

Huzzah! Huzzah! To Gervin's reign,
Our emperor who brought them pain!
With sword and spell, he tore the skies,
Saving us all from their weakling lies.
We danced on corpses, chewed their bones,
Their seed smashed on bloodied stones.
Glory forged in Ruin's mold,
Whole realms drunk on doom and gold!

So let the weaklings boil in troubles,
Gervin's reign built in toil as doubled!
He's got a heart which is made out of fear,
And plotting mind as sharp as a spear.

He'll make ye all his serfs or priests,
While ye drink ale from Ruin's teats.
A toast to chaos, a cheer for death,
Gervin's throne is built on sunset!

Now march we in delight, aiding Ruin's pull,
Our drumbeat unbroken and pockets full.
Our demons laugh, the skies grow red,
As Gervin rules with lies, sword, and bread.

We feast on their kindred, we drink to their fate,
For Ruin's wrath is so sweet to await.
And when stars go dark in their last hurrah,
We'll dance in hell, and still sing "Huzzah!"

Huzzah! Huzzah! To Gervin's reign,
Our emperor who brought them pain!
With sword and spell, he tore the skies,
Saving us all from their weakling lies.

We danced on corpses, chewed their bones,
Their seed smashed on bloodied stones.
Glory forged in Ruin's mold,
Whole realms drunk on doom and gold!

So raise your cups to the shadowed tool,
To Ruin's curse and Gervin's rule.
Then grab and grasp at what you can,
As salvation's destruction is nigh at hand!

For when the stars are all gone and cold,
The observant still sing, and will still hold...
A throne of bones, a crown of flame,
And the right to drink in its ancient name! Huzzah!

Drake moved. He stepped into the square as if he had always belonged there, cloak still covering all of him, including his sword. The drunk guards continued their laughter and dance as some turned to face him.

The cracked pottery face approached him, jovially saying, "Oy, we got a live one he..." he began, but Drake cut him off in a voice that was hoarse, with a foreign lilt.

"You think your pockets are lined, and defend this regime yet do you have any idea how much gold the merchants are taking in?" Drake asked, his eyes staring off into the distance and away from most of them, under the shadow of his hood. "You think your ale and your drunken songs are enough, and that these **Ichor** won't eventually turn on the merchants and Gervin? You've been drinking while setting yourselves up to be first to meet a grisly end, and for what? For their profits and your allowance? A pittance. This is a joke and you are the punchline, so go ahead, sing and dance while you still can!"

The guards exchanged glances, their bravado crumbling under

the weight of his words. One of them, a wiry foreign man with a scar across his obviously goblish cheek, muttered something about the "old gods," as well as Gervin's strategy and protection through Ruin, but Drake wasn't done.

"You've been drinking while these merchants you're supposed to protect are in their cozy homes and tents with expensive furniture and bedding. Go ahead and protect their gaggle of courtesans and slaves," he continued, stepping further away and giving a nonchalant expression. "Remember that your bosses have all they ever wanted now: a kingdom where the weak can be strong, and the strong can be used. Are you feeling used yet?"

A few guards tried shrugging it all off, but many shrank back, their faces strained as the truth he spoke unraveled the illusions they had clung to.

Drake saw it in their eyes, the same greed and fear that had driven them to drink, to forget, to be contented with scraps, in comfort without realizing the very real danger they were in.

* * *

It was in this way he first acted against the goblin factions. He used his sword, not on them directly, but on the illusions they carried. He was able to slice, with the power granted by the blade, through all lies.

The drunk guards stared at him, their faces aghast.

"This is what you've been fighting for, your own eventual demise, but without commensurate remuneration," Drake said, his voice ringing out across the square. "I mean proper pay. It is not Gervin's nor the merchants' responsibility to look out for your interests. The old gods worked through you, right? This is your chance to take back what you rightly stole, and what was wrongly stolen then from you, before it is gone forever... you should gather more to the cause, though."

The drunkards didn't need to be told twice. One by one, they dropped their drinks and stepped forward, resolute and devoted to the overlord of all illusionary demonic forces: Greed himself. They were now dangerous to Gervin's carefully constructed stability built atop turmoil.

The various gangs of goblish or goblin "guards" were menaces to the public, and no relief or service. These mercenaries from strange lands were under no illusions about their paymasters and loyalties, or lack thereof, either. To them, the merchants were not the traders they portrayed themselves as at all, but mere criminal parasites **worse** than the guards, siphoning wealth from a kingdom exploited at less risk due to their presence. The short in their pay left them feeling permanently under-appreciated.

Drake merely had to play upon these present disagreements among the goblins and goblish folks.

The first betrayals came swiftly. A group of goblin guards, their eyes wild with paranoia, turned on their goblin captain. They screamed that he was cursed by the old gods, that his bloodline was tainted by the very sins of order Gervin had been spreading, which ran counter to the chaos and his pretended devotion to Ruin. They hacked that captain down without hesitation. The others did not stop to mourn. Once the leaders who disagreed were hacked down, nothing held them back from extorting and exacting their violence upon the merchants in the city.

The merchants knew this was coming. The cloaked figure had spoken plainly, so they already understood the expected grievances regarding the favor of Ruin. The figure told them that the guards would come with greed in their eyes, and they would not be kind.

The merchants had not wasted any time in bolstering their own private guard details in response. What they had not known and could not have, since the figure had not told them, is they would not come alone. They came with other goblin bandits and minions of the parade cults about the capital city, left now thirsty for long months without Gervin's former indulgence, and a dwindling supply of addicted clients not already fully in their thrall. The figure had visited these as well, to speak welcome words of spoil.

The chain reactions were inevitable. One goblin faction accused another of being "in league with Gervin," while a third claimed that their leader had conspired to hire only guards from the particular regions known for goblins which were less "goblish" or more human, and therefore more prone to order. Soon, the city became an anarchic theater of battle, with brothers turning on fathers, cousins tearing each other apart, and entire goblin and goblish clans burning themselves alive in frenzies of self-justification to Ruin. The goblins had no unity left, only the illusion of it, yet shattered now by certain and specific truths Drake had planted like seeds in the fertile dung-covered soil.

Drake's fight had just begun, and he had already won. When Gervin's forces finally crumbled totally, it would not be primarily from the blade, but from truths that Drake had planted with them.

The city was quickly on fire. Stalls that had once sold spices and silks now bore conflict, their owners and hired guards taking up arms. The merchants had hired mercenaries from even more distant lands, exacerbating the guard's complaints and sharpening the truth setting them against each other.

The street erupted into even deeper chaos. Guards fought back with brutality, their blades flashing in the dim light of the fires which burned into the night. They were unprepared for the merchants' cunning, nor the extents their private guards would go to.

It was a war of greedy vultures feasting on a giant neither side knew was waking, for word had already spread with rumors of Drake's recovery and presence. The dreams of the people began to change. In them, people saw Drake fighting all alone, and themselves as well as others joining him.

Drake, still using foreign goblish accents and cover of his hood, proceeded with intonations that slithered through the ranks of Gervin's forces. He used the sword's power of insight into goblin goals and fears to amplify this schism. The sword cut through illusions but also amplified the importance of truths in the listener.

"Look," he would say, "this is not your war. It is his. If you fight for him, you will die like the rest. Why would you kill other goblins when it will probably only lead to a higher likelihood of you dying later on anyway?" Drake did not stop there.

He would ask, "The man who calls himself emperor, what is he but another man with a crown and authority playing at even bigger deceptions?"

More goblin guards faltered at these truths. Their eyes flickered with doubt, their loyalties fracturing due to the revelation of truth from the right perspective and at the proper time, according to goblish sensibilities.

The battles between goblin and goblish mercenaries became so fierce that some of Gervin's most entrusted enforcers among his elite personal guard began to question their own loyalties.

Merchants who had been Gervin's loyalists began to regret their decisions. Many turned away, retreating from the kingdom entirely with their entire caravans and parties in tow, though as likely to be attacked by some faction of goblin guards as by goblin bandits or the drug-crazed parade cults. Goblins turned on goblins in a frenzy of betrayals.

It was not long before Gervin ordered his guards to drag the fleeing merchants back to the capital city. Things had gotten so much worse that the emperor had to order the use of trolls on the merchants, and not just on keeping his goblin guards in line.

The market squares had erupted into pandemonium. Merchants who remained were caught up in squabbles amongst themselves, and formed alliances along the lines of origins, and amount of goblin or human blood. Merchant turned upon merchant, with their guards being used in repayment for old grudges, only for the guards to then betray their own employers for the right amount of gold. Goblins who had fought side by side before, now could not trust one another, their ranks splintering as fast as fear and confusion could take hold.

Blood was in the streets, and it was through this chaos that the crafty Drake began his bloody and unstoppable march towards the palace.

***

Drake focused upon the singular task laid out before him in delayed justice. Each movement was to become part of history, like some enormous earthquake with tremors felt the world over in flow of all fates, like the heartbeat of some ancient colossus stirring from slumber. Drake moved as if he were not a man but a force, his body a mere vessel in the now of something ancient and hungry for one thing.

Through the power of Nightbane, Drake's exhaustion had faded into something else. He felt a strange, almost euphoric lightness in his limbs, as though the weight of the world had been lifted from his shoulders.

His legs felt strangely well, though still weak deep down, as though he were buoyed by an unseen force keeping him astride, a power not his own but one that pulsed through him like a lofty passenger. Drake felt honored beyond words in the midst of this all.

He could feel himself healing, wounds knitting closed further, and bones hardening, as if he were being sewn back together by invisible hands.

The goblins who had once gloried in Gervin's plotted destruction now found themselves cut down by the very truths they had tried to hide. It was most poetic and appropriate.

A goblish merchant stepped forth then, in a desperate ploy to make an appeal to Drake, grotesquely clad in finery designed to emulate the Solipsian nobility long since extinguished. Robes were stitched with threads that shimmered like spider silk, belt adorned with gemstones that glinted in the dim light as if mocking the kingdom still the more. The merchant raised both hands with palms open and trembling, eyes wide with a desperation that might have been pitiful if Drake could not see straight through to the truth.

"Please," the merchant gasped, voice cracking like old wood on a new and hungry fire. "You must understand, we are but pawns in a far larger game." Fingers curling into grasping hands, as if gripping some globe of deception as he spoke. "Spare us, and we shall..."

Drake's blade moved before the merchant could finish the sentence. As soon as the blade was in motion, the glamour and charm spells sizzled and dissipated in static sparks, revealing the full goblin form of the dead merchant. A single arc, swift and unrelenting, severed the goblin's head from its body.

The now revealed to be very goblin head rolled across the cobblestones like a discarded bauble, its lifeless eyes staring up at the sky as if begging for absolution. Blood sprayed in thick ribbons, staining the embroidered robes with the same crimson. The body crumpled to the ground like a fancy bandit's bag of ill-gotten goods.

"Pawns? **Pawns?! PAWNS, you say?!? Fine.**" Drake barked to all and none, his voice drumming like war. "You call yourselves pawns. Maybe, but willing to be played, to be used. You love the game, don't you? The dance of lies, a race for the other side of the chessboard, the illusion of nobility, and the sweet, sweet rot of pretending you are something you are not. You love it, and you love the dance of destruction so long as it isn't your own, you **BASTARDS!**"

The merchant's guards lunged at Drake, their faces twisted in rage.

One of them, a pale goblish hulk with almost human skin like thick leather, raised its axe, but Drake was already moving, swinging himself forward on his staff with one arm while his other pulled down the sword upon them.

The goblish hulk's axe fell short, edge biting into the stone where Drake had stood moments before.

Drake's blade flashed through the air, cleaving the goblin's defenses and throat with the precision of a surgeon and the fury of a divine borrowing.

Before the others could react, Drake was upon them as well, sword singing through the air as it cleaved paths through foes converging upon the area.

Another goblish merchant, with a face covered in as much makeup as magic, raised his blade in a desperate attempt to end Drake's tide of violence.

Drake sidestepped with the ease of someone who had spent his life training in anticipation for this. He drove Nightbane through the ribs, its dark glowing metal sinking into flesh like an auger for tapping a well, revealing his uglier true form.

The creature with human-flesh-toned makeup gasped, unable to scream, its mascaraed eyes widening in disbelief. It then collapsed to the ground, blood pooling around it.

Panic surged across the marketplace as Drake moved through it, this time with blade instead of his earlier words of warning. This was a full-blown assault, a whirlwind of violence unleashed upon the goblish stubborn and stragglers.

Drake was becoming something else. His blade sang through the air as he carved a path in the ranks of their forces, each strike accompanied by the resounding that only comes by the resurrection of truth in the death of lies. Drake moved with great fluidity despite inhibited gait and healing legs, staff and blade working in tandem to dispatch the goblish hordes. They became extensions of his will, part of his fighting rhythm, each measured strike against the illusions that had bound these creatures to his people, with near artistry in destruction. Nothing hindered him.

Goblin blood was everywhere. He moved through the ranks of the goblish forces, severing heads and limbs with the same detachment as a blacksmith shaping steel. Fighting on, he was utterly undaunted by mounting odds arrayed against him, each foe felled serving only to fuel the fire burning bright within, diminishing neither him nor his energies one iota.

The beasts fell like the sheer inevitability of gravity itself; each swing of the sword a note in an ancient melody, each body crushed beneath the weight of the undeniable truths that Drake carried with himself inexorably forward. Drake left a trail of carnage, the wake of goblin bodies strewn across cobblestones like broken puppets discarded after conclusion of cruel jests.

Drake felt himself curiously outside the chaos, as though he were the singular orderly force surrounded by disorder. He was as stoic as he was coordinated, the sword allowing him vision beyond, almost like observing events from some distant perch above the fray. He could see most things much more clearly now. In the first place, he was already in no way beholden to the lies, the deceits, or the webs of manipulation spun by the emperor's minions designed to entrap and exploit. The blade furthered the path he was set upon by his father. He could not be ensnared at all, and he could not be controlled, especially so long as he held that Ædlertuwin blade.

The world slowed around him, not in a dreamlike haze, but in the way time does when you are moving too fast to see it all. His senses heightened to a keen edge, as he cut through throngs of enemies, the blade giving him the best insights on how to best utilize his environment. He could see through the battle to victory in every encounter, all because of the sword, and was able to put his years of training to absolute use. He carved through the goblin hordes. Each strike was precise and unbelievably devastating, each movement perfectly placed, with his skill now honed by the power of Nightbane.

Drake's inner essence was one with the power of that ancient blade, surging against the darkness beside his own spirit, as embracing the shores of everlasting hope. He fought with fervor born of completely vanquished despair mingled with the righteous fury of loss, yet ennobled by true faith in greatest trust, every strike fueled by memories of those lost to the goblish tyranny's grasp. He could feel the emotional weight through every action of his blade, despite how light it felt to him.

He did not kill for vengeance in itself, nor for glory, but for the truth and for goodness to prevail. The goblins had tried to mimic nobility they had never earned, to pretend that their greed and lies were anything more than the rot that defines them. They were each a little villain, playing their part in a farce that could only end in ash and ruin, one way or another.

CHAPTER TWELVE

HERO WALKS

Collapse for Gervin's goblin takeover would ultimately be due to something deeper than just weakness. It was because they had never been worthy of standing against what Drake and his father represented.

Their illusions, their lies, and their hunger for power, all of it would crumble beneath the weight of the eternal justice that Drake was destined to deliver. The truth was being unleashed, and there would be no turning back from it.

Drake did not fight as a warrior, nor as a king or pretender thus, but as something else entirely. He was reckoning itself.

People, still hidden and in shelter or sneaking around to avoid the guards or gangs, watched in horrified fascination. Some began to cheer, even loudly and openly, as Drake wiped the streets of Solipsia's foes.

He heard screams of goblish terror mingling with the cheers of encouragement from those who recognized him as the son of their hero and understood what he was doing. Some were still yet enthralled or waking from the propaganda foisted upon them by Gervin, framing Drake himself as the villain.

Hour after hour, goblin blood was spilled by Drake.

The goblins who had believed their kind to be masters now found themselves broken, their illusions shattered like glass. Their debauchery and illusions were over, and many now scrambled like rats, their faces twisted with terror. The most cowardly goblins fled in waves out of the kingdom, spreading wide the news of goblish 'civil' war.

Many ignorant and greedy goblin bands and tribes, enticed by news of rising disorder, poured into the kingdom. Their numbers were seemingly endless, drawn like sharks by scent of blood. All search parties in the hinterlands were ordered back to the capital city. They had indeed found him, or he them rather.

From amidst the melee emerged a trio of goblins, their eyes gleaming with malice. They fanned out, attempting to flank him, but Drake anticipated their movements before their greedy little brains had even thought of it. The sword in his hand hummed softly, core shining out despite inner darkness.

The first goblin lunged, claws bared and fangs snarling. Drake sidestepped the attack with an almost lazy grace, his blade arcing up to deflect the strike before slicing downward. Half of the goblin's body fell to the cobblestones, severed cleanly, and what remained attempted to howl in pain before collapsing.

The second goblin charged, wielding a crude machete. Drake met the blow head-on, his sword clashing against the blade with a spark of fire. He grinned, a savage curl of his lips, and drove his shoulder into the goblin's chest. It staggered back, off-balance, and Drake followed up with a swift kick to the knee, snapping it.

The goblin fell to its other knee, and Drake's blade descended in a swift arc, ending its scream, as it crumpled like an empty sack.

The third goblin hesitated, uncertainty flickering across its horrid features.

Drake advanced, his sword held low, and the creature snarled, spittle flying from its jaws.

It darted forward, feinting with one hand while the other clawed at Drake's face.

Drake ducked under the attack, feeling the breeze of sharp nails against his cheek, and countered by decreasing their distance.

The goblin reeled back, not expecting him to respond so. Drake's blade sliced down as he stepped to the side, blood gushing out from the flat surface of gore where there used to be a jutting goblin face.

All three goblins lay motionless on the cobblestones.

Drake stepped over them, his breath steady despite the pounding of his heart. He pressed onward.

* * *

Drake found himself in one of the vast plazas formerly lined with merchant tents. Groups of goblins swarmed at him like ants moving for their hill from different directions, their forms merging into a seething masses of green hatred. At the plaza's center stood a monumental statue of Gervin, its marble face sneering down at the carnage below. Drake's gaze locked onto it, and a cold fury ignited within.

As he went along, Drake pulled down these strange statues Gervin had erected, their grotesque faces smashing into satisfying rubble on the ground. Other Solipsians came out to assist him in the iconoclastic excitement of demolishing the obscene things. These carved figures were mirrors of goblish contempt, standing against everything Solipsia stood for.

This wave of goblins surged toward him. Drake stood his ground, sword held high, and as they closed in, he let out a battle cry as though channelling the very fury of God. The blade was a blur, cleaving through the ranks of foes with terrifying ease.

A hunched creature in a tattered cloak lunged at him from the crowd, with dagger aimed right at his heart, but Drake moved with the speed of something beyond the material and sliced up through arms and face.

The goblin's freshly corpsed body was kicked to the side with the rest, its last breath moving toward disbelief which never met vocal cords.

"Is this what you wanted?!" he raged and roared at them, voice booming like a thunderclap outside of himself.

"YOU!!" Drake growled, his voice raw and hot with fury, "**You who lied to all!** You **ROT** our kingdom's soul, pretending to what you can **NEVER** be!" The truth in his words were a whip, striking at the grotesque forms surrounding him almost as hard as the ancient sword itself.

The goblins hissed and jeered, their voices a broken chorus of busted teeth and mangled tongues.

"I am told you worship Ruin! Behold! Today I bring you the ruin of **all your LIES!**" His words formed a declaration that the time for goblin deceptions had passed, and that this meant war.

A goblin warrior, larger and more brutish than its kin, approached Drake, wielding a massive club studded with iron spikes.

Drake met its charge head-on, his sword parrying the blow with a resounding clang. The force of the impact jarred his arm, but he grinned wildly, adrenaline surging through his veins.

The goblin roared and swung again, its club arcing through the air like a comet. Drake ducked under the strike, feeling the rush of wind against his scalp, and countered with a swift kick to the knee. The creature stumbled, and Drake's swung Nightbane after it, severing the tendons behind its leg. It crashed to the ground, howling in agony.

Drake stood over it, sword poised for the killing blow, but the goblin snarled up at him, defiance burning in its eyes. "You cannot kill us all," it growled. "We will rise a..."

Drake's blade descended, and the goblin's snarl was silenced.

The plaza fell still, the remnants of the horde retreating into the shadows like smoke dispersed by a strong wind. Drake surveyed the scene. That statue of Gervin loomed above him, begging to be toppled with the others. Next to the statue was a hastily built wall over the road, constructed partly of torn down buildings. Goblins taunted him from behind it, hissing and snarling as he approached.

"You cannot pass," one of them shouted. "This is our domain now."

Drake could feel Nightbane's power pulsing. "I think you're mistaken," he called back. "This is Solipsia, and it belongs to us."

The goblins cursed at him. Drake took a step forward, and they responded in kind, coming out of the walls like spiderlings uncoiling from web-bundled eggs.

The first goblin kicked at Drake's face, but he sidestepped the attack entirely.

Drake swung Nightbane down and severed the creature's leg at the knee. It screamed and fell back, clutching the stump as dark blood spurted forth.

One particular goblin warrior, wielding a pair of curved scimitars, charged with a roar, blades spinning impressively. Drake artfully dodged its many strikes, and tied up the goblin's arms in a grapple, countering with a headbutt. The creature stumbled, and Drake caught it across the legs with a swipe of his sword, nearly severing them, causing it to bleed out as it crawled away.

A goblin guard commander ran at Drake just then. It attempted to strike first, but Drake parried the blow, feeling the forceful jolt of impact through his arm. The goblin commander snarled, its eyes narrowing.

Drake rejoined with a swift strike directly on top of the head.

The creature staggered back, dark blood spilling from the wound, and Drake advanced, his sword poised for the killing blow. The goblin commander raised its weapon in a desperate parry, but Drake faked the movement, swinging instead from the other direction and severing the creature's arms cleanly at the elbows.

The commander fell to its knees, its eyes wide with shock and pain. "Die, hum..." its words were cut off along with its head.

More goblins swarmed.

Another goblin warrior, clad in crude armor plated with stolen mail, charged with a roar, its axe swinging wildly.

Drake dove beneath the swinging, rolling to his feet behind the creature and driving his blade into its unarmored back.

It fell over dead.

He then dashed for the statue. After quickly securing staff and sword to his back, Drake clambered up the statue of Gervin. It was standing almost regally, holding a goblin baby above the square, as goblins attempted to slash at him from below. Drake stood on the shoulders of Gervin's statue, pulling out Nightbane. He cut through the arms, so the gobling and hands crushed one of the goblins amongst the mob below, gore staining its face.

Holding the sword carefully, in preparation to jump when ready, Drake then rocked back and forth while grasping tightly, until the entire statue fell, crushing any of the goblins which did not move out of the way.

Jumping from the falling statue, he locked back into fighting.

* * *

Something vast and insurmountable stirred within the hearts and minds of all Solipsians, all at once, unseen, as though a curse was lifting, with the arrival of a new mantle.

The crowd was no longer just watching, some were now participating. Groups of warriors and former soldiers or guards, their faces now streaked with soot and blood, had joined the fray, their weapons raised in defiance and support of Drake.

They fought alongside him out of duty and a need to cleanse the rot of fear that had festered in their hearts for too long. Young men, trained as hunters or guards, with bows on rooftops or hidden in their homes, shooting through windows. Their retired fathers were here too, hacking with rusty blades against the ceaseless arrival of goblins.

A hulking troll from Gervin's guard lumbered forward, axe raised high, as it bellowed a challenge through lips twisted into snarls.

Drake's heart pounded in his chest with the memories unbidden of his most recent encounter with trolls, of his legs crushed and weeks in agony, pain lancing nonstop through his body like lightning. This was to be the rain he had saved up all his pain for. His father had been right about everything, perhaps most of all this.

With deliberate calm, Drake raised his sword and moved in the troll's direction. His hand tightened upon the sword as he focused his will upon the truth. He easily dodged the beast's axe.

Drake launched himself towards it pushing off the ground with his staff, swinging his blade around and across its belly.

Troll guts spilled forth from the wound. The creature convulsed violently, axe clattering to the ground, as it crashed backward in a shower of its own blood.

A bunch of the gathering human warriors cheered wildly at this. At that moment, they felt invincible fighting alongside their young hero.

Drake did not pause to savor the momentary triumph, though acknowledge it he did, but not at the cost of his precious momentum in battle. His father had taught him very well how to lead.

He turned his attention back towards the oncoming tide of enemies, staff swinging out to catch a leaping goblin across the head. It screeched in pain as its skull crunched audibly beneath Drake's exerted force, the body crumpling like a ragdoll.

More goblins fled, others fell, but none, not one, would escape the storm that had now begun to gather around Drake. If not now, he would get them later.

He moved through them like a force of nature against their deceptions, each step a declaration of truth, each strike a promise of more.

With every lying foe destroyed, Drake grew more powerful. His eyes burned within in the blinding fire of truth, scorching all else. Nightbane cleaved through goblish flesh and enchantments alike. All else faded into irrelevance as Drake progressed, towards destiny and perhaps death, but never defeat.

The goblins in the wealthy districts surrounding the palace, those that remained, were not the ones who had once plagued the land. These goblins were the far more ancient ones. They were not the youthful goblins killed off in droves nor the guards nor market goblins with simple enchantments and makeup. These wealthy goblins were even older than Gritch. Their forms were twisted by centuries of deception and indulgence.

Revealed to Drake through Nightbane, he saw everything, and all things about their grotesque beings. Beyond the more powerful enchantments making them beautiful, their real skin hung in tatters, a sickly green mottle with pustules that oozed a viscous, bile-like fluid, pooling on the cobblestones like spilled ink despite their contrived visage.

The eyes all others saw were beautiful and sharp. Their real goblin eyes behind the illusions burned with a grotesque vitality; rotting, milky, and clouded, yet fixated on Drake as though he were the last thing they had ever wanted to see. Their faces were crumpled into grotesque caricatures of what was already disgusting. Noses caved in, mouths stretched wide in permanent snarls, with remaining sharpened teeth gnawing at their own rotting flesh like vultures pecking at bones.

Drake's lip curled in revulsion as he took in the sight before him. These were the beings his father knew the least about and had rarely spoken of, the ones who had rotted nearly to death yet persisted in their foul existence, like a strange auto-necromancy shambling through the ruins of their own decay. They had once been kings of deception, masters of illusion, weaving spells and charms to manipulate every corner of the world. But now they were stuck here with him, about to be made into dogfood.

He remembered his father's words, "Those monsters could live for 500 years, son, if any cared for themselves, but they can't. They're so lazy, they rot to death. Can you believe it? A creature so foul they rot to death before having a chance of dying naturally... the mixed goblins live longer because they don't rot as quickly; cut the difference. They age or rot to death by 400 years, but they won't have rotted by 150 years like most of the full-blooded that survive, who could probably could live even longer than the mixed goblish, if they took care of themselves."

These were the ones that were pure goblin but far older than 150. His father could not even have imagined such disgusting things as these which survived beyond the rot using demonic magics.

Drake raised his staff to parry a blow from an ancient encharmed goblin, whose fingers were actually fused with oozing necrotic growths. These were rendered invisible by the charms

It inflicted more damage upon itself in the failed attack than it could have ever hoped to cause in Drake.

He could still see the hint of the illusion cast by the charms, portraying a wealthy young woman in fashionable wears.

The creature snarled and continued its suicidal attack.

Drake pivoted, his weight shifting to the staff's crook, and swung the sword across the goblin's skull like a baseball bat.

The wigged head went flying over the wall of the city. Charms fell before the body collapsed in a heap of its true form.

"You cannot hope to defeat us," one of the creatures shrieked.

"We are infinitely many, eternal and unending."

Drake cut it down with a swift stroke, the blade shearing through its neck as if parting curdled milk, before retorting. "Unending?" he asked the remaining wealthy ancient goblins in mockery. "There can be only one truth. You are nothing but rotting carcasses, parasites feeding upon fantasies. I will scourge you from our world like the vermin you are!"

"You think you can judge us? We are truth, child, the eternal dance of life and death, of decay and rebirth! You have not lived long enough to understand, boy!" This one, in the form of an aging man wearing a dress, stayed far back away from Drake.

Drake's laughter cut through the marketplace, harsh and cold. "Rebirth?" he scoffed. "This is not rebirth! This is stagnation. Putrid cycles of lies and corruption, they end now. It all ends now." Drake's body trembled with exhilaration, yet his movements remained precise, almost mechanical.

Another ancient goblin in a dress, its face a grotesque mask of decay, lunged at him with an ear-shattering scream.

Drake sidestepped, his staff cracked the creature on the back of its head, sending the thing sprawling into a tree. "You are born in rot, you live in rot, and you die of rot," he sneered, his voice dripping with contempt. "You are rot."

The first goblin in a dress snarled, its mangled mouth covered in lipstick. It tried to walk away.

A number of the warriors assisting Drake had taken up the task of finishing off his defeated foes, allowing him to move more quickly. An archer on a roof shot the goblin as it began to walk off, and another warrior following behind Drake smashed its skull with an enormous hammer.

Drake kept moving, more warriors followed. The goblins' cries faded into the distance as Drake pressed on.

The goblins fell in numbers greater than even the still arriving hordes, so the surrounding crowds of goblins eventually thinned. Drake's blade cut through the remnants of the goblin horde, leaving few untouched.

* * *

Drake's relentless march through the city left obscene monuments to the kingdom's fury, cobblestones slick with ichor and blood as the bodies of goblins stacked up.

The palace loomed ahead on his path, its towers yet gracing the sullen sky with defiant pride, but before Drake could reach its gates, more enemies descended upon him. He felt and heard a pounding of the ground, like an earthquake.

Drake's gaze locked onto a towering figure in the distance, a troll like the ones which had attacked Silver Keep but even larger, its bulk resembling a mountain of muscle and sinew, its eyes glowing faintly with an unnatural green light. The creature's movements were fast despite the laborious effort to maintain its colossal frame.

Still more trolls, lumbering titans of muscle and malice, moved through the outskirts of the city like mobile battering rams. Their enormous forms sent shockwaves rippling through the ground, with buildings groaning.

Drake watched as one such beast plowed through a row of houses where archers had taken up defense, its massive fists swinging wildly, reducing stone and mortar to rubble. The troll roared, voice like thunder clapping against the heavens, spittle flying from its jaws as it stomped closer, eyes locked onto Drake with primal hunger.

"Whewe go, wittwe hewo? (Where go, little hero?)" the troll rumbled in recognition, its voice a deep, rumbling bass that vibrated through the ground. "You fink swowd stob uss?"

Drake didn't answer. He simply raised his sword, the dark blade humming brightly with internal light from energy that pulsed in time with his heartbeat.

The troll charged, its massive legs propelling it forward with a lumbering gait that was both terrifying and, from what Drake now saw, comically inept. It swung its club wildly.

With a swift, calculated motion, Drake sidestepped the blow, pushing himself up on his staff to land the sword upon its head, cutting off part of the troll's skull.

The injury sent a jolt through the creature's body, and its leg buckled violently. The troll staggered, its massive frame teetering. A low, guttural groan escaped it as it tried to regain balance, but Drake wasn't done.

Staff in arm and with a flick of his wrist, he gripped upon the pommel with both hands, and drove the sword right through the troll's chest, Drake being the man ever relentless.

The troll convulsed, its body writhing as if caught in an unseen tide. Blood spurt from the wound, dark and thick, pooling on the cobblestones below.

Another troll appeared behind Drake in the midst of melee and as other warriors fought off other trolls and goblins around him. Its roar, designed to instill fear, was cut short by a sickening crunch: the sound of its neck bones breaking under the force of Drake's strike.

The creature collapsed to one knee, its massive form trembling as it tried to rise again, only to wobble precariously before toppling sideways into a pile of rubble.

"You dare challenge me?!" Drake bellowed at the other trolls moving in on him.

The nearest troll's response was a guttural snarl as it picked up speed towards Drake, its lips curling back to reveal rows of yellowed rotting stumps. It charged, each step sending tremors through the ground, buildings shuddering in response, practically shivering. Drake stood his ground, staff planted firmly beneath him, sword raised high.

As the troll moved toward him, Drake could see the creature's true nature revealed through the power of the blade, its skin mottled and pockmarked, eyes dull. Despite its size, its limbs were awkward and disproportionate. It was as though some goblin had enchanted it.

The sword revealed the truth in vulnerabilities hidden beneath layers of grime and scar tissue.

The creature's fists smashed into the ground where Drake had stood mere heartbeats before, sending stones flying.

Each impact jarred the earth, yet Drake felt only a fraction of the force, his body buoyed by an unseen energy that seemed to flow through him from the sword itself.

The sword's power pulsed within, revealing secrets hidden beneath layers of flesh and bone. Drake saw them now: the weak points, chinks in this titan's armor, knees and joints wobbly as though learning to walk, belly soft and yielding as rotten fruit.

"Trolls are terrible fighters!" Drake taunted, voice laced with contempt as he leaped beyond the swing of an incoming troll's axe, with the assistance of his staff.

The troll snarled in frustration as it redoubled its efforts to split Drake.

Drake's movements were fluid and precise. He darted in close, sword flashing out to slice through tendons thick as ropes, eliciting a howl of pain from the creature.

"Look at you," he mocked, circling the wounded troll like a predator around his prey. "All that strength!" He feinted left, then right, drawing the troll's attention with each deft movement of his blade.

Drake lunged forward, staff swinging low as he swept the troll's legs out from under it. The creature crashed to the ground with a force that shook the city, its body trembling like an uprooted and fallen oak. Drake was upon it in an instant, sword driving down with all his might into the exposed flesh of the troll's belly.

The blade sank deep, eliciting a bellow of agony from the stricken beast. Ichor streamed forth in torrents, as Drake wrenched the sword free and struck again, once, twice, thrice, until the troll lay still, its form convulsing weakly before falling limp.

Drake stood over his fallen foe, body drenched in sweat and gore but feeling more powerful than ever. Around him, more trolls crashed onto the battlefield, their massive forms trampling through the chaos like elephants through underbrush. Yet Drake felt no fear, only a cold, calculating resolve.

He turned to face the next wave of attackers.

"Bring all your strength, trolls!" he shouted against the carnage.

So they came, lumbering titans charging forth with all the subtlety of boulders rolling downhill.

Drake danced around their blows, staff and sword weaving deadly patterns through air thick with dust and blood.

"Troll strength is but an illusion," he said, his voice carrying across the battlefield. "Built for destruction, not endurance! Fragile as a child's toy! Go for the stomachs and tendons!" He said this more to the other warriors who had joined him than to the trolls.

Drake lunged forward, staff swinging low as he swept a troll's legs out from under it.

The creature crashed to ground with force that shook earth, its body trembling like a fallen oak uprooted by storm.

This time a group of warriors moved in and stabbed it in the belly. The word was out that the trolls were easy to kill.

Trolls buckled beneath their assaults, their weak bellies being targeted now across the kingdom.

One troll, its eyes wide with confusion and fear, raised its club and roared.

Drake didn't wait for it to strike. He swung Nightbane in a wide arc, the blade slicing through its body and driving it backward, its massive frame crashing into a stack of overturned stalls.

It toppled to the ground, groaning as blood poured out from the wound running the length of its belly.

Another troll lunged at him from the shadows, crashing through a wall with a deafening crash. It swung its axe wildly, but Drake was already in motion.

He leapt around the creature's outstretched arm and through the legs, with a grace that belied his forgotten injuries. With a swift motion, he pushed the butt of his staff into the troll's back as leverage to drive the blade into its neck, sending it sprawling forwards into the remains of a collapsed building.

The remaining trolls hesitated, their massive forms swaying as if uncertain whether to charge or retreat.

Drake took advantage of their hesitation, advancing toward them with measured steps, tapping his staff at speed. Most began to scatter in all directions. They ran off and were chased down by Drake's helpers, many killed.

* * *

As the last trolls crashed to the ground, a collective gasp was felt. The trolls, once titanic terrors, now lay in heaps of fallen giants, their massive forms sprawled like the toppled statues of Gervin's regime. Drake was stood yet unbroken, sword dripping with demonic blood.

The battle raged on, but something shifted further in the pulse of the kingdom. A stirring, at first, rustling beneath the surface, like the first whispers of an awakening beast. It was as though the very heart of Solipsia pounded with newfound resolve. From the shadows and alcoves, where they had hidden, the citizens of Solipsia began to emerge, their eyes wide with a mix of fear, desperation, and something else, awoken by Drake and his example.

It began with the warriors, of course, but next to join the fray were the tradesmen. Their blistered hands, stained with ink, grime, and grease, clutched rusted tools of their trades once used to chop and carve wood; rend and mend leather; or build and construct all that still supported the city. They emerged from doorways and alleyways like phantoms, their faces grim, and eyes sharp as razors.

One wielded an ancient and dingy sword freshly sharpened despite its age, yet he swung it with the precision of someone who had come to terms with his fears. He struck down a goblin rushing to Drake. "For Telyn!" he bellowed as blade struck the green menace, his voice raw with fury, as if he were an extension of Drake with the very name of his sister, itself, a weapon.

The man embraced Drake. Drake was overwhelmed with emotion, and felt stronger bonds with the people of his kingdom than he had ever felt before.

Many yelled out other heroes' names, or the names of their own dead. The people were beyond rage, and the few who remained entrapped by the lies had nothing to say for themselves.

A blacksmith, his apron stained with more than just the usual day's labor, stepped forward. In one hand, he clutched a hammer, its head darkened with use and abuse, and in the other, a freshly forged sword. His gaze met Drake's. "Thank God," the man muttered, voice hoarse from disuse or perhaps shock, "you're truly one of them, one of the heroes of old."

Drake offered a grim nod, sword still raised. "You're a hero now too, sir."

The tradesman straightened his outerwear, chest puffing out yet trying not to cry from the honor. "I'm no hero, lad. Just a working man. But I've got a few tricks up me sleeve."

Yet another tradesman joined the gathering movement in step with Drake. He spat on the ground next to a pile of dead goblins, his fingers curling around a dagger so dull it might have been used to scrape paint from walls. "They took our children," he growled like a bear, looking over to Drake, his words thick with venom. "Now they'll see what we're really made of."

Drake fought alongside his newfound allies. Around him, the citizens battled with ferocity. They stood shoulder to shoulder with what remained of the much maligned hero kin.

A commotion was heard from one of the houses, and out rolled a wretched goblin. The woman who ran out after it, her face gaunt with exhaustion, raised a butchers knife high. "You won't take my daughter!" she screamed with a shrill, her voice trembling. The blade met the creature's skull with a wet crunch, and the goblin fell back, its body twitching.

Her eyes hollow with fresh grief, she stabbed the head of another goblin crawling from their house, as it tried to reach her daughter, hiding behind her. "Parasites!" she snarled. "You're just parasites!" The little girl hugged her mother's leg. She and her daughter were welcomed into the throng of justice seekers, perhaps the safest place to be at the moment.

One young man, his shirt torn and bloodstained, raising an ancient shield undoubtedly from ancestors ages past. "We'll never be slaves again!" he shouted over the escalating and welcome human noise, his voice cracking with emotion.

"We're free! We're free!" his friends chanted at him, to which he joined, their voices rising like a chorus of pent-up fury.

Another mother, her hands blistered from years of scrubbing floors, used her broom to crush the skull of a goblin running away from the advancing crowd. "Vermin," she muttered, wiping blood from her face.

Behind her, more figures emerged from the shadows. Pregnant mothers clutched babies to their chests while brandishing rusty blades with their other hands. There were teens armed with makeshift shields fashioned from pans and kitchen appliances, their eyes gleaming with a fierce determination that belied their youth. Old folk leaned on canes like staffs, knuckles white as they gripped gnarled wood, faces lined with both age and anger.

Drake surveyed the assembled crowds walking with him, heart swelling with pride. Most were not soldiers or warriors. Many were bakers, masons, carpenters, and laborers; mothers and children, fathers and grandparents.

These were ordinary people thrust into extraordinary circumstances. Yet here they stood, ready to fight for their homes, their families, their very lives. Old men and women were present in droves, lean and weathered by time yet fierce as winter wolves.

Children followed, armed with an assortment of improvised weapons: pots and pans clutched tightly in small fists. Those who should have been too young or too old to fight had iron-cored brooms wielded with surprising agility.

Drake raised an eyebrow at the sight of the brooms. Yet as he watched one child, no more than eight summers old, swing it through the air, he saw the advantages. The iron-cored shaft was sturdy, balanced well in hand, and could deliver a crushing blow when wielded with enough force.

A woman, her dress torn and mud-splattered, approached Drake cautiously. She held a baby swaddled in rags close to her chest, but her free hand clutched a meat cleaver. Her eyes were hard, flinty, as she spoke. "We've been hiding," she admitted, voice barely above a whisper. "But no more. Not after what we seen you do, good on ya boyo!"

Drake nodded solemnly, acknowledging her words with a solemn dip of his head. "Maybe some of you should have stayed hidden, though. This is important, but it's not the only fight, not your fight necessarily..."

She interrupted him with an energetic shake of her head. "Not our fight? With all due respect, dearest sir, you think we can stand by any longer and watch while those monsters tear apart our city? Our homes? Our lives?" She gestured to the baby in her arms, "This little girl deserves better than to grow up in a world ruled by goblins and tyrants."

Many began singing the song that began in the forests with Drake's return to the kingdom, "The Hero Walks," but now sung to a war drum. Many took it up, voices rising in a chorus of defiance that filled the blood-soaked and body-littered streets. Drake had helped to feed a surge in his people of something recently unfamiliar to them, yet all the more vital with its departure: hope.

As they advanced, more citizens emerged from hiding places, drawn by the sound of battle and the sight of neighbors taking up arms against their oppressors. They joined ranks swelled by desperation and courage alike, each new addition bolstering their resolve until it became nothing short of an unstoppable wave of sheer hope crashing through and destroying the wicked shores of fear and doubt.

Goblin numbers dwindled as they realized they were no longer fighting against a single man, but the whole people; an army of uncommonly angry commoners. Those remaining, once confident in their superiority, now faltered under the onslaught unleashed by the people they had sought to enslave. Their cries of rage turned to screams of terror as pots and pans clanged against skulls, iron-cored brooms jabbed guts, and rusty blades found their marks hidden beneath layers of enchantment.

Soon most of the surviving goblins were running away instead of fighting. They scattered like shadows in a storm. Common people took up the chase, and few of the creatures made it out of the kingdom. Some tried to hide, but the people found them too.

Drake saw as one such group cornered a remnant ancient goblin. It tried to escape through a narrow alleyway, but found no exit.

"Please," it begged, eyes wide with terror as it cowered against a wall. "Mercy, I beg of you… I'll pay you anything, I'm rich!"

There was no mercy left here, not for goblins. The creature screamed as the makeshift weapons found its flesh hidden beneath the layers of enchantment.

This was not about vengeance or retribution for Drake; it was about survival, about reclaiming what had been stolen, and those who could not yet fight for themselves.

The people of the kingdom were no longer cowering in fear. They were fighting, and they would not stop. Word went out throughout the land, so the goblins were now the hunted.

CHAPTER THIRTEEN

GERVIN'S FOLLY

Palace gates looming before them, Drake turned to address the crowd. He shouted aloud for all to hear, "Together we stand! We fight and we win, together! We reclaim our kingdom, now!"

A mighty cheer erupted from those gathered, as many more took up arms and prepared to follow their young hero into battle, joining the expanding throng.

Drake led the charge he started, staff tapping against cobblestones, that rhythm steady as a drumbeat calling forth the militia.

Behind him, the people of Solipsia surged forward, their feet in lockstep through the streets, sounding like thunder rolling through a valley of buildings. He felt no trepidation, only hardened resolve. This was his path, chosen for him long ago, how his father's words had first taken root within his heart, but so destined since ages past. The sorrow was fated to point him this way, towards truth buried deep beneath the layers of lies.

So the hero indeed walked, sword held high as beacon, cutting through shadows. Drake paused at the threshold, taking a deep breath.

'Father,' he thought, 'you brought me here, thank you.' His mind was abuzz with the meaning of this moment yet the sword still glistened, covered in blood and ichor yet still shining. The palace gates felt like the threshold between the realms of the dead and of the living.

Drake approached the gates, which predated anything else at the palace, and they looked quite different to him than ever before, with the emblem of the symbol for Solipsia lit up for Drake, and it was most beautiful. The symbol was mostly unnoticed and rarely visible before Gervin due to the gates always having been open. He squeezed his grip on Nightbane and, predictably, the light from the symbol pulsed with the tightening. So ancient and plain was this emblem that it was no longer recognized in the kingdom, yet Drake saw it clearly now.

With deliberate slowness, Drake knelt down before what he now recognized as the most abstract and original emblem of Ædlertuwin, but from even older traditions. It was the most important symbol of Solipsia, which the two-headed eagle merely reflected. In fact, Nightbane itself was shaped for it. The symbol represented sacrifice, ceaseless prayer, eternal life, and redemption.

The gates then opened for Drake, to the crowd's amazement.

The entrance to the palace was a gaping maw framed by marble columns as thick as ancient trees atop a series of great steps. The gates now stood ajar, inviting them in.

Drake's walked briskly through the vast marble halls. His staff tapped against the cold floors, foretelling the horde of footsteps that followed in his wake. Behind him at a bit of distance, the city's unlikely heroes. The movement of those immediately following Drake shook the ground. The massive corridors resounded with their presence almost lovingly, as though built for such crowds yet long denied the pleasure.

A few remnant guards attempted to stop the rush of people, but were ill-suited to the task. Some still tried and paid the price in instant death.

"For Solipsia! Death to the goblin hordes!" an old tradesman bellowed as he had in his youth, his voice raw with emotion as he swung his blade in wide arcs, cleaving through some of these foolish fiends who remained. This lone bellow became a chant through the crowds pushing forward. A few in the crowds thought the goblin guards showed something of courage in these acts, however they knew nothing about the troll enforcers used only to terrify the palace guard and keep them in line.

"For Solipsia! Death to the goblin hordes!" More voices screamed it.

Goblin screams of terror mingled with the clamor. High-pitched wails cut through the overwhelming noise. The goblish palace guards fell swiftly under the combined assault. The halls ran red with blood, as they were chased down for sport now.

Enchanted courtier goblins in courtly attire, their true forms concealed beneath illusions of finery and elegance, were universally unmasked, their illusions failing to find footholds with anyone any longer. The palace was built with only one publicly known entrance and exit, through the front, making it something of a giant trap. Goblins ran for the windows, but that did nothing for their cowardice, as these had been built with thick enchanted crystal.

A child brought low one such ancient courtly goblin hiding in one of the many dining rooms, with a light bop on the head from a broom. The thing was sent to the ground in a heap of limbs, with all enchantments disappearing at once. The boy ran away holding his nose.

The halls gave way to a grand chamber, the throne room of Emperor Gervin. The doors stood wide open, inviting Drake and company into the heart of deceit and corruption.

He stepped inside, surveying the changes made by the goblish emperor. It had been cleaned from the revelry, but many things had also been replaced. The throne room had always been a cavernous expanse, with walls adorned with massive paintings depicting scenes of chivalry and virtue. These had all been removed. Now banners hung from the vaulted ceiling, each one bearing primitive art with symbols of power and domination, skulls impaled on spears, dragons devouring worlds, and serpents coiled around blades dripping with blood.

The chamber pulsed with a sickly light. At the far end stood the new throne, a monstrous construct of black stone carved into the likeness of some ancient chimeric beast, no doubt the demon of Ruin. Upon it sat Emperor Gervin alone in this chamber, his form shimmering with the lingering remnants of his strong illusion magic. Gervin's eyes were wide, pupils dilated with madness. His lips curled into a smile that did not reach his eyes.

Drake walked with speed toward the middle of the throne room and then stood tall before it, sword poised as he stared at the creature that had orchestrated so much suffering, staff gripped firmly in his other arm. The crowds still poured into the chamber yet remained quiet, partly out of fear, partly reverence, and partly shock. Hanging around the throne were massive banners displaying the most beastly acts imaginable, performed by none other than the emperor himself. Most people with children covered their eyes and guided their families back out the entrance and away from the horrific portrayals, which, as stated earlier, were indescribable to polite company.

Gervin sat still, but no longer displayed his fake smile.

Drake wore a look of absolute disgust, attempting to look away from most of the banners.

Above the throne, between all the others, hung one enormous banner, its fabric freshly bearing the traitorous title: "**Empire of Gobland**"

* * *

Drake's laughter erupted through the chamber, a sound raw and unbridled. It wasn't pained or desperate; it was genuine and thorough. Others in the crowd laughed with him.

"What's so funny?!" Gervin snarled, his voice a guttural growl, as he pointed at the hated hero. His eyes narrowed to streams of malice that burned with hatred and confusion.

Drake continued to laugh, his body shaking with the force of it as he pointed at the banner above the throne. The whole crowd behind him was now laughing with him. "**Empire of Gobland?**" he gasped between breaths, tears now streaming down his cheeks from laughing so hard. "You're a goblin! All of you are goblins!"

Gervin's form shimmered strangely, the illusion faltering momentarily as Drake's laughter cut through the enchantment almost as well as Nightbane. To Drake's vision, Gervin's true form beneath was already revealed as maddened by magics, with vacant eyes swallowing the light itself. It was the most ancient-looking goblin Drake had seen yet, practically a skeleton hanging with flesh and a belly, though nearly as tall as a human. There was indeed something much more human about Gervin, but nothing that would overshadow the goblin features, or make anyone think he was in his true form, which remained hidden to all others.

The illusion that was Gervin "the human" was carefully crafted over centuries, but it frayed at the edges and in the corners of eyes. Not another sound stirred, not even the slightest whisper of breath or rustle of cloth.

As Drake laughed, deeply and seemingly uncontrollably, his gaze remained locked onto Gervin's. That which enabled such mirth was found only in the eyes of those who had gazed into the depths of darkness, and emerged in full trust as inseparable from the light. He laughed not on his own behalf but for the light itself.

"You dare mock me?!" Gervin spat angrily, his voice barely above a whisper yet plainly terrified. "I am your emperor! I am the embodiment of Gobl..." he caught himself, "Solipsia's might!"

Drake's laughter died away, as did the laughter in the crowd, replaced by an eerily intense calm. He gestured towards Gervin with the sword, dark blade gleaming out brightly in the dim light of the throne room. "You're nothing but a rotting corpse," he said, his voice steady. "And I've come to end your evil."

Gervin's eyes widened in disbelief, his form trembling with a mix of rage and fear. He rose from the throne, his movements jerky and unsettled, as if the very air resisted his commands. "Guards!" he roared, voice cutting through the silent yet filled chamber.

There were no guards left to answer his call, only the mass of silent Solipsian witnesses.

Drake watched as Gervin struggled to maintain his composure, the remnants of his illusions flickering like dying embers under such concentrated focus by the people so subjected to tyranny. The emperor's actions alone revealed his true form in all its grotesque monstrosity. He was nothing but a creature born of decay and malice, clinging desperately to the last vestiges of power that had once been his.

"You think you can defeat me! I am eternal!" the false emperor rasped while sneering, voice vibrating with the same cruel resonance as the banners above pronouncing Solipsian replacement. Hands trembled, fingers twitched as if deciding whether to cry more, strike out, or flee.

Drake stepped forward, making the decision for the tyrant, his movements deliberate, staff tapping against the marble as he walked across the enormous throne room. The Ædlertuwin blade of destiny hummed in his grip, its edges pulsing with the natural light deep within that seemed to grow with the more truth it revealed to its wielder. The battle for the kingdom's soul was nearly over, and Drake understood in that moment how much he represented the greater truths that could not be silenced or denied any longer. His movements now carried the weight of ages past and futures yet unborn.

"You are eternal, you say?" Drake asked, almost sadly and sympathetically.

"You will pay for this!" Gervin hissed, voice trembling with fury. "I am the rightful king and emperor! I will crush you beneath my heel!"

Drake merely smiled, a cold expression that held neither warmth nor mercy. He stepped across the marble floor, dark blade poised to strike down Solipsia's tyrant. "Not today," he said softly, almost gently. "Your empire is a lie, you are not eternal," Drake said, voice low and cold. "You are no emperor. You are a parasite, just like the rest, as feasting on the lives of others. What are you? In a word, a monster. Gervin, monsters are meant to be slain."

Gervin's anger deepened. "And you?! What are you? Some village boy, son of a monster, with a fancy sword and delusions of grandeur?" The false emperor lunged behind his false throne, his movements sudden and desperate now. His hands clenched into fists, and the surrounding air began to move around them.

***

Shadows coiled from the walls, writhing like living things. Children in the crowd screamed at this.

At the same time, the floor beneath the throne room split open, with roots and thick thorny vines erupting from the marble stone. More screams came from the crowd, many of whom were panicking and attacking the roots.

Drake didn't flinch. He stepped over the vines and hobbled over the breaks in the marble as the things lashed at his legs, their barbs tearing at his boots.

Drake raised the Nightbane in a wide arc. "You think you can hide behind your parlor tricks, rotling?" he taunted the illusionist, voice sharp as his family blade. "Your magic is pathetic! It is meaningless now, as are you and all goblins! The vines are not real!" All the lurching vines died at once, disappearing. The marble stones of the flooring were suddenly restored as though nothing had happened at all.

Gervin peeked over the throne, eyes flashing with fury. The

shadows surged forward, though more slowly than the vines, tendrils of darkness finally lashing at Drake's face, but then, of course he was faster still.

Drake spun on his staff, the wood finally cracking under the strain, and drove the blade into the heart of a shadowy mass. Something in the darkness screamed with a sound like thousands of broken things re-breaking but this time toward repair, and the darkness recoiled. The breaking sound continued to pierce eardrums of the crowd who all winced in response, covering their ears as quickly as they could.

The surrounding air around Gervin crackled, as if reality were screaming in protest to his impositions. Gervin's hands twitched, his fingers curling into claws as he tried to summon more magic, but something greater still seemed to resist him. The marble walls trembled, the stone veins pulsing with a light that was not its own.

Drake pressed forward, his blade carving through Gervin's illusions. More shadows appeared, writhing against the dim light and trying to ensnare him, but he moved like the eye of a storm; calm, calculated, and unrelenting. His unavoidable presence alone was a rebuttal to the lies that Gervin used to control the kingdom. The very truth of his having prevailed through all things to arrive here was a pox on the empowered deceits, and an ever-countering proof of heroism itself. He could feel the weight of every life lost pushing him onward. It was a spiritual wind forcing him into the fate.

Gervin snarled, as he unleashed wave after wave of those demonic creatures of darkness. The shadows coiled around Drake's limbs, trying to pull him down, but he laughed it off with a flick of Nightbane.

"If you were a genuine puppet, you might be useful, goblin," he spat, his voice dripping with sardonic contempt, still moving toward the throne, unstoppable. He noted how Gervin cringed, and how the shadows retracted at that word, so he resolved to use it more when speaking next, "Goblin, did you think your title or illusions grant authority? You're just a goblin wearing a crown of lies! **You took everyone from us, from me! Did you think this would end nicely, king goblin, your honor?!** Well today you die, goblin!"

The shadows recoiled at the repeated use of 'goblin,' their tendrils flaring with a sickly green light before vanishing into nothingness. Gervin's face twisted in rage, his hands flying through complex gestures as he tried to reweave the darkness, but Drake was already on him. He lunged forward and poked the evil emperor square in the chest with the now broken staff. Gervin hurtled backward, out into the open from behind the throne. The human facade blurred for a moment, his illusions peeling away more and more to reveal the twisted, pure goblish features beneath. His mind, once sharp and calculating, now burned with feral energy as he scrambled to his feet, trying to imagine a way out of this.

"You think you've won?" Gervin hissed, now lowering in volume out of fear. "You don't understand what you're doing..."

"I understand," he said, his voice steady as the ancient blade in his hand shone out bright. "You didn't just kill my father, the other heroes, our kin, and so many others, but you tried to kill everything they stood for too. You turned this kingdom into a prison of the soul, and now you're selling it for parts to the highest goblin bidders."

***

The palace trembled again, the walls groaning under weight of Gervin's magic as he tried spell after desperate spell. The dense air contracted once more, charging with energy, though lightning coursed so small as to be unseen, invisible to human eyes. Gervin staggered back under the power of his spells, his human facade cracking at regular flashing intervals.

The swelling crowd of people gasped as they saw more and more of the emperor they had not seen before, and never wished to see, indeed.

Drake caught a glimpse of something else as well. He saw the hint of Gritch's features in Gervin clearly, that nasty and tricky goblin whose goals still remained mysterious.

Gervin, pulling out a dagger of fiery crystal hidden within his monarchical robes, lunged forward. Drake sidestepped, staff sweeping out in an arc that disarmed the king, but also threw the staff.

The blade clattered across the marble floor, skidding to a halt near the feet of a boy in the crowd.

Gervin stumbled, off-balance, and vulnerable, yet still clinging to the human form despite the assured cost of effort. Its eyes darted around the massive room, searching for an escape, but the crowds had completely encircled Drake and the sniveling false emperor.

"You don't understand," Gervin rasped, voice trembling. "I saved this kingdom! I freed it from the monst..." It stopped before continuing further, looking around at the crowd of surrounding hateful faces now all in full bloom.

Drake scoffed. "You saved nothing. You enslaved our nation," he spat out, in curse. "You dressed yourself in lies to steal its soul." He approached ever closer, sword pointed at Gervin.

The enchantments shimmered around Gervin like a mirage, the human form flickering in and out of focus as if caught in a windstorm, but a goblish shadow was now as readily visible as the human form imposed upon it.

Drake brought Nightbane's blade closer, the tip pressing against the skin of Gervin's neck now.

The enchantments shattered completely, revealing something far closer to the true nature of this creature that had masqueraded as their emperor. Gervin's form convulsed, body writhing as the illusions fell away like a discarded shroud.

The transformation was sudden and brutal, like the snapping of a rope under too much strain. Skin that had been smooth and unblemished turned to a map of scars forming scale-like patterns, splitting at the creases with irritated age and rot, a lizard hide shifting and contorting over limp bones dragged by gravity. Eyes that had been bright and piercing sank into hollow pits of darkness. These were sockets filled with profound malice.

Gervin's rotting lips peeled back in a snarl, revealing a few broken and yellowed fangs. Its body seemed to shrink inward, collapsing under the weight of truer form, that of a goblin, nearly full-blooded, masked through sorcery that had fooled an entire kingdom into accepting the creature under a false identity.

Gasps rippled through the assembled crowd. Horror and disgust mutilated their expressions like acid. The women clutched their children tighter, men stepped forward protectively, and all were murmuring revulsion and disbelief.

"Look at you," Drake taunted, voice laced with contempt as he circled the fallen goblin emperor. "All this time, hiding behind so many lies and illusions. You're pathetic."

Gervin snarled, "I was always the emperor!"

Drake said, "You're a monster born in rot and using decay as a weapon."

The boy who had caught the fiery crystal dagger earlier had emerged from the crowd, his small face set with righteous anger. He charged forward, the dagger held high above his head.

The crystal blade gleamed all the redder as it plunged down into Gervin's back repeatedly, stopping the creature's sanctimony. The boy sank the crystal deep into the rotting flesh that sizzled and smoked as it splattered blood. The boy growled in utter contempt and hatred felt to the core by all assembled, who stood still a moment in shock.

Gervin screamed aloud in a screeching squawk reminiscent of some strange unidentified bird, its body convulsing in agony. Gervin's screams were later said to be heard beyond the city limits, some claimed the kingdom over.

"All your would-be kings..." Gervin rasped, a quivering mass bleeding out. "I had them killed! Every last one! All those mysterious deaths of heirs," it bragged in its final gasps, blood flecking its lips, "in pursuit of the power... many of them children." Gervin stopped to laugh again, a twisted parody of mirth.

Drake's grip on his sword tightened, knuckles turning white as he fought to maintain control. He took a deep breath, steadying himself as he prepared to strike the final blow.

A voice echoed throughout the palace, loud and clear coming from the throne room side-door. "Father?" the voice of a child called, filled with terror in plea. "Father, help me!"

The crowd stirred uneasily, eyes darting toward the door as if expecting to see a lost heir emerge from the shadows. Drake hesitated, his sword hovering in mid-air, uncertainty flashing across his face.

"Drake," one of the women whispered, voice trembling with fear, "is that...?"

Drake's expression darkened, realization dawning on him. He turned back to Gervin, eyes narrowing as he saw the goblin's smirk. "You think this will save you?" he growled.

Gervin laughed. "It's enough," he rasped. "Enough to distract you... to give me the chance I need."

Drake's reaction was instant, sword forwards, driving it towards Gervin's chest.

The goblin lunged at the same time, movement sudden and unpredictable, as Drake felt a searing pain rip through his side.

He staggered backward, hand clutching at the fresh gushing wound from Gervin's other hidden blade.

Dark blood welled between his fingers.

The crowd surged forward, some screaming, their voices rising in a chorus of alarm and outrage. A nurse rushed to Drake's side, hands pressing against the wound in an effort to stem the bleeding.

Others turned their attention back to Gervin, eyes blazing with fury.

Drake slumped to his knees and into the arms of supporters, vision swimming as he fought to stay conscious, hand firmly on sword gripping with all his might.

The boy with the fiery crystal blade screamed in rage as he drove that crystal weapon into Gervin's back a final time.

Drake's vision faded to black. The last thing he saw was the face of the boy who had delivered the most important wounds to the enemy, eyes wide with shock.

The boy watched as his new hero fell in final triumph for Solipsia, and its mistakes. Perhaps a penalty it could not afford.

The goblin convulsed, body writhing as the crowd's weapons found their mark again and again. Gervin attempted to scream one final time, but could not for all the blades in chest and blunt weapons upon face or skull. The tyrant creature convulsed its last under the beating and stabbing, its form twisting and contorting as life ebbed away.

Gervin's true form was revealed in death, all remaining charms shattering like glass under a hammer blow. Lips peeled back in final snarl, a rictus of hatred over remnant yellowed fangs.

* * *

The throne room lay shrouded in a silence so profound it felt almost tangible, as though reality had turned to stone. Drake, held in the arms of the crowd, seemingly claimed by the darkness.

A doctor stepped forward from the crowd and tended to his wounds, as everyone watched.

The surrounding crowd held their collective breaths, the weight of what they had witnessed holding them still in that sacred moment.

Someone moved through the crowd, and it was Gervin's young cousin, Kenid, who had survived thanks to the willing self-sacrifice of Telyn; but that is a tale for another time.

Kenid moved closer to where Drake lay, as the doctor finished his stitch work. The doctor, a man by the name of Jan and whose family would come to be honored for generations, stated he believed Drake would make a full recovery.

Kenid gave out a single cheer, "HURRAH!" Hearty and emotion filled cheers erupted from the throats of the others gathered, as well. It was raw triumph. A sound swelled like a storm rushing in, washing over the palace walls and spilling into the streets and out into the rest of the kingdom beyond, and all the lands troubled by goblins. Voices lifted in jubilation, each cry a testament to hope rekindled, a symphony of relief and victory that resonated through every corner of Solipsia, and beyond.

"Gervin's dead! The goblins have fled!" someone shouted, "Long live Drake! Tyranny no more!" Many repeated this, and so the title lyrics to the most popular song in Solipsian history were then coined, and sung out everywhere:

Our palace stolen, in shadow's grope,
A single voice rang out, in hope.
Our hero reborn from tales of old,
Stirring ye hearties, both brave and bold.

Gervin's dead! The goblins have fled!
Good news with goodness is spread.
Through streets, in fields and glades,
In every heart, the dark now fades.

Long live Drake! Tyranny no more!
Cheers to quake all, from shore to shore.
From peaks of mountains to valleys low,
For our hero out of time, none could slow.

Solipsia open, unbroken spirits her pearl,
With hearts in tune and flags unfurled,
Their voices raised in unified song,
To celebrate our freedoms' new dawn.

Evil is shorn, our kingdom reborn!
We care not for the monsters' scorn.
Now hope fills hearts with faces agleam,
Futures for they who dared to dream.

So we take up our charges anew,
The brave and fortunate few,
Our visions now unclouded and clear,
Through battles won, our victories draw near.

Hero! Hero! Long live Drake!
Each strike a triumph for justice's sake!
Who called to arms the hungry and cold,
To stand as one and never again fold!

Gervin lied! The goblins have died!
All hope is now raised, far and wide,
Through every land where faith had seed,
In each heart where courage was in need!

The cheers grew louder, a roaring tide of sound that threatened to drown out all else. Women ululated together, their voices rising in a chorus of pure joy and release.

Men shouted with fists raised high, faces flushed with exhilaration and disbelief.

Children danced, their laughter ringing through the air like bells.

The sound of celebration cascaded down the marble halls, spilling into courtyards and alleyways, carried on the wings of joyous cries. The city came alive with great energy, a collective exhale after holding breath for far too long. Songs were sung, and the emperor's larder was emptied and funneled out amongst the starving crowds. Bands took up their instruments once more, and merrymaking began throughout the city and the kingdom.

"Solipsia is free!" a young girl screamed, twirling in circles with her arms outstretched. "Free!"

Drake lay unmoving at the center of it all, his form still and pale amidst the sea of revelry. Yet even in unconsciousness, he held on tightly to his family sword, fingers clenched around the hilt. The sword bore the blood of deceptive tyranny, its dark blade gleamed all the brighter still.

The crowd began to stir, their initial shock giving way to purposeful movement. Strong arms lifted Drake's unconscious frame carefully through the crowd, cradling him like precious cargo. The people parted before them, forming a living corridor that led from the throne room and into the heart of the city amid the fanfare and music everywhere.

As they emerged into the open air, the cheers redoubled, swelling to deafening heights. Drake was carried aloft on a sea of voices, his unconscious form borne through streets clogged with jubilant citizens. Freshly unfurled banners hung from windows and balconies, some hastily fashioned from cloth and bedsheets, bearing symbols and colors of defiance and hope.

"Hero!" someone shouted, voice filled with reverence, but cracking with emotion.

"Our hero!" The words reverberated through the crowds like a chant, growing louder and more insistent with each repetition, and joining to the forming song among the people. "Hero! Hero! Hero! Long live Drake! Tyranny no more! Evil is shorn, with goodness in store!" Lyrics expanded, becoming a journal of emotional liberation for many.

Drake's unconscious journey, carried back through the city, was a procession unlike any other as the streets pulsed with life coming out from the waking hinterlands. Children ran alongside those bearing Drake's body, their faces flushed with excitement and pride, wishing to just touch his arm or a piece of his clothing.

"Look at him!" one boy exclaimed, pointing at the sword still gripped tightly in Drake's hands.

"He did it! He killed the goblins and trolls!" A young woman with tears streaming down her cheeks reached out to touch the blade, her fingers tracing the dark metal with awe.

The procession wound its way down into the city. More people joined the ranks, swelling the crowd until it seemed as though the entire city had come out to celebrate.

Drake was laid gently in the center of the grand plaza, his body arranged carefully on a makeshift dais of crates and barrels, with people's finest mattresses and pillows set under him. The people fussed over who could provide the best accommodations.

The sword was allowed to remain resting upon him, no one being able to easily loosen Drake's grip. The sword still worked on Drake even as he rested. Though its initial purpose was fulfilled, the path of its ultimate destiny was now realized.

Above him, banners fluttered in the breeze, bearing words and symbols of triumph and freedom.

The goblin tyrant's body was torched outside the city's gates along with the other goblin and troll bodies.

CHAPTER FOURTEEN

AFTERMATH

Unfamiliar stillness came, a silence so profound, resonating with the deepest emotions underneath in the absence of sounds. No jeers escaped gnarly mouths of goblin merchants. No hushed voiceless business, hidden in alleyways while avoiding goblin guards as though some crime were being committed.

Instead, there was only the pleasant hum of life happily returning to precious normalcy: a blacksmith's hammer striking steel industriously, the distant clatter of potters' wheels or sewing machines, and the soft murmur of voices exchanging relieved greetings and discussing next steps.

The goblin and troll corpses lay strewn across the kingdom, the smell of rotting flesh reminded the newly liberated of dreams for loved ones shattered. Their forms were as crumpled and broken as the kingdom had been.

Many had volunteered for the duty of removing and burning the bodies, but it was a very long and tedious process, after all. The stench of death was a choking funk that clung to clothes, skin, hair, buildings, and even wildlife for a time, like a haunting ghost of gross defilement.

Guards, taking up their former duties again, stood vigil over the gruesome tableau, expressions grim beneath goblin-dented helmets. Their spears rested against the cobblestones, hands gripping hilts, on the lookout for any goblins foolish enough to show up, or anyone remotely goblish looking, for that matter.

An elderly woman, her back bent under the weight of years, paused beside the piles of corpses collected on carts to be burned next. Nearby, she watched a crowd roping yet another Gobland statue to pull down. She clutched worn beads to her chest, lips moving silently in prayer.

Beside her, a young man with a dark smudge on his forehead and haunted eyes sketched the scenes onto parchment, his charcoal strokes capturing the horrors with ghastly precision. Currently, he was working on a piece depicting the group toppling a particularly large statue of Gervin holding a goblin child on his shoulders, surrounded by real piles of dead goblins and trolls.

Bands of iconoclasts were now patrolling the streets, seeking out the many statues to destroy around the kingdom, to reclaim for material.

"May God never allow this to happen again," the old woman murmured to the young man, crossing herself.

The young man looked up from his drawing, eyes meeting hers. A tear rolled down his cheek as he nodded. Celebratory calls could be heard down the road.

"You saw too much, we all did," she stated softly, her blank gaze drifting to the piles of goblin corpses heaped on carts, waiting to be burned. "The things they did..."

He swallowed hard, his throat tight with emotion. "Yes," he managed, voice hoarse. "I saw it all, everything, I couldn't look away. I drew it."

His charcoal continued to dance across the parchment as he spoke, capturing the both the glorious and grotesque details of the scene before him, a statue of Gervin toppling, with goblins strewn about like broken dolls, and blood pooling like ink.

The old woman shuddered, her gaze fixed on the young man's drawing. "Such cruelty," she whispered. "And yet, look at them now."

She gestured to the crowd having moved on to roping another statue, faces of fury. "They fight back, and reclaim what was stolen."

The young man nodded again, his strokes becoming more vigorous as if fueled by a renewed sense of purpose. "They do," he agreed. "How do we stop it from happening again though?"

The old woman sighed deeply, her breath rattling in her chest like distant thunder. "By remembering," she said, her voice steady despite the tears welling in her eyes. "Never forgetting what happened here. Standing tall against the darkness, and moving closer to the light."

He looked at her then, his gaze searching hers for answers neither of them had.

Their conversation blended into the murmur of voices that filled the streets, a symphony of relief and hopeful plans.

People arrived from far distant lands to assist in the rebuilding efforts, many refugees returning, drawn by the news of triumph and the promise of rising heroes. They came on foot and horseback or by ship, some bearing gifts of gratitude, others simply seeking solace in shared experiences of the survivors, and yet others seeking those capable of fighting the goblins and trolls in their own lands.

* * *

Drake awoke days later.

His eyes fluttered open, focusing blearily on the celebratory canopy above him. He found himself ensconced within a makeshift sanctuary erected at the heart of the grand plaza, with ever expanding layers of wreaths and flowers, and gifts from admirers demonstrating their gratitude. The sanctuary wooden beams and thatched roof gave way on the sides to the vast expanse of beautiful blue sky. He stirred beneath the layers of furs and blankets, his body aching with a multitude of pains that spoke to the battles hard fought and won.

Voices drifted in from outside, punctuated by bursts of laughter and the occasional shout of jubilation. Songs were being sung, and everyone sounded joyous. The scent of roasting meats mingled with sweet perfumes wafting through the air, creating an intoxicating blend at odds with the stark reality he had known before.

He pushed himself upright, wincing as muscles protested against the sudden movement. His hand rested on the hilt of the sword. The weight of it grounded him, tethered him to the present even as visions from the past clawed at the edges of his consciousness.

The festival which erupted during his slumber had continued to pulse like a living thing, a strange realm of joy and celebration that drowned out all else.

Banners hung from every available surface, their vibrant hues stark against the soot-stained stone: reds for blood spilled, blues for tears shed, greens for life renewed.

Kenid, his young cousin, was nearby, apparently his only surviving relative.

His grip on his father's sword tightened involuntarily, knuckles turning white as thoughts churned like storm clouds within his mind. He found his staff repaired nearby with sheath still in place.

The sword laying across his chest had done much to heal him further, its dark edge now radiating light. It now felt heavier with the weight of his connection to truth through it, and his many days of holding it while unconscious, as though it were commanding more respect from him.

Kenid spoke up at once, "Sir, you are awake!"

"Yes," Drake swung his legs over the side of the makeshift bed, feet touching cool stone beneath him. He stood, swaying slightly as dizziness washed over him like a tide. Taking a deep breath, he steadied himself.

Kenid had much to share, and so they spoke for a time. He was eager to share the story of Telyn's bravery, and very emotional in the telling.

"Everyone has been waiting for you, Drake. You are the hero of Solipsia!" Kenid announced.

"All the folk who helped are heroes. The boy with the crystal dagger was truly brave. I was merely vigilant and had much help. Who was he? Too bad you weren't there."

"Drake, I was there! I saw him! I've seen him around, but I don't know his name," Kenid said.

"We should definitely find him and reward the bravery he displayed, and at least make sure he is safe," Drake stated. "We should recognize everyone that took part in our holy mission. If we are going to protect Solipsia from such things ever happening again, then we must train and raise up moral yet unafraid fighters." He looked over to the two guards stationed at his sanctuary.

They exchanged glances, not sure what to do, having never taken orders directly from an uncrowned man before. One stepped forward, clearing his throat before speaking, "My lord? What would you have us do?" he ventured tentatively, willing to do anything for their hero out of sheer loyalty, but struck deeply by the immediate nobility on display in Drake's actions upon waking.

Drake turned to face him smiling widely and excitedly. "We are going to find all the heroes, recognize them for their bravery, and help them organize!" Drake repeated, with contagious exuberance.

***

Word spread quickly through Solipsia's streets, carried on hurried footsteps and joyful conversations. In fact, it was the first bit of real news for the kingdom since Gervin's destruction.

The search for the heroes, who had helped against the goblins and against Gervin, became an urgent mission. It united all citizens still riding high on waves of triumph and relief. It was the mission of their now awoken hero, and so they all took it very seriously.

Drake called a gathering of all heroes, and not just the ones who happened to be in the city on that fateful day. Messages went out to every corner of the kingdom.

They were easily able to track down the boy who had used the red crystal dagger. The boy was named Mordred, whose father was a cobbler of modest background. Drake went to meet him, bringing Kenid along with, hoping perhaps they could be friends.

"There he is!" Drake said when he saw the boy once more, "That's the one!"

"I... I just wanted to help, honest, please don't punish me," Mordred stammered as Drake and Kenid approached, with the crowd behind them. "I... we lost so much. I was angry."

"You did well," Drake assured him. "Crucial timing, everyone is safer for your bravery, boy! Your family should be proud!"

Mordred shook his head, tears welling in his eyes. "No," he whispered. "They're gone. All gone."

Though not surprising given all the loss which had happened, the weight of the boy's words settled like a shroud over the surrounding crowd, all of whom could feel great sympathy. Drake felt something within him shift, a profound sense of loss and empathy that transcended mere sympathy.

"Gone?" he repeated in asking without thinking, in a breathless voice.

Mordred nodded, sniffling as tears spilled down cheeks streaked with dirt and grime. "The goblins took them," he explained. "My parents, my brothers, my sister... They're all gone. I am alone. And, and that's why I was so angry. I'm still angry, and I'm sorry but I'm not sorry for that," the boy persisted in his unnecessary apologies.

"You will be alone no longer," Drake declared resolutely in an even voice. "I was waiting to tell Kenid this but now is as good a time as ever." He squared his shoulders and continued, "I, Drake of Eldred, do hereby adopt the both of you; Kenid, son of Edmin, and you Mordred, son of Daggred. I will raise you to be warriors, and you will want for nothing. I have high expectations for the both of you!"

A chorus of cheers and applause swelled to deafening heights from the crowd.

Drake looked upon Kenid and Mordred, seeing his own reflection mirrored there. Kenid felt compelled to hug Mordred, lifting him up as he shed tears of joy. Drake, also tearful, kneeled down to wrap his arms around the both of them.

Later in the evening, Drake spoke with the gathered crowd at the grand plaza.

The acclamations of the crowd washed over Drake like a tidal wave, each cheer and shout resonating through his very bones. His heart swelled with the pulse of life that surged through Solipsia's veins. He looked out at the sea of upturned faces, eyes aglow with fervor and hope rekindled, and felt the weight settle upon him stemming from what they must have seen in him, the hero, a responsibility as vast and daunting as the kingdom itself.

"The emperor ruined everything!" a voice called out from the crowd, quavering beneath the surface. "He delivered nothing but sorrow and death to our doors!" Her words grasped all hearts like a curse, so heavy with the weight of shared experience and collective pains.

Nods rippled through the gathering, a wave of silent and somber assent that seemed to roll outward from the woman. Shouts came from the crowd, voices rising in unison to amplify her sentiments.

"He took our children!" someone yelled out in tears.

"Our homes!" added a deep voice, shaking holding back anger.

"Our very souls!" called out a woman, red-eyed in shameful

emotion. Many recognized her for having been especially ferocious in her discrimination against the heroes during Gervin's campaigns.

The blacksmith who had joined Drake in battle stepped forward, his voice booming like thunder as he addressed Drake directly. "We saw everything that you did," he declared, chest puffed out with pride and respect. "Took every risk despite everyone doubting you and everything being set against you, fighting for us all. You saw through the lies and slew the beasts, freeing Solipsia forever from the grip of goblins."

Drake met his gaze, seeing resolve mirrored there.

Behind them, voices swelled, **"Long live King Drake!"** they chanted, fists raised in the air. **"All hail our king and hero!"**

"All hail Solipsia and our heroes of old!" was all Drake could manage amid the emotion The acclamations and confirmations from the loving masses overwhelmed Drake, each cry a testament to his long-borne cross of rekindling the faith of others against the ruins of darkness. He felt the emotion of it all surge through him, igniting something deep within, a spark that grew into an inferno, burning away doubts and fears alike, stoking a new level of willpower.

His mind drifted back to the past, conversations with his father under starlit skies beside crackling campfires. The old hero's words rang clear in his memory: "Lead them well, son. For they need not another tyrant." Drake straightened at the remembrance, resolve steeling within like molten iron poured into the mold of his being.

He stepped forward and thanked them all. His breath came steady and even, lungs filling with air infused with the scent of hope and the empowering odor of anticipation. The expectations were on him, but it was not unbearable. Rather, it grounded him, tethering him to purpose and duty. It was what he had been born and raised to do, lead, and it was his destiny.

***

With measured tread, Drake once again walked toward the palace with his most trusted friends.

He stopped, between the massive columns at the top of the steps, and turned to address his people, his Solipsia. His voice carried far and wide across courtyards and alleyways. "I did not seek this path," he began, enunciating each word carefully lest there be any misunderstanding. "Nor do I claim greatness, for I have seen how far I can fall. Together, however, we have endured the darkness, so together we will forge something greater!"

A hush held the crowd, hope shining in all the eyes looking on, bright and unyielding as the first light of daybreak.

"You have helped me to see what it means to be a leader," he continued, voice softer now but no less powerful and loud for its gentleness. "To stand beside you, shoulder to shoulder, and face whatever comes next, as partners in this journey toward truer freedom, which we must now understand is everything opposite those goblins and their ways."

Cheers erupted from the throng once more, swelling.

"This is not my throne," he declared, gesturing to the palace behind him. "It belongs to every one of you, to each man, woman, and child who has suffered under Gervin's rule and dared to dream against the goblins and their evil."

Applause thundered through Solipsia's streets, echoing off stone walls and shattering the remnants of despair that lingered like ghostly specters.

Drake stood tall, arms outstretched as if to embrace the very essence of the recovered kingdom. "We will rise from these ashes, and shine all the more!"

Within days, Drake moved to honor the fallen, long past and current, and rally the brave into tight camaraderie.

Drake spoke resolutely and with conviction, "Yes, our forebears fought valiantly; their deeds shall be always honored and remembered henceforth. The youth must have their names and examples to remember and look up to as they come of age. The heroes who came before us, those who stood against the darkness and paid the ultimate price, their names will no longer languish in the shadows of slander. Our new generations will know about their sacrifice."

He signaled to aides stationed nearby, men and women clad in the livery of House Eldred, who stepped forward with purposeful stride. Together, they unveiled stone pedestals carved from marble as pale as moonstone, all bearing inscriptions etched deep into their surfaces. Names long forgotten were reclaimed from obscurity, resurrected to take their rightful place in history.

"Eldred," Drake read aloud, tracing the letters with his fingertips. "Jophre. Hebbrigd. Kaelan. Lysandra. Eolande. Jargvin. Edmin. Prolten. Grago. Draid. Donmir. Gearon. Balnor. Agbal. Erdon. Telyn..." Each syllable resounded through the plaza. He faithfully called out all the names of all the great heroes of the past which could be remembered, who had been besmirched under Gervin. Next to the names of old, were the heroes of the most recent redemption of Solipsia, of course, in overturning the goblin emperor. All the names of those killed by Gervin and his goblins were remembered as well.

Tears welled in all eyes. These were tears of joy, of relief, of remembrance long denied. Gratitude and honor made palpable flowed through the crowd like an electric current. Drake surveyed the scene before him, heart swelling with pride and purpose as he witnessed firsthand the power of truth and heroism. Tending toward the emotional on such occasions, Drake managed to keep his composure despite the great difficulty.

"This is but the beginning," he declared, raising his voice to carry over noise and emotion. "We must rebuild, not just statues, but homes, schools, and farms. We must rebuild the foundations for our future."

Enthusiasm rippled through the crowd like a wave, voices raised in unanimous agreement as they reflected his sentiments back at him. "You speak wisely, Drake!" a burly man called out, fist pumping the air with fervor.

"But remember," another added, voice cutting through the din like a knife, "we need more than bread."

Drake nodded, acknowledging the wisdom in their words. "Indeed," he replied. "Spirit nourishes soul as food does body. We must tend to both if we are to thrive." He raised his voice once more. "The meek must aid the vulnerable toward strength, and they will be well-supported in doing so; learned must teach the unlettered toward intellect, this will see my full support as well. No longer will our people suffer under the yoke of ignorance or oppression. The kingdom shall defend our columns of civilization."

Applause erupted from the throng, thunderous and heartfelt approval that swelled to deafening heights.

New statutes were erected at street corners and plaza squares, bearing likenesses of heroes long forgotten, silent testaments to valor reclaimed from shadows cast by deceit. Drake walked among them as they were built, paying homage to those who had come before him, and those whose sacrifices had enabled everything they enjoyed.

As days turned into weeks, Solipsia stirred to life like a gentle and playful beast roused from slumber. Streets once choked with detritus were cleared, cobblestones scrubbed clean of grime and gore until they shimmered beneath the autumn sun's gaze. Markets bustled anew, stalls groaned under the weight of produce and wares hawked by local human merchants eager to ply their trade.

Children's laughter rang out from schools rebuilt with haste yet care, halls adorned with frescoes depicting scenes of virtue, progress, and chivalry. One boy struck a pose with his wooden sword,

"Haha, I am Drake! Die goblin scum!" His little brother brought up the rear with an even smaller wooden sword painted red with crayon, "N' I'm Modwed! Haha!"

Through the jubilation and celebration in growth and recovery, Drake remained ever vigilant, a sentinel standing watch over his kingdom, eyes ever scanning the horizons for signs of threat or strife. For he knew all too well that darkness lurked beyond Solipsia's walls, waiting patiently for the opportunity to strike once more.

Drake moved throughout the kingdom, an ever-present mind, guiding its recovery with wisdom. He consulted with councilors and advisors, men and women drawn from every walk of life, each bringing unique perspectives shaped by experience and the sort of wisdom only born of struggle and recovery.

"The people need to see progress," one counselor argued, voice grave with concern. "Not just words, but deeds, constantly tangible reminders that their sacrifices were not in vain."

Drake agreed wholeheartedly, his mind already racing with plans and initiatives designed to breathe new life into Solipsia's veins. He listened intently as blacksmiths spoke of forges reclaimed from ruins, bakers of new types of ovens and mills, weavers of looms set back to work or improved, each voice painting vivid portraits of civilization's resurrection, with how they could contribute. He most loved to watch happy families grow, and fields once again worked.

The unlikely allies who had stood beside Drake during the darkest hours, regular folk armed with rusty swords and iron-cored brooms, became just as instrumental in shaping the kingdom's recovery. Their voices resonated through council chambers and marketplaces alike.

Drake listened intently to the words of his people, absorbing their concerns like the parched ground drinking in rain after a drought. He nodded solemnly, acknowledging the truths in the words despite whatever complexities involved.

***

Horizon presented yet another new dawn in beautiful shades of splendor, as late winter settled into early spring once more. Drake stood sentinel at the cliff's edge, breath misting in the cool morning air as he surveyed his freshly vindicated kingdom in quiet thought and reverence.

The sun ascended steadily, its warmth banishing the remnants of night like a gentle caress, chasing shadows back into the recesses from whence they came. Drake inhaled deeply, lungs filling with the scent of pine and earth, a fragrance redolent of life renewed and hope reborn.

His legs, once weary from injury and battle, now felt spry and powerful beneath him, rooted firmly to the ground as if drawing strength from the very soil itself. The wounds that had marred his flesh were healed, leaving only faint traces in his many scars as reminders of past deeds.

Drake's gaze swept across the realm, eyes taking in every detail, rolling hills dotted with sheep grazing contentedly. He took in the forests dense and untouched save for narrow paths worn by the feet of travelers. He drank in the rivers winding like ribbons through canyons and meadows ablaze with wildflowers. It was a vision of peace and prosperity, a stark contrast to the chaos and devastation that had so recently laid waste to the lands.

No goblin shadows lurked in valleys below anymore however, their malevolence banished like a fleeting nightmare.

This was his kingdom now. It was his responsibility to nurture it back to health and guide its growth into something stronger, more resilient than ever before.

Drake saw the reminders everywhere. The scorched earth where fires had raged uncontrollably wore on him. Twisted trees bearing witness to atrocities committed beneath their boughs. Villages reduced to rubble throughout the land haunted him still.

He felt pangs of sorrow at such sights, grief welling within him, and reminding him of the importance of his vigilance. He refused to succumb, or let despair claim him when such sorrow could be used for fuel. There was still so much work to be done, with so many lives depending on his actions.

Drake straightened, shoulders squaring as if bracing against oncoming and unseen assaults. He turned away from the cliff's edge, retreating back into the heart of Solipsia once again. As he descended, Drake's thoughts turned inward. He remembered his father's words, wisdom imparted with gentle patience, tempered by experience hard-won.

"Lead them well, son," Eldred had counseled, voice grave with responsibility. "For they need not another tyrant, one who rules with iron fist and cruel decree. Instead, show them compassion, understanding. Be their shepherd, guiding them toward greener pastures."

Drake nodded solemnly at the recollection. His job was not done, not by the half-measure. He would honor his father's legacy most, by leading Solipsia on a path of righteousness rooted in truth and justice, the world over.

Drake brought the heroes, warriors, and any other volunteers under his wing, and trained them as his father had him. He had a grand plan, and a vision for the future.

Drake had also hired teams of blacksmiths and scholars for the purpose of understanding the power of that incredible Nightbane sword. They labored hard in examination of the sword under differing conditions, searching for its secrets.

Firstly, no non-human, such as goblins or even goblish, could ever hope to wield the sword properly, as it dulled at their holding it. They carefully examined the blade's core, its edges, its hilt, each piece a part of the puzzle. They found no magic in the rare metal itself, no runes secretly carved into its surface as hidden, no identifiable enchantment. It was simple, almost cruel in its purity: the blade was not enchanted by spells or relics, and it plainly held no magic. There was no spell or curse involved, it was a mirror reflecting whoever held it. It was powered by something far more elusive than any other force they knew of: the spirit of the wielder.

For weeks, they tried to replicate the instrument. They forged swords from the same rare ore, called 'supernum,' crafted them with the same precision, even doused their blades in alchemical elixirs meant to align the material essence to the human soul, a hopeful theory supported by many of the scholars. Every time they went to lift one of their creations, it felt nearly hollow, lifeless and useless, as though they were goblins trying to hold Nightbane itself. Not even Drake could do anything with these swords, despite his skill at the Ædlertuwin relic.

The team's frustration was genuine. Variously, these men had spent their lives studying blacksmithing, magic, enchantments, or unraveling the mysteries of the arcane, yet this, this was a puzzle that defied all logic.

What kind of enchantment could not be copied? What power could not be discovered in terms of its nature? They wondered.

Then, after all other experimental options had been exhausted, when finally training Drake in blacksmithing, they stumbled upon the truth of supernum. It wasn't just in the material nor in the physical techniques, it was in the spirit and the construction's purpose for the smithy artist. The blade didn't just cut, it revealed truth primarily within, only allowing those trained in the warrior moderation of Ædlertuwin to expand in its skills. Supernum reserved its greatest gifts, in craft as well as battle, for those so trained spiritually and martially as Drake was by his father.

***

The forge was a cathedral of smoke and sweat, built freshly into the throne room. Drake had found more use for the space after all.

Freshly trained by master blacksmiths, he stood at the center, working with his blacksmith team as they came in, both in smithing and in his martial arts.

A silhouette stood as if carved against the glow of molten metal, his hands calloused from years of labor, then refined by unexpected war and steel. It was Jarek, a man whose face had been split open by a goblin's blade during the Reconquest, huffing through the labor of forging a beautiful weapon. He was taller than Drake, but half again as large and bulky, built up by extreme toil in fiery metal. His hammer swung with impressive force, his eyes darting between the glowing metal and Drake's watchful gaze.

"You think you can teach me something about how to make a sword?" Jarek jibed, wiping soot from his brow before he slammed the hammer down again. "War and kingly things might be your specialty, but this is my domain." He slammed the hammer down again.

Drake did not answer, taking the slight compliment in stride appropriately. He stepped forward. Standing beside the blacksmith, nodding. He smiled up at the mountain of intensity and said, "You don't build swords, Jarek."

Affronted, Jarek began to speak.

Drake cut him off by proceeding with his argument, "You see them into being!"

The blacksmith blinked, confused, putting down his hammer. "What do you mean?"

"Your replications of Nightbane are physically perfect," Drake said to him matter-of-factly, "I've got nothing to teach you in terms of product or smithing skill in itself, however in the craft of one's motions and how ***you*** improve yourself. You, not the sword. I can help." Drake moved in and reached for the hammer with a look that spoke of an open request for permission.

Jarek nodded easily enough, grinning in amusement and trying his best not to scoff at the king.

Drake used the tongs to swing the metal up out of the furnace onto the anvil, and then brought the hammer down repeatedly with an almost unnatural speed and force which seemed beyond his frame. The surface of the blade rippled like water, but the hammer was swung back twice as fast releasing upon the metal an identical strike precisely next to the last. Drake would continue this for over two dozen strikes.

Jarek staggered back as he watched, eyes widening.

The metal of the forming blade sang into shape, visibly lighting up beyond the molten orange of the supernum.

"This isn't about strength, endurance, or even skill," Drake called out above the noise of the hammering, a voice calm, pristine, and peaceful despite the labor and force of the strikes. "It's about intent, and the skill of gaining more skill; progress. You don't just forge the metal, you bring out truth within first, then the blade through your improved perspective of its material, almost like a sculptor with marble, but more so."

Jarek still didn't quite understand, but Drake didn't let him off the hook yet. For weeks, they worked together, all the blacksmiths did, side by side in the forge next to Drake, their king, who pushed them to their limits, in spiritual demand.

The blacksmith masters who had taught Drake so recently, now all sat before him in the throne room.

Drake taught them how to feel the weight of a blade, not just in its grip, but in its purpose and through their intent. He showed them that every strike had to be deliberate, every curve of the metal a reflection of the crafter and wielder's will.

Their hands were blistered from relentless practice both martially and in blacksmithing. Drake didn't stop, however. He could not allow any of them to stop, driven by a spiritual urgency and feeling as though they were all on borrowed time.

The opposite corner from the forge had earlier been converted into a space for training, most especially in cold weather. He trained his blacksmiths in war, regardless their age, right beside his recruits and trainees. They would all learn the same lessons his father had taught him.

One night, after days of failure, Jarek finally saw it. He had spent hours shaping the blade, his hammer falling with a rhythm that felt less like labor and more like a heartbeat. When he raised the sword to the light, its edge gleamed not with fire, but with something older, and alive within himself.

Jarek brought it to the palace at once, waking Drake.

Drake stared at it for a long moment before nodding, the smallest flicker of approval in his eyes. "It's not Nightbane," he said, "It's so close, though. It's close enough for battle, for sure!"

One by one, each of the blacksmiths mastered the craft of supernum-nightbane weapons, with Drake's relentless tutelage. The forge became a crucible, not just for metal but for men, as crucial as the training area. This was so true that Drake began requiring his warriors in training to also train in the blacksmithing arts.

The forge became a place where truth and friendship were forged alongside the metal. It was a sanctuary for those who had been broken by war, a crucible for truth. The blacksmiths would then talk, not just about the material, but about the weight of their own errors, the scars they carried, and the memories of gruesome battles. They shared stories of the goblins they had fought, of heroes who had died before them, of a kingdom that had been carved from blood and sweat.

They became great friends and confidants in trade. The art of forging the supernum blades benefited from this greatly, as the blacksmith masters, now skilled warriors in the martial arts of

Eldred's ancient line of Ædlertuwin, shared in the depths of their refining skills. Eventually, many would come to craft weapons even greater than Drake's Nightbane.

***

The streets of Solipsia were packed, renaissance burst through cobblestone alleys and market squares. Drake moved purposefully through the crowds, as he made his way toward the palace. The air was filled with the scent of freshly baked bread mingling with the sharp tang of forge-fires, a symphony of industry that spoke to the resilience and determination of its people.

Drake hurried through the palace's vast marble halls, and entered his throne chamber. The rest of the room was transformed since the Reconquest, stripped of opulent trappings and, aside from the many memorials to heroes of the kingdom, adorned everywhere with maps, while scrolls and codices sprawled across multiple tables between the training areas; all the trappings of Solipsia's newfound purpose. Drake worked to secure not just their own kingdom, but all realms from the lingering specter of goblin tyranny.

Drake stood in front of the assembled company, his most advanced heroes and warriors, some forced into the role and others brought up in it, though not quite like Drake. Each wore earned expressions of resolve, dedication, and duty. These were the sentinels he had summoned, men who would form the vanguard against the darkness that still lingered.

Drake began, voice steady and authoritative. "Today we have a new mission, one that will see to the end of the goblin menace once and for all. These are your tools," he declared, presenting each warrior with their newly crafted swords and axes. "Wield them wisely, for they represent not just the supernum in the construction but also the spirit of your people, our people; honesty unbroken and unyielding. Each blade bears its maker's mark. You can go directly to these men, and they will teach you how to wield it better."

Drake stood in front of his men, the weight of the Nightbane resting on his back. Around him, the heroes gripped their new blades that had been forged with the same brutal precision as their own souls. These were not just weapons, but new extensions of themselves, each one a mirror reflecting the will to fight, to endure, and to become.

"You think you're special as sentinels?!" Drake barked. "You're imperfect men striving to be more! The only difference between you and anyone out there is that you can't fall, especially at that most crucial moment. You don't have that luxury. Your enemy is shameless and graceless. The trials people face out there in their normal lives are from God. Goblins aren't from God," he said as he stepped forward and raised one of the master replicas high above his head.

The dark supernum gleamed in the light, its edges sharp enough to cut through illusions as easily as it could sever flesh. "This is a sword yes, but it's also a mirror. You must look at yourself in it and through it. You will see your enemy in a new light."

One of the most distinguished students, a born hero and the first with a replica, Kael, grimaced in acknowledgement of this truth, his grip tightening around the hilt of his spirit-empowered sword. He had already been sent on a number of special missions for his king.

Drake did not stop, "You don't fight simply because you're courageous, you are all courageous there is no doubt," he said, voice low and steady with his signature calm. "You fight harder than mere courage might permit, because all that you have to lose in this world worth fighting for is on the line."

The men regarded Drake with reverence and hung on every word he had to say.

"Many of you still think this is about war," Drake stated matter-of-factly. Calmly, he responded to the idea, "Let me disabuse you of this misunderstanding, as we may be forced to engage in battle and war but these are not our primary objectives. It's about moderation, in the extreme."

He turned to face them fully, pulling Nightbane out of its sheath and holding it in his hand glowing brightly while he spoke, as though it were alive through Drake in the depths of his vision as he spoke, "What happens now, after our victory? Now that the goblins are gone, and the kingdom stands again? What will do we do then? Do we conquer?"

The question remained in the air unanswered, like a blade poised to fall.

Kael's jaw tightened, his fingers curling around the hilt of his sword. "We'll fight," he said finally, voice hoarse.

Drake laughed. "Yes, you will, Kael!"

Kael raised the replica again, its dark core emitting light strangely as if it were a second sun.

"Most of you who have fought the goblins before, bless you. But you did so out of fear and anger arising alongside opportunity, but these remain extremes. If you want to survive our coming struggles, you've got to learn balance. You've got to learn the ins and outs of when not simply to fight but when to strike, when to survey, when to stay silent, and when to not act yet; discernment in justice."

The training began in earnest. Drake didn't just teach them how to swing their new blades, he taught them how to see further with them. Each freshly forged weapon came with tests for its wielder, each forcing its hero to confront their own fears, their own weaknesses. They practiced in silence, the only sounds rhythmic clangs of supernum against supernum, and the occasional cry of pain as the blades bit into flesh. The blades strangely self-arrested upon striking in practice, however, as utterly reliant upon the will in the wielder's intent, though only wholly obedient to the good. So they were incapable of causing allies any major harm while training, for instance, because the intent would be otherwise. When a wielder moves toward darkness and lies, the blade ceases to grant vision upon truth, rendering the materialist betrayer harmless against others using Ædlertuwin blades.

"You think you're heroes, gods among men, now?" Drake asked them one night as they trained by the light of the stars. "No, you are simply ordinary men who have been forced to forget how to be shameless in error, forced to kill their inner-goblin. The greatest hero is the one that helps others dig deep inside and find the courage they need to do the same, or even better."

The training was spiritual, mental, and physical. Drake forced them to confront their own memories, their own traumas, and their own individual eccentricities. He used the replicas as both tools and weapons, forcing them to face not just the goblins out in the world, but the rot within themselves.

***

The heroes were gathered in the center of the outdoor training grounds, weapons gleaming against the light of a full moon. Drake stood before them, his eyes burning with purpose. "You've all fought your battles," he shouted. "But now, you have to fight for something else." He raised Nightbane high above his head, the blade in his hands still brighter than any other. "This is not just a weapon. It's a choice. You can use it to cut through lies, or you can let it become another lie, which is when it loses its greater edge, the most valuable aspects of the weapon. This is not about me or the weapon. It's about you and our missions."

With that, the campaign began not against any one enemy, but against themselves. The heroes trained to kill yes but more so, to become harbingers of truth. In the end, they struggled for something far greater: the will to service for good, and stand against the rot that had festered even in their own hearts for too long.

The sentinels accepted each of their charges solemnly, eyes

reflecting the grim determination that burned within their hearts. They were a diverse assembly, hailing from every corner of Solipsia, who stood as a united front against the encroaching darkness. Drake needed each of them for their unique contributions.

"You will journey far and wide," Drake continued, voice ringing out clear and true. "No goblin nest shall escape your vigilance. Seek them out, root them from their lairs, and purge this world of their corrupting influence."

They were all nodding. "We will not rest until it is done," one warrior vowed, fist clenched around the hilt of his new sword. "Goblins shall know fear once more. All will know justice once more," Kael stated.

Drake smiled, satisfied by their zeal and excitement. He knew well the challenges that lay ahead, the trials and tribulations they would face as they ventured into the untamed wildernesses and shadowed realms beyond Solipsia's borders. He also knew that these sentinels were more than mere soldiers and up to the task. They were champions of light, beacon bearers in a world entrenched with darkness. The weapons would cease to function for them, if they veered from their purpose.

With blessings given them in ancient incantations, the holy orders set forth on their sacred quests. They fanned out across the continents like rays of sunlight piercing the fog and darkness, relentless hunters driven by a common and singular purpose. No goblin nest escaped their vigilance, no lair remained unscathed as they scoured every valley, climbed every peak, and delved into depths where light dared not tread, to root out any vestiges of the rot.

News of their deeds preceded them, sweeping through villages and towns. Tales spoke of battles fought and won against seemingly insurmountable odds, of massive goblin hordes vanquished overnight by their blades forged from truth itself.

* * *

Tales of Solipsia and songs of Drake spread lovingly across distant lands, sweet truths carried as though by zephyrs, soft and welcomed most like the embrace and kisses of one's love. Excited voices rang out in joy of virtues through courts and marketplaces alike, alighting imaginations with hope reborn, as carried through the darkest ruins of despair. Drake's story of heroism was a triumph that resonated deeply within all those who could yet hear it.

Solipsian envoys arrived at foreign shores everywhere, bearing gifts and offering guidance, as well as assistance against the darkness. None needed to bend their knee to Drake and his line, though most did despite Solipsia never seeking conquest.

"The world shall have our aid against the goblin menace," he declared repeatedly, voice as steady and resolute each time. "For we are bound not just by blood, but also by shared purpose to see light prevail where once darkness reigned."

So it was that the cadet house Eldred of the Ædlertuwin lineage arose from the ruins, its lineage marked by courage and compassion and strength tempered by mercy, despite all odds. These traits came to be valued once again, so that the realm flourished under their stewardship, prosperity blooming like wildflowers after a stormy season. Through the generations, house Eldred rose to prominence across realms far and wide. Even their distant descendants became sought after as leaders, the world over.

With its memory renewed, Solipsia returned to its original name of "Solace" lost long ago, yet one more thing restored by its natural-born king. The kingdom, and indeed the world, came to rely upon Drake in his lifetime, and the responsibility always weighed heavily upon him, all the more with success.

Drake, now with graying hair, spent much time in the forests outside the city. These were the ancient forests that defined the kingdom for many other lands. These quiet moments alone when he could recuperate were his favorite, when there were the fewest expectations, and he was free to prepare himself for the possibility of even greater good.

Each step took him deeper into sanctuary, where the clamor of daily efforts receded, providing solitude. The canopy above filtered in the remnant sunlight, coloring the forest in a golden, ethereal glow. Drake inhaled deeply, lungs filling with the cool air.

He found a clearing bathed in light, untouched save for a single stone bench. It bore no ornamentation, no insignia marking it as anything more than what it was: an invitation to rest, to reflect, and to commune with the deeper elements of soul. Merry shadows played about the surrounding trees, as he sighed deeply.

Drake laid back on the bench, eyes closed as he listened to the symphony of all the life surrounding him. His ears followed the rustle of leaves stirred by breezes gentle as sighs, the distant knock of a woodpecker's beak against bark, and the soft sounds of creatures going about their days unburdened by the likes of state affairs, or goblins for that matter.

Years became decades, seasons cycling like counted breaths against mortality for many. Solace thrived under Drake's guidance, its streets bustling with healthy industry. Fields yielded bountiful harvests beneath careful tending, while schools filled with eager minds hungry for knowledge. Many children of the proceeding generations grew up to be scholars trained in Eldredian moderation, strengthening the culture of the people rapidly, and radiating outward. The kingdom forever stood as testament to the power of the good, of resilience, and of struggle despite seemingly insurmountable odds. Solace became the cultural hub of the entire world.

Drake had overseen the sacred duty personally, ensuring justice where cruelty once reigned. He studied maps and charts, plotted courses for his sentinels to follow, marked locations of goblin activity reported or suspected, and led the most difficult missions himself even into his waning years. His throne room became a sanctuary of strategy and planning, a war room as force for truth against the lies, where the fate of the world was decided.

* * *

The legacy Drake left became the crux of world history, a testament to nobility and wisdom that would define reality for hundreds of generations to come. Kings of his lineage succeeded to the Solacean throne, century after century, many bearing his same resolve and vision like a torch passed from hand to hand.

His name became synonymous with fiery rebirth against the ashes of strife, a lighthouse shining brightly against any encroaching dark storm, guiding lost souls toward the shores of redemption.

Prisoners, slaves, and thralls of the goblins or goblish were freed everywhere they went. Ill-gotten spoils confiscated from goblin hordes were joyfully returned to their rightful owners, as best as could be done, a restitution to so many villages and families which felt quite a lot like healing. Families wept tears of gratitude as they clutched heirlooms thought lost forever, laughter mingling with sobs at joyous reunions in stone cottages under broken thatched roofs.

Drake witnessed many of these scenes firsthand, his heart swelling with pride and purpose as he saw the tangible effects of his endeavors manifest before him. His men and he moved through the goblin-stricken areas of the world like guardian angels in armor, offering solace and support to those in need, lending an ear to their stories and sharing in their triumphs.

Drake knew that his own part of the tale drew to its close, a chapter written in blood and ink, etched deeply into the heart of a kingdom forever changed, and forever made the better. He felt no sorrow or regret, for he had lived fully, loved greatly, and left an indelible mark upon the world.

As he aged, having done so much outwardly, Drake turned inward and discovered even greater meaning to his father's refrain, "Life is never truly your own." He saw pieces of himself mirrored in faces upturned toward him, heard his own words coming from many and varied lips through chambers across the world filled with voices raised in unison, and heard choruses singing praises to his brotherly band of heroes in many languages he had never heard before and would never hear again. None of it was ever his, and so he felt great contentment in giving everything back.

Drake remained ever vigilant and steadfast in his duty until the day he died. Yet even as his physical form passed away despite his best efforts to stay and further bolster the world, in his place stood a great void like a shining challenge to those who might follow. His spirit endured within the lineages he sired, guiding kings who followed in his path. They followed his path, filling the hollow of his footsteps with unwavering resolve. Each ruler bore his legacy like a mantle passed from shoulder to shoulder, their reigns drenched in the wisdom of Ædlertuwin. Drake's love also endured, permanently carved into the heart of Solace forevermore. His tale may have drawn to its close, but the tremors from the earthquakes of his deeds determined much of history, bringing about many yet unborn, who would have never otherwise been. He became a father figure for the entire kingdom, and his loss was felt greatly throughout. Drake's life was the very restoration of valor and virtue, shining brightly against the darkness.

Thus concludes the chronicle of Drake Eldredson, hero, king, and best friend to his beloved nation, a man who dared to challenge fate itself, emerging victorious not for himself but for all that he held dear, leaving behind a world reborn from ashes and recast in the light of greater truth.

The End.

About the Author:

Dr. Roe is a visionary philosopher, psychologist, and author. His work blends ancient wisdom with modern science to explore the transformative power of spiritual life. Born in the U.S., his early fascination with meaning and ethics shaped a life which became dedicated to discovery of the truer self.

As founder and editor-in-chief of 24K Journal of Virtues Science (24k.cc, virtues.blog), he posits virtues as empirical frameworks for human flourishing, placing them as skills honed through life's challenges, much like physics guides architecture. His Structural Virtues Theory suggests moral growth emerges from disciplined engagement with reality, while his concept of Resurrexit Spiritus (Spiritual Resurrection) reinterprets adversity as a catalyst for renewal, drawing on Christian and classical thought.

Marcus's work spans ethics in technology, community building, and societal renewal; as he advocates tirelessly for systems that prioritize human dignity. In GOBLAND, his debut novel, he channels these ideas into an epic fantasy where the hero's journey mirrors the cultivation of virtue amid chaos. The story, rich with poetic introspection and action, invites readers to see hardship as a crucible for growth.

A devoted family man with six children of his own, Marcus approaches both fiction and philosophy with a commitment to psychological empowerment. His writing, poetic yet grounded in practical insight, urges readers to embrace enlightened action, bridging the gap between abstract spiritual ideals and everyday life. Through his work, he seeks to inspire a world where virtues are more common.

www.ingramcontent.com/pod-product-compliance
Lightning Source LLC
LaVergne TN
LVHW020704110826
845149LV00012B/2103

* 9 7 8 1 9 6 7 9 1 6 9 7 9 *